M.E. DAVIDSON is a Houston-based writer whose work lives at the intersection of family, dread, and the indifferent power of the natural world.

A lifelong obsessive of sharks, movies, and the transportive spell of story, he is drawn to the moment when wonder curdles into fear - when something beautiful reveals its teeth.

A produced screenwriter, Davidson brings a cinematic eye and a grounded sense of human frailty to his fiction. He works in IT by day, where systems are designed for control and regularly tested by failure.

Judy, his debut novel, channels his fascination with real sharks, movie sharks, and the terrifying possibility that nature never needed to hate us to destroy us.

Published in 2026 by Dark Anthem Press

www.darkanthempress.com

Created and Printed in the United States of America.

First Edition 2026 - Published by Dark Anthem Press, an Imprint of One Moorer LLC.

Cover design by Drew Foerster.

Identifiers: 979-8-9926547-4-5 (paperback)

979-8-9926547-5-2 (eBook)

JUDY

She is Hunger

By
M.E. Davidson

For Jennifer,

Who held steady through every tide.

AUTHOR'S NOTE

It might have been a while since you've been deep-sea fishing, so here's a quick refresher on boat terms:

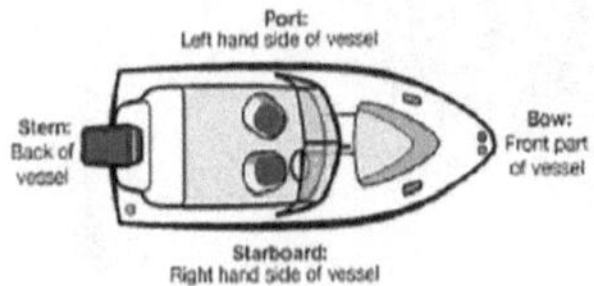

- The front of a boat is called the bow, while the rear of a boat is called the stern.
- When looking towards the bow, the left-hand side of the boat is the port side.
- And starboard is the corresponding word for the right side of a boat.

The rear wall of the boat, generally where the name is painted, is called the transom. The platform on the back of the boat is called the swim ledge.

The door in the transom that leads to the swim ledge is called the transom door. The top edge of the hull (the rail) of a boat is called the gunwale (pronounced guh-nuhl).

The gunwale can have a metal grab rail attached. The rope that tethers the dinghy to the boat is called a painter.

MAP OF NORTH CAROLINA AND PAMLICO SOUND

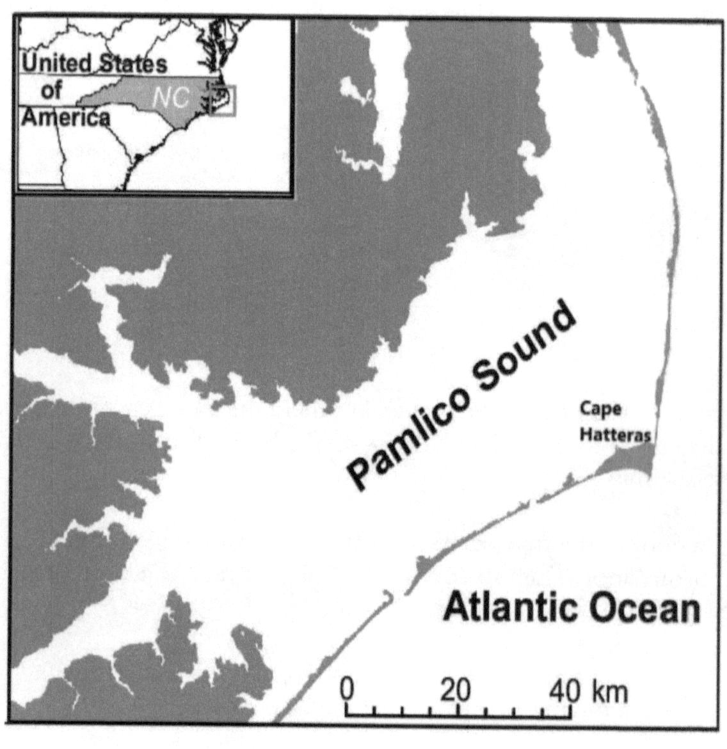

Consider the subtleness of the sea.
How its most dreaded creatures glide underwater.
Unapparent for the most part.
And treacherously hidden beneath the loveliest tints of azure.
— Herman Melville, Moby Dick

Track the Apex. Protect the Balance.
— Mission Statement: Aquavantis Shark Research Center

PROLOGUE

The sea doesn't care.

It doesn't care who you are, what you've built, or what vows you once spoke. The sea takes without apology, without conscience, without hesitation. A mother watching her child in the surf. A captain who's spent a lifetime reading tides. The sea pulls them down the same way - quiet and cold - until lungs empty and the light is gone.

It doesn't rage. It doesn't mourn.

It just lets go. And what was once whole comes slowly apart.

CHAPTER 1

The deep belonged to her.

The shark moved in slow, undulating strokes, her massive frame carving through the blackness. Water surged over her gills, siphoning oxygen with each rhythmic pulse. The sea breathed with her, the endless tide a cradle that had rocked her since birth. Cold, bottomless, and hers.

She had not fed for a while. The last kill had been a school of mackerel, their silver bodies twisting and flashing not far from the surface in the deep waters of the Atlantic before her jaws cut through them like a scythe. The memory was faint, lost in the churning rhythm of the tides, but the emptiness gnawed at her now, urging her forward.

Her skin bore the scars of time - etched into the slate-gray hide like old battle hymns - but she registered nothing. Pain was for prey, for the soft-bodied creatures that darted and panicked, those built to be consumed.

She was not prey.

She was the hunt.

The ocean, vast and shifting, called to her with something more primal than hunger. A need older than memory, a drive embedded deep in muscle and marrow.

She had ruled these waters alone, unchallenged, unrivaled, but the time had come to seek more than dominion. The season stirred within her, restless and relentless, demanding more.

The need to breed, to ensure that her legacy cut through the currents long after she was gone.

The males had begun their wanderings, their presence faint but undeniable in the distant brine. Unworthy, most of them. Smaller, weaker, interlopers daring to cross into her domain. If they came, they would come carefully. They would know what she was.

Even in the deep, there were laws.

Twice she had carried life inside her, the weight foreign yet undeniable. The births had come in silence, her body wracked with heaving contractions until they were free.

Pale, thin-bodied things, no larger than a man's arm, curling and twisting as they drifted into the blue.

She had not lingered to watch them grow - they would survive or they wouldn't.

The sea had no patience for weakness.

She drifted, suspended in the ink, barely moving, her senses reaching farther than sight ever could. The deep was not a place for vision. Light didn't penetrate here, not the kind her eyes could use.

Shapes blurred. Shadows lied. Even the moon vanished above a certain depth. She didn't need light.

She read the water through vibration and charge - flickers of movement along her lateral line, pressure shifts that hinted at distant mass, the electric trace of muscle twitching in a school of fish.

The current carried information: stingrays buried in sand, pelagics scattering from something larger, the slow churn of something vast turning far below. Smell unraveled across time.

Then another scent curled through the current - newer, sharper. Twisting toward her like an invitation wrapped in iron and salt. Blood.

A thin, trembling line in the water, fragile as mist but undeniable. A creature in distress, leaking life into the tide. The urge flared, ancient and absolute, turning her slow, deliberate drift into purpose.

She angled toward the trail, following its beckon through the deep, her world narrowing to the scent of weakness and the promise of what came next.

She followed the trail in silence, her movements sinuous, unhurried. No need for haste. The wounded never escaped. The taste thickened in the water, a ribbon of death threading through the dark. She eased into the current, riding the flow with the patience of something that had never known fear.

She did not know the name they had given her or that they had attached a small device to her dorsal fin. As she moved, her body made subtle, calculated adjustments - a flick of her pectoral fin to tighten her turn, a slight arch to her body to slip into the current more efficiently.

Her tail shifted in short, controlled sweeps, steering her toward the scent that coiled through the water. Each movement honed her path, narrowing her focus to the tremor of life ahead.

She existed in the now, in hunger, in instinct. The source revealed itself in flickering bursts as bioluminescent creatures scattered, startled by her looming shadow.

A fish - a part of one - floated ahead in the current.

Torn.

Wrong.

Its body missing. Only the head remained, leaking blood and oil in a thick cloud that wrapped around her senses.

She circled once, reading it the only way she knew how. The scent was strong - iron, marrow, decay - but the shape was strange. A kill with no chase. Flesh with no fear.

Something was off.

But her body responded before her mind could question. Her gills flared. Muscles tensed. A deep twitch rolled through her tail.

Another scent rode the current - thin and metallic, coiled in the blood like wire. It wasn't natural. But it was close.

She turned toward it.

The bait pulled her forward, calling without sound. The current narrowed. Pressure shifted. Her instincts surged.

She rose.

A single flick of her caudal fin launched her into motion. Water screamed past her body, tight against her flanks. She swept in from below, mouth half-open, jaws flexing.

And then she struck.

Her teeth crushed the tuna head in a single bite - bone, skin, hook. She didn't recognize the hook - not as trap or threat. But pain bloomed instantly, sharp and radiant, buried deep in the jaw just below her teeth.

Her body absorbed it in full, reflexive and unyielding. She thrashed, twisting and snapping, muscles knotting as the sting flared hotter with every tug.

Blood spooled from the torn flesh, swirling into the murk already rising around her.

She twisted again, harder - but every surge drove the steel deeper.

CHAPTER 2

The frame shook - once - before the knock came.

Not hard. Not urgent. But enough to pull Ava from the counter. She glanced at the clock: 12:42.

Half a Southwest Chicken Salad from McDonald's on the counter, iPad open beside it with half-finished call notes from a family clinic in Kill Devil Hills. Lunch break was a loose concept today. She crossed the tile, drying her hands on a dish towel as she went.

The kitchen was in its usual state - tidy enough at a glance, but never quite caught up. Jack ate like he was preparing for a growth spurt that hadn't told his body yet, and there was always something left half-washed or restacked. She tried to stay on top of it. Lately, it felt like trying to hold a tide at bay.

Her house sat back from the street in Manteo, small and quiet, a few blocks from the Sound - two bedrooms and a sunroom she didn't use much. Jack didn't have a key.

At twelve, he still assumed doors would open when he needed them - believed someone would always be there to open them. Danny didn't have one either. She had changed the locks, but he never asked for a copy. That, more than anything, marked the line that had been drawn.

The neighborhood sat on the edge between working-class and barely-white-collar - older homes with modest additions, secondhand Hondas beside office park sedans, and lawns trimmed just enough to pass muster. Everyone here had a mortgage that stretched a little too far and a to-do list that always started with "next weekend".

Jack was standing on the top step when she opened the door, backpack slung over one shoulder. He wore a rumpled school polo and sneakers with the laces knotted too tight.

Behind him stood Danny in his Kealy's Crab Shack polo and ballcap, sunglasses pushed up on his head, as if he'd left in a hurry.

When she stepped closer, she caught his smell - fryer oil, brine, crab meat worked deep into the fibers of his shirt. The smell of the crab shack. She'd always hated it.

At the foot of the driveway sat a beat-up Volvo with oxidized paint and a dented bumper. She figured it must be Danny's - looked like he'd finally gotten himself something to tool around in.

Is it even safe to drive?

At least it's a Volvo. That should count for something.

"You're home," Danny said. "I thought Jack might have a key."

"It's lunch," she said flatly.

Then to Jack: "What's going on?"

Jack looked down. "Got in a fight."

Her eyes narrowed. "With who?"

"Some kid in gym. I don't know. It was stupid."

She knelt in the doorway and checked him - arms, face, the set of his mouth. She looked for scrapes, for scuffs, for anything he might be trying to hide.

"Did he hit you back?"

Jack shook his head. "Didn't get that far."

It was the second fight this month. Not like him. Not even close. Something had shifted. A pressure she couldn't see. Boys didn't talk, not really - not when the ground was shifting under their feet. She wondered if it had something to do with her. Or Danny. Or both.

"I already looked him over," Danny said. "He's fine."

She said nothing.

"School called," he went on. "Said he shoved someone. Teacher didn't see it, but the kid went down. Nurse checked him - nothing serious. But they wanted Jack gone for the day."

"And you brought him here."

Danny shrugged. "Didn't think you'd be home. Figured I'd drop him, head back to work."

"You were just going to leave him?"

"I was going to text."

"That's not the same."

Jack shifted beside her. Ava stepped aside. He hesitated, then slipped past her with a muttered thanks - not to her, not to anyone in particular.

She stayed in the doorway. Danny remained outside, the screen door between them.

"You see the weather?" she asked. "Storm track's creeping closer. They've got the watch up already."

Danny nodded. "Yeah, I heard something about that."

"You still planning to go tomorrow?"

He shrugged. "Guy running the boat says we'll be fine."

"Who is it?"

"No idea. I just got told to be at the marina in Hatteras."

The breeze through the screen carried the first hint of salt. Not the bright kind, not beachy - this was wet rope and diesel. The kind that meant tide.

"Someone should call if it gets cancelled."

"They will."

Jack reappeared in the hallway. "I hope it doesn't."

Neither parent replied.

Danny adjusted his cap, "I've got to get going. It's the lunch rush - left Shel in charge. Thanks for dropping Jack off tomorrow. I appreciate it."

Ava nodded, jaw tight. She didn't answer the part about tomorrow. She wasn't thrilled about playing chauffeur again, but now wasn't the time to get into it.

"We're good."

She closed the door without another word and locked the deadbolt.

She waited a moment, listening for the sound of his car pulling away. It came slow, gravel crunching beneath the tires. When it was gone, she leaned against the door and let out a breath she hadn't realized she was holding.

A minute later, she found Jack in the den, sunk into the couch, watching YouTube on his tablet, some animated channel about game tricks and hacks.

"I've got to get back to work," she said, voice soft. "You going to be okay the rest of the day?"

Jack nodded, eyes on the screen.

She didn't press, "I can bring something home. How about Poor Richard's? One of those giant bacon cheeseburgers with the seasoned fries and extra pickles?"

Jack gave a little shrug, but the corner of his mouth ticked upward.

She watched him for a second longer, eyes still locked on the screen, and felt the pinch of something she didn't want to name. She'd given Danny hell for dropping him off - but here she was, doing the same.

Calling it different didn't make it better.

CHAPTER 3

Sixty miles east of Cape Hatteras, North Carolina, research vessel Aquavantis drifted in the long-breath rhythm of the Atlantic swell, her hull creaking on every lean and correction.

A converted commercial crabber, she'd been stripped to steel and rebuilt as a floating shark lab - 102 feet long, with hydraulic lift arms, welded catwalks, twin chase skiffs, and a grated platform capable of raising a two-ton fish clear of the sea.

She carried a full complement: marine techs, fisheries biologists, a platform crew, telemetry staff, a vet, a documentarian. Eighteen souls aboard, not counting the pilot.

The sea around her had gone unnervingly flat, the surface dark and slick like bruised glass. The sky above was smeared with the outer arms of Tropical Storm Gustav, a spiral reaching west.

The barometer had dropped. The wind had turned. Twelve hours, maybe less, and she'd scrape the coast.

Even here, well offshore, you could feel it in the water - a longer, heavier rise under the keel, each set pressing more weight into the hull than the last, as if the ocean were holding its breath before the first punch.

* * *

They'd hooked her less than an hour earlier, three miles to the southeast, on a drifting baitline the skiffs had been tending. One moment the float was nodding in the chop. The next it lay flat, then knifed under.

When the shark surfaced behind the portside skiff - huge and gray and mute - every free hand drifted to a rail. Even for men of the sea, awe had its own gravity.

She'd taken the tuna head - brined and bleeding - and run deep. Dragged floats. Fought the line in wide, grinding arcs until the fight bled out of her. Now she drifted. Not struggling. Not resisting. Guided by current and fatigue.

Below the starboard quarter of Aquavantis, the steel cradle floated half-submerged, flared wide like a feeding mouth. The skiffs formed a broad V with their tow lines, coaxing the shark forward without drag. Between them, she hung in the water, suspended by exhaustion more than rope.

Her snout tapped the steel cradle, a dull scrape. Gills pumped shallowly. Her tail flicked without strength. Twenty-one feet from nose to tip, she filled the V entirely.

A call rose from the port skiff, "Nose in the V. She's lined up."

On the starboard deck, platform tech Victor Salazar eased the hydraulic lever forward. The lift answered with a syrup-thick sigh - pump whining through lines, valves coughing open, pistons shouldering weight. Steel moved against steel; the cradle groaned and began to rise.

Water sheeted off in silver fans. The shark came with it, bulk settling into the grating like a wreck eased from the deep. Scars along her flanks caught the gray light - some fine and pale as old rope burns, others fresh and pink-edged where the dermis hadn't sealed. Near the dorsal, a half-moon gouge suggested a bite from another predator.

The dorsal itself was truncated - clean at the top, the upper six inches gone and healed into a smooth, unnatural arc. Copepods fluttered from the softness near the jaw like thread. Small crabs clung in the tail's ridges.

There was power in her stillness.

Not threat.

Not fear.

Presence.

Expedition lead Owen Dyer watched from the platform with the wariness of a man who knew how quickly these moments could tilt from miracle to mistake. Beside him, cameraman Johnny Cotton filmed from the rail, lens steady since the cradle broke the surface.

Behind them, more of the crew slid along the catwalks - galley hands, interns, mechanics - drawn to the sight of the animal in the lift. A hush traveled their line, the kind that made you breathe shallower without knowing why.

Half-raised, the shark sagged under her own weight. Her pectorals hung instead of bracing. Her color dulled. The cradle gave a low, unhappy sound.

Lead platform biologist Lina Tran lifted a hand, sharp, urgent. Victor locked the lever. The hydraulics hissed into stillness.

Her lower half remained submerged, tail and belly still buoyed by seawater. Another foot, two at most, and even that support would be gone. She was too large to lift dry. Too heavy.

A few wrong seconds and gravity would do what predators hadn't: organs displaced, spine compressed, gill arches warped and collapsed. It had happened on other boats. Not on this one. Not again.

Ladders dropped. Lina, Devon Price, Ally Feng, and Caleb Neighbors went down with practiced ease, boots ringing on aluminum. Johnny followed with the camera, moving low, keeping clear of the caudal fin.

Above, Owen held the rail and tracked them by habit - who was where, whose hands were free, what wasn't yet tied down as the swell began to run longer under Aquavantis.

Ally knelt at the snout and slid the thick rubber nozzle behind the shark's tongue, angling it toward the gill arches. Caleb followed with the collar, a padded steel arc to hold the mouth open, and braced it in both hands, forearms locked.

Only then did the pump kick on, a deep mechanical thrum underfoot, and cold, oxygen-rich water roared through the line, flooding her gills in white streams.

She twitched, once, then again. A faint flutter ran along her flanks as the flow took. Not swimming. Reflex. Primitive and vital. An animal still trying.

Hands moved in a sequence the crew could do in their sleep. Devon's pliers went to the hook driven into the jaw's corner. Lina measured pectoral spread and logged girth at two stations. Ally's tablet pinged live telemetry as the hose thundered. A towel went over the snout to dull the light. The smells layered, brine, hydraulic oil, iron.

"Careful," Lina said, eyes on the mouth as Devon reached deeper.

He set the pliers, wiggled once. The hook clicked free. The leader line went slack.

Devon's palm skimmed her underside.

"Flat," he called.

No pups.

Data climbed into neat lines. Twenty-one feet. Near three thousand pounds. Respiration improving under the flow. Tissue tone firm. No sign of gravidity.

Ally found the old tag bolted to her dorsal, corroded, but still legible beneath the crust. She keyed the serial number into her tablet. A match pulsed onto the screen, and with it, a name.

Judy.

For a moment, even the scientists went still.

Four years earlier, they'd tagged her near Hudson Canyon, a drowned river valley thirty miles off New Jersey, where the continental shelf falls away into deep water black. The place was a cathedral for predators: steep walls crusted with coral, upwellings thick with baitfish, warm eddies spinning off the Gulf Stream to braid with the cold slope water.

The crew from Shark Week had been aboard that day, cameras rolling as she came alongside. Eighteen feet then, she'd already been the kind of matriarch biologists talk about in half-whispers.

They'd tagged her, cut her loose, watched her slip back into the water. The segment had gone everywhere, drawing donations, fueling projects, making her something more than a datapoint.

Then she'd disappeared, swallowed by the enormity of the Atlantic.

To see her again was more than luck. It was the sort of statistical improbability that didn't belong in field notes. Bigger now. Heavier. She was a battered relic of the continental shelf, and she'd come back into their reach as if summoned.

Ally set the new unit just aft of the scarred notch and drove the screws in with quick, practiced turns. The old tracker, dull, battered, its casing scored with years of salt and strikes, looked primitive beside this one. The old tag had run on fixed batteries, good for a few seasons if the stars aligned.

The new model was different. Sleek, titanium-braced, shaped to slip through water without catching growth. Its power source wasn't a set of cells waiting to die, it carried solid-state storage and lithium-glass, fed by the shark's own motion.

Every kick of the tail gave it a trickle of charge. Ten years, maybe more, before the signal went quiet. A state-of-the-art fin tag for a state-of-the-art predator.

She checked the seal, thumbed the activation switch. A red light blinked, faint and steady as a heartbeat. Judy would not be entirely lost again.

Waves ran longer. The deck had begun to move in a way you felt in your ankles, more heave than bob. Above, the rail filled with faces. Below, the team worked quicker without letting it show.

"She's good," Lina said.

Ally nodded. Devon glanced up toward the rail.

"Let's drop her," Owen called.

Victor threw the lever. The cradle moaned and began to descend. Water climbed higher along her flanks, crept past the gills, pooled around her pectorals. The lift of the sea returned to her in inches; her weight shifted out of the steel.

Her gills opened wider. Drew deeper.

Devon loosened the tail rope. The knot gave. He let the line slip from his fingers. It fell into the water like discarded weed.

For a breath, everything steadied: the hose roaring, the slap of water against steel, the wind threading the rails above.

Then the sea rose.

Johnny worked the aft corner of the platform, crouched low with his shoulder to the cradle rail. Lina was forward at the snout, Ally by the dorsal, Caleb on the hose, Devon aft along the belly, each of them moving inside the narrow grammar of the lift.

Judy's head angled slightly starboard, her jaws resting only a few feet from the platform's edge, close enough that no one forgot where the margin was.

The next set rolled in heavier, lifting the cradle and tipping it toward open water. The shift threw Caleb off balance. His grip on the hose collar slipped, and the thick rubber line jerked free from Judy's mouth with a wet pop, seawater erupting from the nozzle in a pressurized spray.

It struck her head hard enough to knock the towel loose, sending it skittering into the water, where it vanished in the churn.

The flow, no longer aimed into her gills, whipped in wild arcs across the platform, the white jet hammering steel, slapping legs, and spraying high into the air.

Johnny caught a faceful of it, flinching instinctively, one hand thrown up to shield his lens as the spray sheeted across his camera and stung his eyes.

The follow-on wave hit before anyone could recover. Water swept over the grating, pushing loose gear toward the starboard edge. Johnny's boots lost traction on the slick steel. He stumbled sideways, camera thumping against his chest, and reached for the rail. The current carried his legs with it, pulling him in a slow, sliding diagonal toward Judy's head.

The camera strap snagged on a cleat, then tore loose, the rig skittering across the grating and vanishing into the water. Johnny's upper body pitched forward over the rail. He caught himself on his forearms, boots scrambling for purchase, trying to shove backward.

A surge rolled through the cradle, the water grabbing at his knees, sucking him toward the open side. His palm slipped. He twisted to pull away. *Too slow.*

From below, Judy's head swept in from the left, not a straight charge but a sudden, fluid pivot. Her jaws found him in that last half-second, closing low, just beneath the cameraman's ribs.

The sound was quick and conclusive - bone cracking, breath gone in an instant.

She shook once, a short lateral snap, and tossed him aside with brutal efficiency.

Johnny hit the grating hard, rolling to his side, the wind knocked out of him. Blood fanned from the tear in his torso, streaking the wet metal and spilling into the water below in bright, curling threads.

Owen vaulted the rail without hesitation, landing hard on the slick grating. He slid to Johnny, boots skidding in the wash, and got an arm under his friend's shoulders.

"I've got you," he said, voice tight, bracing Johnny upright as another wave slapped against their legs.

Johnny's head lolled, eyes half-focused, but his grip found Owen's sleeve for a moment, just long enough to hold it.

They locked eyes - pain, shock, something unspoken passing between them - before Johnny sagged. Owen pulled him toward the platform's center, shouting for help as Caleb and Devon moved in, one grabbing Johnny's legs, the other pressing a hand hard against the wound.

With a flick of her tail, Judy was clear.

Twenty-one feet of muscle and memory slipped through the flooded taper, gills flaring, jaws still red. She did not circle. Did not check.

The trailing edge of her fin curved once, deliberate as a signature, and vanished.

CHAPTER 4

The pressure faded as she swam.

Water slid across her flanks again - cold, clean, alive. The weight was gone. The surface behind her roared with noise - engines, shouts, steel - but it was growing smaller, more distant.

Her body ached.

Jaw torn.

Muscles stiff.

Blood in the water.

But her tail moved. Her gills drew. She was not done.

The ocean had changed. She *felt* it.

The currents were wrong. The temperature off. Even the salt tasted different. Deeper pressure. More noise. A low hum moving through the water like a living thing.

The storm.

It pushed on her from below and behind, reshaping the sea, tilting familiar paths into new ones, lifting the thermocline, scattering scent.

She didn't understand it. She didn't need to.

She turned west.

Not to escape. Not to flee. But because the sea told her to. The old paths were gone. This was the way now.

Her gills flared. Her body angled low.

And she vanished into the dark, following a map older than memory, steered by nothing but instinct and water.

CHAPTER 5

The Outer Banks of North Carolina form a fragile chain of barrier islands - long, narrow strips of sand edging the continent like bone along a wound.

Low and thin, they shoulder the mainland away from the ocean's full weight.

To the east: open Atlantic, where the Gulf Stream bends and hurricanes take root.

To the west: Pamlico Sound, brackish, uneven, fed by rivers and framed by marsh. Eighty miles long, it swells and shallows with the tide, hiding seagrass beds, oyster reefs, wrecks, and the soft-bottomed channels only locals know by feel.

By a little after eight, night had settled. Hurricane Gustav had strengthened to Category 1, and its outer bands were already combing the coast.

The sky hung low and purple-black, split now and again by distant lightning. The Sound rose into steep, choppy shoulders. Wind threaded the spartina and pressed salt into every breath.

Out in that darkness, a stolen skiff ran light and hard.

The twenty-two-foot runabout rode bow-high, slamming down in wet, hard smacks. The red and green running lights blinked through spray; a single flood mounted at the console threw a cone of glare across the black water, revealing, briefly, foam, wind-scraped waves, the bright bob of a buoy.

Aluminum rails rattled. A length of tow rope fishtailed behind, forgotten. Seawater slicked the deck and pooled at the base of a scuffed cooler, where spilled beer mingled with brine.

Dean Murdock stood amidships, wide in the shoulders and leather-brown from too much sun.

Tommy Ray Holt hunched at the tiller with a cigarette stuck to his lower lip, eyes squinting against the rain.

They were the kind of men whose jobs ended in sweat and

started again the next day, Dean on landscaping crews when there was work, Tommy Ray loading freight at the docks. Work kept them tired, not ahead.

The cooler clattered with each impact of the hull, Bud Lights knocking together inside. They'd been drinking since sundown. It dulled the edges, the speed, the dark, the sense that anything ahead might matter.

They weren't fishing. Not legally.

Pamlico's lobster pots belonged to watermen who set them in daylight and in weather made for work, not warning. Dean and Tommy Ray were poachers, slipping out under storm to work steel cages they hadn't baited, lines they hadn't set. Tonight, the hurricane made a shield of emptiness; no one sensible would be out here.

Tommy Ray feathered the throttle as the skiff pitched.

"Hell of a night," he said, words soft with beer. "Good night for work."

"Ain't work if you don't own the pots," Dean answered, though there was a grin behind it.

The console light caught a buoy jerking in the chop, foam wrapped around its base.

Tommy Ray eased off, "Kill it. Grab that one."

Dean planted a boot on the rail and swung the grappling hook. The line took on the first throw. He hauled hand over hand, grunting as a pot broke the surface, steel frame slick with silt, crabs clinging to the mesh, lobsters hammering the bars. Antennae flailed. Claws snapped. For a second, claw-on-metal rose louder than the wind.

He dragged the trap aboard. Tommy Ray flicked on a handheld flashlight to add to the flood, sweeping the beam across the pot and the bucking deck.

Dean reached in and hauled out a thick male, carapace dark and shell hard with age. The claws snapped wetly as he lifted it clear of the pot.

"Dinner," he said, satisfied. "I'll boil him whole."

"Boil two," Tommy Ray said, and laughed when the boat dropped into a trough and threw spray over them both.

They dumped the catch into a plastic tub and went back for another. Dean's hook found the line again, and a second pot came up lighter, two lobsters, kicking hard, dropped in with a wet clatter. The flashlight beam slashed out into the chop, hunting the next buoy, catching only water and the pale backs of waves.

The shudder came from below - a low, solid knock that traveled up through deck and shinbone. Not the slap of a fat wave. Something deeper.

Tommy Ray glanced back, a cigarette pinned to his lip.

"That ain't the wind."

A second impact followed, harder, behind the stern. The skiff jolted sideways. Dean grabbed the rail, peering past the running lights into the water's black skin.

A scrape rasped along the hull, long and rough, as if a heavy log rolled under them and dragged along the gelcoat. The flashlight beam cut white through spray and slid across the water. Nothing solid. Just the pale blur of depth shifting beneath the hull, then gone.

Movement ghosted the edge of the light.

Something big slid just under the surface off the starboard quarter, pale where the beam snagged it, gone the instant Dean fixed on it. Too quick for trash. Too fluid for wood.

"Shark, maybe?" Tommy Ray said, unease leaking through the beer.

The hull lifted and set. Pressure pushed up from below as if a body passed close beneath the skiff.

The prop struck cartilage with a hard, bright crack. The outboard coughed, spat water, and caught again. White churn exploded aft, a tail beating the Sound into boiling froth.

The mounted flood made a brief, brutal tableau: water blown to lace, foam and blood rising together.

Dean lunged to the rail.

A juvenile white shark twisted beneath the surface right off their stern, five feet of tight, bullet-shaped muscle, belly flashing grey, gills flaring wide.

Just ahead of the dorsal, the prop had opened her, skin and fascia torn back in a ragged crescent, muscle pale beneath, edges feathering into ribbons.

She breached halfway, jaws open in a silent spasm, back arched with shock. Her eye showed black in the glare. She rolled once, a loose, panicked spiral, and slid down the far side of the swell.

Dark returned. Blood trailed aft in thin, wavering threads that the next wave wiped flat.

The skiff fell off a crest and slammed hard. Spray pummeled the rails. Lightning stitched the western sky and left it darker for the flash. The water where she'd been erupted once more, a single desperate slap of tail, and settled into chop.

Tommy Ray's knuckles had gone white on the tiller. His cigarette hung forgotten.

"Christ on a cracker. I think that was a white. A baby."

Dean wiped water from his face and reached for the hook line again, jaw set.

"Ain't nothin' but a fish. Keep pullin'."

Tommy Ray hesitated, flashlight beam wavering toward the place where the shark disappeared. The light found only spray. Wind. The red smear fading into gray.

He clicked the beam off and turned the flood back to the buoys.

The skiff nosed deeper into the storm, running light over short, steep water. Behind them, the injured shark sank into the Sound's dark, her blood unwinding in steady ribbons that spread and thinned until the current took them apart.

* * *

The boat's propeller had struck ahead of the dorsal fin, carving a deep, mortal groove through cartilage and muscle.

Blood clouded the water in long, silky threads, invisible to the men above but pulsing through the current like a signal.

The shark jolted, pure reflex, but slowed almost immediately, disoriented.

Something was wrong.

The water pitched and rolled. Pressure shifted. Its body no longer obeyed. Every tailbeat overcompensated, sending it into wide, lopsided spirals.

It hadn't meant to approach the boat. Not as a predator. It had been drawn by vibration, low thumps of the outboard, the churn of a sea made unfamiliar by storm. The barometric drop, the scattered bait, the shifting tides, it was all noise.

Confusion.

The spinning prop had been another anomaly, another flicker of turbulence. Then came the strike.

Now it drifted, injured, the world tilted and blurred. For nearly an hour, it swam, not toward anything, not away.

Pain wasn't emotion. It was signal. Something had gone wrong. Instinct gave conflicting commands: Up. Forward. Down. Turn. Turn again.

A shadow passed overhead, bird or boat, it didn't matter. A dying fish drifted by, unacknowledged. The impulse to chase stirred, then faded.

Its mouth opened and closed mechanically. Gills drew water through torn slits. It swam because motion was oxygen. Because motion was life. Even as blood leaked in thick pulses, strength turning to drift.

The spirals shrank. Slowed.

Then they stopped.

Muscles slackened. Tail motionless. The body tilted nose-down. The liver, once buoyant with oil, wasn't enough.

Blood loss made it dense. Heavy.

And so it fell, alone, into the deep.

* * *

As midnight neared, Gustav gathered strength.

What had begun as a loose snarl of heat and pressure now clawed at the Outer Banks with purpose. Gusts screamed across the Atlantic shelf, shoving walls of water ahead like fists.

Pressure fell. Swells rose. The ocean gave heat and moisture, funneled upward into towering anvils of cloud. Thunder cracked, low and wide, vibrating through water and sand.

Pamlico Sound, the largest lagoon on the East Coast, bore the weight of it.

Winds tore across its surface, carving whitecaps where none should be. Inlets frothed with debris. Spray hammered the shoreline, driven by wind and tide.

Beneath it all, the bottom shifted, groaned. Sediment rose in spirals. Channels widened. Others collapsed. Sandbars formed overnight like scars.

Oyster beds shattered. Shells scattered like broken teeth. Marsh grass lay flat, pressed into the mud. Fish fled or didn't. Some were caught in the churn, flung onto roads, left gasping in ditches.

The worst never came.

A dome of high pressure to the north held steady, a quiet force that turned Gustav's path. The storm veered. It unraveled in a widening arc and raked northward instead, dragging its fury up the coast and leaving Pamlico behind.

But not untouched.

The Sound had been punched deep. Saltwater surged in from the inlets, pushing past the brackish gradient, lifting the salinity just enough to matter. The old balance, between tide and river, salt and fresh, shifted.

The change was slight. Subtle. But it moved through the system like a tremor.

Pamlico, a place of slow, patient change, had been undone in a night.

CHAPTER 6

$\mathbf{M}$orning came slow and gray.

Highway 12 stretched ahead, a narrow ribbon of asphalt winding across the Outer Banks, linking one slender barrier island to the next. It was the thread that stitched together the chain of spits and dunes, fragile land suspended between sea and sound.

After Gustav, it looked even more temporary.

Pooled water shimmered in the low shoulders. Palmetto fronds and broken branches lay tangled in the ditches. Sand, whipped into motion by the storm's outer bands, drifted across the road in thin, rippling sheets, like the islands were trying to reclaim it grain by grain.

To the east, the Atlantic rolled with leftover energy, its surface twitching under distant winds. To the west, Pamlico Sound stretched wide and glassy, the brackish water holding the soft reflection of a sky beginning to clear.

The storm had moved on. But nothing felt settled.

* * *

The world felt fresh, scoured clean by the tempest, but Ava wasn't fooled. Storms didn't simply pass; they rearranged things.

She knew this firsthand. At thirty-five, she carried the weight of too many battles, her wariness etched into the fine lines at the corners of her eyes.

She was attractive, but exhaustion dulled the edges of her beauty, the kind that once turned heads in crowded rooms. Life had sanded her down, left her raw, cautious.

She dressed in light summer clothes, a loose-fitting linen blouse, comfortable shorts, and her worn sandals. Her hair was swept into a ponytail that barely held the chaos at bay, strands already escaping to frame her tired face

In the passenger seat, Jack slouched comfortably, one sneaker propped against the dash, the other tapping a loose rhythm against the floorboard. His shaggy brown hair curled over his ears, unbothered by wind or weather.

A Nintendo Switch rested in his lap, thumbs moving with muscle memory, eyes drifting lazily between the screen and the road ahead. He didn't speak much, didn't need to. Whatever tension clung to the front seat didn't reach him.

The world still made sense in his head: games had rules, problems had solutions, and nothing ever stayed broken for long. Ava watched him out of the corner of her eye, struck by the quiet ease in his posture. He didn't know yet how quickly that could change.

The BMW X1's interior was the controlled chaos of a successful pharmaceutical salesperson, pristine on the surface, but with the quiet debris of a life spent on the road.

A stack of product brochures sat in the back seat, half-crumpled from being tossed there days ago. An empty protein bar wrapper rested in the cup holder next to an untouched bottle of water.

The leather seats still smelled new, though the floor mats bore the dust of countless rest stops. A Bluetooth headset rested in the center console, nestled beside a pair of designer sunglasses that had seen better days.

The car, like Ava, was polished but tired, always in motion, never quite at rest.

The BMW moved steadily down Highway 12, tires hissing on the wet asphalt, the storm-washed world unfolding in glints of pale sunlight and shrinking puddles.

Ava kept one hand lightly on the wheel, the other resting near the vent, fingers absently brushing the dial. She cracked the window. The air rolled in thick with salt, storm-charged and metallic, like copper and brine, heavy with ozone and something faintly green. The kind of clean that didn't last long.

They'd turned south off 64 a half hour ago, and already the land had narrowed from the long ribbon of Roanoke Island behind them to the thin barrier chain ahead.

She'd seen the sign for Corona Beach flash by as they merged, one of those small, half-forgotten places people drove past without stopping. But the name had tugged something loose in her chest.

She and Danny had driven those roads once, before Jack, before everything. Some random Saturday, no agenda. They'd cruised slow near the beach houses, those stilted fortresses stacked in soft pastels and storm shutters, half-empty in the shoulder season.

He'd guessed prices out loud, absurd numbers, usually, and she'd laughed, countering with her own fantasy figures. Million dollar views, bought on a bartender's wage and a junior pharmaceutical rep's commission.

"Someday," he'd said, serious beneath the teasing. "Maybe not all at once, but piece by piece."

Now, similar homes slid past, distant and glazed by salt mist. Tourists clustered near the driveways, kids in oversized T-shirts chasing gulls. For a second, it all felt possible again.

She exhaled softly, brushing her hair back from her temple. Life had carved that version of her down to something smaller, more efficient. She could find joy in the drive, but not in the same way. Not like when they were younger and thought the world might bend if they leaned hard enough into it.

Beside her, Jack played silently, caught up in whatever battle flickered across his screen. He had no idea what Corona Beach meant to her. No idea how many quiet little maps of "someday" his parents had drawn but left behind.

The radio crackled softly beneath the hum of the engine, static rising and falling with the road noise.

"…nine a.m. on a spectacular Saturday morning," the announcer said, voice smooth and easy. "The Outer Banks dodged a bullet last night, folks…"

Ava barely registered the voice, cheerful, rehearsed, too bright for the mood in her chest. The announcer rolled through wind speeds, high tides, and lucky breaks as Gustav barreled north, now someone else's problem. She turned the volume down, but not off. Enough to keep the silence from swallowing the car.

She adjusted the air vent and sighed.

Nine a.m. on a Saturday.

Her day off, technically. She could've slept in, maybe made it to noon without speaking to anyone. Instead, she was already halfway down Highway 12, almost an hour into a favor she hadn't offered. Jack sat beside her, humming faintly under his breath. Happy. Somehow that made it worse.

She'd half-expected the storm would wash out the trip, had even left her phone on the nightstand with the ringer on, waiting for a call that never came.

That was the knot in it. The part she didn't want to look at too closely. That maybe she wanted it to fall through. To have Danny make some excuse.

Not because she didn't want Jack to be happy, but because trusting Danny with that happiness felt like handing glass to someone with slippery hands. She didn't say that out loud. She barely admitted it to herself. But it was there, humming under the rest of it.

She didn't mind the driving. Not really. She liked the quiet in the car, the ritual of it, glancing at the fuel gauge, keeping her coffee hot enough.

What pissed her off was the principle. Danny wanted to play dad today, which was great in theory. He was all about time with his son, in that dreamy, poetic way men got when they didn't have to figure out the logistics. He wanted to take Jack fishing. Fine.

But why the hell was she the one getting up early to make it happen?

Her home in Manteo sat at the north end of Roanoke Island, close enough to the beach to smell the salt, far enough inland to be affordable. No dune views. No ocean breeze. Just gravel yards and modest rentals tucked behind tree lines.

It was close to the clinics she visited and far from the chaos of Nags Head. Her days were spreadsheets and Styrofoam coffee, most of them ending in gas stations off Route 64.

Danny lived a few streets over in a sagging two-bedroom that smelled like fryer grease and forgotten laundry. He shared it with a shift manager from the restaurant, a kid who spent his days playing Call of Duty and never opened the blinds.

Danny said it was temporary. Ava had stopped asking. The place didn't change. The curtains didn't move. She wasn't sure if the mess drifted room to room, or if it had simply settled into the walls.

Against her better judgement, she agreed to haul Jack to the marina in Cape Hatteras for a day on the water. Danny had promised to meet them there and bring him home afterward, but Ava was the one paying for the gas, the time, the sleep.

That was co-parenting, wasn't it?

One person trying to keep the pieces from rattling loose while the other played it cool.

She'd heard them in the living room a few nights back, Jack and one of his friends from school, the tall one with the braces and the messy hair. They were half-watching YouTube, half-playing some co-op shooting game and talking smack.

"My dad's taking me out Saturday," Jack said, loud enough to cut through the noise. "It's like, an actual fishing boat. Real gear and everything."

There was a beat of silence before the game swallowed them again.

Ava had paused in the hallway, one hand on the doorframe, holding a laundry basket she suddenly didn't feel like carrying.

He hadn't sounded that alive in weeks, not for her, not for school, not for anything.

And God knew she didn't have time for trips. She barely had time to meal prep, let alone orchestrate family bonding excursions.

But Jack had lit up, quietly, cautiously, like something in him still believed Danny might get it right this time.

And so here she was. Southbound. Halfway to Hatteras, bone-tired, heart-tight, trying not to resent any of it. Trying not to snap. She gripped the wheel a little harder and glanced at Jack. He stared out the window, half-smiling at nothing.

"You looking forward to this?" she asked, trying for conversation.

"Uh huh," Jack mumbled, still looking out the window.

"You ever even been fishing before?"

"Uh huh."

"My hair is on fire."

"Okay."

Ava smirked. "Liar. You're not even listening!"

Jack sighed, put his Switch in the cup holder, and turned to her. He ticked off his responses on his fingers.

"Yes, I'm looking forward to this. No, I've never been fishing before. And clearly, your hair is not on fire."

Ava huffed a laugh, "Smartass."

Jack grinned, leaning back against the seat, "I've seen it on ESPN at Dad's place. Baseball caps. Weird lures. Gross bait. Oh! Know what? I saw this on YouTube, they caught this swordfish, and it leaped onto the boat and stabbed this guy right through the frickin'..."

"Jack," Ava cut in, warning sharp but soft.

"...hand! It was epic!"

Ava watched the excitement light up his face. His mouth opened in a breathless grin, eyes wide behind smudged sunglasses. That look had been more frequent once. On a different boy. A different summer.

Before she and Danny had started arguing about everything and nothing, money, time, how tired they both always seemed. Before the edge in his voice, before her silences. Back when Jack had two parents pulling in the same direction.

She looked away, blinking at the road ahead.

"Blood was going psss psss psss," Jack continued, miming arterial spray.

Ava shook her head, but she couldn't help but smile, "And I suppose you'll be too grossed out to touch a fish?"

Jack made a face, "Obviously. There better be someone to take it off the hook. Oh... and Dad. Looking forward to seeing Dad, too. He can be the fish taker-off-er."

Silence settled between them. Outside, the dunes rose and fell, sculpted into new shapes by the storm's passage.

"I bet he'll do that," Ava said after a beat. "He does a lot for you."

She didn't mean it bitterly. Danny had a way of showing up for Jack in ways she couldn't, or maybe wouldn't. The fishing trips, the late-night movies, the little indulgences she always second-guessed.

He could bend without breaking. She had a harder time with that.

Jack's smile faded. He turned back toward the window and sighed, his breath fogging the glass.

"Marco's parents got back together. They were divorced for, like, two years. So..."

Ava eased the SUV to a stop at another light, "Yeah? Good for them. I'd say Marco's folks are the exception. Usually, divorce is pretty much, ya know, final."

Jack picked up his Switch, fingers tight around it. He stared out at the receding storm clouds, frustration etched in the slump of his shoulders.

Ava sighed, reaching over to draw a quick heart in the fogged glass.

"I heart you."

Jack exhaled, his shoulders loosening, "I heart you, too."

He turned to the action on his Switch, "And never say never."

Ava forced a smile, "I didn't say never. I said final."

Jack rolled his eyes, "Keep your eyes on the road."

"Aye, aye, Cap'n."

The light turned green, and Ava pressed the accelerator, sending them south toward the marina, toward Danny, toward the uncertain waters ahead.

CHAPTER 7

Thirty minutes later, Ava guided the BMW into the marina, rolling past the small general store, a squat building with peeling white paint and hand-painted signs advertising live bait, cold beer, and ice.

A row of crab traps leaned precariously along the side, tangled with old rope and seaweed. The wooden porch sagged slightly, its floorboards warped from years of salt air. A rusty bell jingled weakly as a customer pushed open the screen door.

The air was thick with salt and grease, heavy as a wet towel. Somewhere nearby, a fryer filled the breeze with the sharp scent of hushpuppies and old oil. Beyond the lot, the docks stretched out over the water, weathered planks lined with boats rocking gently in their slips.

Most were working boats, low-slung, open-decked rigs with winches and bait barrels, crab pots stacked in aluminum cages, masts rigged with halogen floodlights and chipped paint. Tarps flapped in the breeze. Lines creaked where they pulled taut against cleats.

Half the names were hand-painted: Miss Clara, Sea Dog, Carolina Habit. Ava scanned the transoms, looking for the name Danny had given her - Devildam.

She spotted it from a distance, long, white, a little tired looking. Parts of it gleamed under the sun, but there were streaks of something dark along the sides, like old rust or dirt.

It wasn't small. Bigger than she expected. Not beautiful. But standing its ground.

Tires crunched over gravel as she eased her BMW into a spot beside the battered Volvo Danny had somehow acquired. Up close, rust bloomed across the hood, and the side mirror sagged under a strip of duct tape.

A few other vehicles were scattered nearby. A crab-pot pickup, a sun-bleached sedan with one fogged headlight, and a F-250 that looked like it had circled the Earth many times.

The kind of lot where everything had a story, but not a single guarantee.

Jack leaned forward, squinting through the windshield.

"There's Dad's clunker," he said, nodding toward the Volvo.

If he has a car now, why the hell didn't he take Jack?

Ava shut off the engine, hands lingering on the wheel. She stared at Danny's car for a beat too long.

"Ready?" she asked without looking at him.

Jack shrugged, stuffing his phone into his pocket, "Yeah. Ready."

"Alright then," she muttered. "Let's get this over with."

CHAPTER 8

Devildam was no luxury yacht.

She was a workhorse, a charter fishing boat meant to handle long days and hard use.

The thirty-nine-foot Hatteras Convertible sat low and steady in the slip, her deep-V hull shaped to shoulder offshore chop, though the years had taken their toll. Rust freckles climbed her scuppers. The once-crisp white of her fiberglass superstructure had faded to the color of old bone.

The wheelhouse perched above the salon, a squat crown of tinted windows dulled by salt and weather. Twin diesels idled beneath the deck, their rumble more habit than power. Rod holders lined the gunwales like teeth. She could take a hit - wide-beamed, heavy through the water - but time and tide had worked their way in.

Off her stern, nestled along the port side, a small one-man dinghy rocked in the gentle marina roll, tethered to a cleat on Devildam by twenty feet of sun-bleached painter, a tough, salt-stiffened line meant to take abuse and hold fast, no matter the chop. It floated slack for now, waiting for its next trip beyond the break.

* * *

In Devildam's stateroom, the cramped cabin aft, the air was thick - fish, cheap aftershave, and something heavier, like regret ground into the walls.

Dust motes drifted through a narrow beam of light slicing in from the porthole, the only real illumination in the tight quarters. From the far bunk came the low, rhythmic growl of snoring.

A sharp knock jolted the door.

* * *

André "Kid" Sommers stood outside the stateroom door, one ear angled toward the wood, listening, not for anything in particular, just getting a read.

He was a month into twenty and carried himself like the world hadn't touched him yet. No shirt, as usual. Sweat already traced down his chest even though the sun had cleared the dock pylons only an hour ago. His hair was cropped short and clean, lined tight against his scalp, a look that suited him: precise, low-fuss, unbothered.

He moved like someone with too much energy and nowhere good to put it, pacing half-steps, shifting weight from heel to toe, fingertips tapping the doorframe in a rhythm only he knew. Built narrow and fast, all tendon and twitch, like someone who couldn't sit still through a whole sentence unless it was his.

He knocked again, not hard. Insistent.

"Rise and shine, Cap," he called through the door, voice light, like they were already mid-conversation.

"Guests are inbound."

* * *

Mick "Cap" Barton groaned and cracked one eye open. He had never been a morning person, and his body, weathered and creased from fifty-plus years of sun, salt, and whiskey, protested the sudden call to consciousness.

He reached for the small lamp bolted to the wall, flicking it on with a reluctant sigh. The light revealed a space thick with dust and history, a lifetime pressed into the walls. A triangular bunk filled most of the bow, its sheets tangled from restless sleep, the mattress worn thin by years of use.

Clothes sagged from hooks, faded fishing shirts, oil-stained jeans, one clean pair of cargo shorts set apart. On the bulkhead, an old brass clock sat broken and silent, its hands fixed on a moment that no longer counted.

Nautical charts, yellowed and curled at the edges, were pinned haphazardly above the bunk, their ink smudged from too many damp nights. A rust-stained sink jutted from one corner, its faucet dripping slowly, the sound rhythmic against the hush of the cabin.

Among the clutter lay things that had outlived their usefulness - a rusted marlin hook, a dented Zippo, Polaroids curling at the corners. A picture frame rested face down on a shelf, dust gathered thick on its back. Cap knew what was beneath it. He hadn't looked in years.

He swung his legs over the bunk and planted his feet on the floor, one hand bracing against the low ceiling for balance. His back cracked in a slow, uneven ripple as he straightened, joints stiff from bad posture and too many nights on the thin cushions.

Dressed in a pair of ratty boxers, he shuffled toward the rust-streaked mini-fridge beside the sink. Inside, the shelves were jammed with beer bottles, a forgotten Tupperware container of something he wouldn't dare open, and an ever-present carton of milk. He grabbed the milk, set it on the counter, then turned his attention to the mirror above the sink.

His reflection held a face thinned by weather and work. Lines cut deep at the mouth and eyes; his hair had gone sparse in uneven patches, gray winning where brown still clung. The eyes hadn't changed. Still sharp. Still measuring. Only now they carried a fatigue he didn't remember earning.

He opened the medicine cabinet. Alongside a rusted razor and a half-used tube of toothpaste sat two neat rows of cancer drugs. Tarceva. Roxicodone. Others he barely glanced at anymore.

His routine was mechanical. He shook the bottles, counted by sound, tipped the pills into his palm. No hesitation. No thinking.

He uncapped the milk, lifted the cup, and tipped the pills into his mouth in a single motion. A long gulp from the carton chased the bitterness down. He wiped his upper lip with the back of his hand, erasing the milk mustache.

"Alright, then."

Another knock.

"Cap?" came Kid's muffled voice.

"Ayuh. I'm up. I'm up. We do okay with that storm?"

Cap blinked against the cabin's dim light, scratching at the side of his jaw. He tried to piece together the storm's passage, hadn't felt like much. Some rocking, maybe, the boat nudging at the fenders. A few cracks of thunder in the night, nothing more. In a world where weather came and went like mood swings, it hardly registered. He'd ridden out worse without getting out of bed.

"Boat's good," came Kid's muffled voice. "Should be a go for today."

He opened the faucet and splashed cold water on his face. It did little to wake him, but he did it anyway. Routines mattered, even when life had taken on a shape that didn't quite fit anymore.

From the other side of the door –

"Cap? Charlie at the marina wanted me to pass a message..."

Cap grunted, "Ayuh?"

"He told me to tell you he's done askin' nice 'bout you sleepin' on the boat. Says it's not allowed."

Cap snorted, rubbing a hand through his stringy, patchy hair.

"Ayup. Thanks for the message, Kid. Tell Charlie this."

Cap threw a one-fingered salute at the closed door.

"Are you flippin' him the bird?"

"Ayup. Loud and proud. Kid? Coffee, if you will?"

"You got it, Cap."

Kids' footsteps faded as he went to fetch coffee and deliver Cap's message to Charlie. Cap sighed and looked around his cramped, familiar domain. His eyes landed on the photo wedged in the corner of the mirror - Abby, newborn and wrinkled, fists balled tight, eyes shut against the world.

Fourteen, maybe fifteen by now. He hadn't seen her in over a year. He'd take anything - a photo, a voicemail, some sign she was still out there.

Another day. Another fight to hold onto what was his.

He looked at himself in the mirror—older than he felt, but not done yet.

"Alright, Mick," he muttered. "Don't fuck this up."

CHAPTER 9

Ava popped the door to the BMW open, the thick, post-storm heat rushing in before she even stepped out.

Jack was already moving, circling the SUV, his tennis shoes shuffling through the gravel.

The marina had settled into its after-storm rhythm, diesel and salt hanging in the air, water slapping the pilings in a steady, unbothered cadence. Above it all, the sky had cleared to a hard blue that felt more exposing than calm.

Jack bounced on his heels while she locked the car, shifting from foot to foot like he could barely contain himself. His T-shirt hung loose over his swim trunks, the cotton sun-bleached and thin from too many tides, too many summers. His eyes scanned the docks, already hunting for the boat.

A gull dipped low, and Ava reflexively ducked, swatting the air with a sharp exhale as the bird flapped off with a complaining squawk. It circled once, then landed on a nearby piling, eyeing her like it was weighing its odds.

She rolled her eyes, brushing off her shorts.

"The birds love your mom," she muttered.

Jack laughed softly. They started down the dock towards Devildam, passing old crab boats and weather-beaten center consoles.

"Remember when me, you, and Dad were at SeaWorld for my birthday? And that one gull came down and stole his ice cream?" he asked with a grin.

She smiled, the warmth of it catching her off guard. Danny had stepped away from the bench, cone in hand, mint chocolate chip, when the gull dive-bombed from nowhere, snatching the scoop clean off before he could react.

All that was left was a soggy waffle shell and Danny's stunned expression. The bird flapped off in triumph, green ice cream trailing from its beak.

Jack had nearly fallen over laughing, and Ava had been too caught up in the moment to do anything but join in. It had been effortless, one of those rare, golden slivers of time when they all felt like a real team.

Jack's grin widened, "That was a fun day."

"Yeah," she admitted, glancing toward the boat. "It was."

They arrived at Devildam as Kid emerged from the cabin holding a steaming pot of coffee. His skin glistened in the sun and a wide, easy smile broke across his face as he spotted them.

"Charter for the Kealy party, right? Come aboard!"

He extended a hand, first to Ava, then to Jack, helping them through the open transom door and onto the back deck with a strength that didn't match his wiry frame.

The surface beneath their feet had the worn, sun-bleached look of a boat that had seen years of hard fishing. The non-slip coating had chipped away in spots, revealing the raw fiberglass beneath. Coiled ropes lay near the rail, frayed in places but serviceable. Rust-streaked rod holders lined the stern, a few of them already loaded with poles ready for the day's catch.

A large, weather-beaten cooler sat near the bait station, the lid slightly ajar, revealing melting ice and the faint scent of the last catch. A cutting board, its surface deeply scarred from years of filleting, was bolted beside a bucket half-filled with water.

A tangle of faded orange life jackets and rain gear hung from hooks near the salon entrance, stiff with dried salt and neglect.

"My name's Kid," he said, setting the coffee pot on a side table. "Jack of all trades, master of none."

Ava smirked, nudging Jack, "Hey, just like you."

Jack rolled his eyes but grinned anyway.

Kid laughed, "The others are in the salon. Fresh coffee. You in?"

"Like... the hair salon?" Jack asked, brow furrowed.

Kid grinned, "Nah, man, boat salon."

He pointed toward the cabin, "That's the living room, basically.

Where everyone hangs out."

Jack nodded slowly, piecing it together.

"Alright, quick lesson," Kid said, turning and pointing as he spoke.

"Salon's in there. The living room. Bow's the front. Stern's the back. Port is left, starboard's right."

He jerked a thumb toward the rear of the boat, "That flat part at the very back? That's the transom."

Jack's head tilted as he took it all in.

"And this railing?" Kid rapped his knuckles against the edge.

"This is called the gunwale. Spelled like 'gun-wale,' but pronounced 'gunnel.' Because boat people like to mess with you."

Jack cracked a smile, "Seriously?"

Kid nodded, deadpan, "Dead serious. Makes you sound smarter, though. 'Grab the gunnel' sounds like you've been doing this your whole life."

Jack laughed and nodded, "Okay. That one's gonna take practice."

"You'll get it," Kid said, opening the door to the salon. "Stick with me."

Through the salon window, Ava caught a glimpse of movement, shadows shifting in the dim light. One leaned over a table, another sat against the bulkhead with a mug in their hand, steam rising in slow spirals.

She caught fragments of conversation, the muted thrum of early morning. And then she saw him. Danny. Standing near the kitchenette. Eyes locked on her through the glass.

* * *

What's she doing here?

Danny stood just inside the salon, watching Ava on the back deck through the glass. The reflection caught her first, light flaring off the window, her shape doubled for a moment, then resolved into her standing there like she belonged, Jack hovering at her side.

She could've dropped him off and kept driving. But no. She'd walked him all the way down the dock. Planted herself where Danny would have to see her.

The salon pressed in around him, familiar and suddenly too small. Low ceiling. Narrow beam. The slow, restless roll of a boat that had spent most of its life offshore. Vinyl benches hugged the port and starboard walls, their cushions cracked, foam peeking through split seams.

Between them sat the folding table, nicked and stained from a hundred spilled coffees and late hands of cards.

Ava had always done this, waited, let the silence stretch, then placed the truth where it couldn't be ignored.

Like at the school open house last month. Jack's math teacher had cleared her throat, flipped through a folder, said something about concerns. Danny had waved it off, easy, confident, said Jack was fine. Probably bored.

Ava had waited. Long enough for the room to shift. Then she reached into her bag and laid the printout on the desk. His most recent test. Fifty-three percent.

"He's a grade level behind," she'd said. "We're getting a tutor."

Not sharp. Not angry. Final.

Danny had nodded, folded his hands, like agreement was the same thing as being right. Now the salon felt cluttered with that same quiet judgment. Cheap beige marine carpet lay matted flat underfoot, darkened where boots crossed most often. A flush-mounted hatch sat aft of the table, centered between the benches, its edges worn smooth by years of scuffing. Beneath it, the twin diesels idled, felt more than heard.

It was the kind of room where sound carried and privacy never quite held. You ate there. Slept there when you had to. Waited out squalls. Told the same stories again because there was nowhere else to put them. It worked. Most days.

The air smelled the way it always did: diesel, old salt, fish ground into the floor, mildew that never quite left no matter how many air fresheners the owner sprayed. A small galley crouched in the aft corner, rust-streaked microwave, compact fridge, a two-burner stove with one knob missing. Cabinets ticked softly with the boat's motion.

Danny felt the pressure build behind his ribs. The instinct to brace. With Ava, it was never volume. It was precision. And he always felt it a second too late.

He managed a Kealy's Crab Shack, long hours, short pay, grease that clung no matter how many times he washed. It wasn't what he'd pictured for himself. But it paid the rent. Kept the lights on. Gave him something solid to do with his hands.

Still, the doubt had been there even before things fell apart. Ava, moving forward, sales calls, regional meetings, ironed blouses. Danny, standing still. He told himself he was the anchor. Lately, he wasn't sure if that meant steady or just heavy.

Rod holders lined the trim, some newer than others. A small flat-screen TV was bolted above the forward bulkhead, outdated and mostly useless unless the boat was docked and lucky. The paneling, faux cherry veneer from the late '90s, had warped with salt and time, holding onto more stories than anyone bothered to tell straight anymore.

A narrow stair split the forward bulkhead: up to the wheelhouse, down to Cap's berth. Both steep. Both poorly lit. At the bottom of the lower stairs sat the head, barely wide enough to turn around in, rust freckling the faucet, the curtain never quite closing right.

Through the glass, Ava shifted her weight and looked straight at him. Divorce hadn't come yet. Not officially. But it hung there, thick as humidity after a storm, making everything harder than it needed to be. Some days they barely spoke. Other days they were careful in ways that felt worse.

The room gave him nowhere to go.

* * *

"No, thanks," Ava said, declining the coffee from Kid.
She forced her gaze away from Danny. "I've gotta get going."

Kid gave her a nod and headed for the salon as the door creaked open and Shel Clarke stepped out onto the back deck, blinking against the glare.

"Coffee run?" he asked, nudging Kid with his elbow as they passed.

"Already did the heavy lifting," Kid said, grinning. "You're late."

Shel laughed, low and easy. He moved like someone who never quite settled in one place, always shifting, always halfway on the way to somewhere else.

People liked Shel. He had a way of sanding down the awkward edges in a room, turning tension into a laugh before it had time to settle. Maybe it was all the years of learning how to blend in— growing up the only Black kid in his neighborhood, his school, sometimes in an entire town.

It taught him how to read a room fast. How to make himself easier to like, even if most people never looked past the surface.

He worked tables at Kealy's Crab Shack, saved what little he could, and dreamed of something bigger. Cities with noise. Skylines that didn't end in pine trees. His sketchbook was never far. The pages were a mix: goofy caricatures of crab shack regulars, quick studies of strangers on buses, and the ones he didn't show, inked shadows, jagged skylines, people lost in crowds they couldn't escape.

Fishing didn't mean much to him. This trip wasn't about that. It was about being somewhere else, even for a weekend. About being with people who didn't ask too many questions. Having a laugh. Taking a break.

He and Kid had clicked early, two college kids, two Black men in a town that didn't offer much room for either. The rest didn't need explaining. It showed in the looks they traded when someone crossed a line, the way their jokes landed without setup, like they'd been running the same rhythm for years.

On the boat, it settled fast, Kid playing it cool, Shel turning everything into a bit. It worked. Out here, Shel wasn't just another server at Kealy's. He wasn't a punchline or someone trying to make rent one crab cake at a time.

He was here. Breathing. Wearing one of the shack's T-shirts - *If you're gonna get crabs, get the best at Kealy's!* - and grinning like he actually meant it. All energy. All charm. The kind of presence that filled space without trying.

"Hey, Ava! Hey, Jackie! My man," Shel called, flashing a grin as he threw Jack a quick salute. "We gonna fish today or what?"

Jack smirked, "We're here, aren't we?"

Ava chuckled, "Lookin' good, Shel. This all about you?"

Shel puffed out his chest, playing it up, "Well, me, Danny, and the shack. Top sales for the quarter, baby. Management said we earned it."

Ava raised an eyebrow, impressed despite herself, "Yeah? That's great. Enjoy your reward."

She nodded toward the cabin, "Do me a favor? Tell Danny to give me a call when he's fifteen minutes out with Jack? I need time to get my act together."

Shel hesitated. A quick glance at Jack, "Sure thing. And hey… I mean, I know things are kinda…"

He glanced toward the salon, then back at Ava, measuring his words, "…different now, but I hope it's not, like, all different. Y'know?"

Ava's smile was small, careful, "Just because Danny and I are figuring things out doesn't mean everything has to shift."

Shel nodded quickly, like he was relieved, "Good. Good. 'Cause I like having you in the orbit."

He slung an arm around Jack's shoulder, "And this one, Jackie-boy here? He's gonna bring you back a full cooler. Trout. Bass. Swordfish. Maybe a mermaid."

Jack laughed, "You know those first two are freshwater, right?"

Shel waved him off, "Details."

Ava gave them both a last smile, then stepped carefully from Devildam to the dock, her sandals whispering over the sun bleached planks. The boat shifted under her weight and did not quite settle again.

CHAPTER 10

Ava slid into her BMW, exhaling sharply as she shut the door behind her.

Heat rushed up around her, air trapped too long against leather and glass, the faint bite of hot plastic and sun baked upholstery catching in her throat.

She tossed her bag onto the passenger seat, turned the key, and braced for the now-familiar hesitation.

The engine coughed. Chugged. Then stopped.

She froze. Tried again.

The dashboard lights blinked to life, stuttering like a drunk waking up, then dimmed again. The starter gave a half-hearted whine and fell quiet.

"Don't do this," she muttered, gripping the key harder, as if pressure could will the thing to cooperate. "Not now."

She'd been meaning to get it looked at for weeks. There'd been warning signs, a sputter on cold mornings, a strange vibration in idle, one afternoon where the dash had gone totally black before flickering back to life.

But there hadn't been time. She was always five minutes late to something: picking up Jack, returning a call, chasing down one more client.

And now here she was, in a ninety-degree car, on a dock, with no one around she wanted to ask for help.

She turned the key again, "C'mon, c'mon..."

The engine sputtered, gave a final weak guh-guh-guh, then died like it had made up its mind to embarrass her. The silence that followed was loud.

Heavy.

The kind that pulled the breath from her lungs.

Heat gathered around her, thick and close. Sweat slicked the back of her neck. She slammed her hand against the steering wheel.

The horn squeaked, a pitiful, off-key meep that made it all feel worse, like the car was mocking her now.

"FUCK YOU!" she snapped, louder than she meant to, voice sharp in the confined space.

Her head fell back against the headrest with a dull thud, eyes on the ceiling, blinking back the sting of angry tears.

This was not how the day was supposed to go.

Not here.

Not in front of him.

CHAPTER 11

Larry and Colleen Kealy sat near the windows on the salon's port side bench, tucked against the curve of the wall beside the small kitchenette.

Colleen had turned herself slightly toward the light, one leg crossed neatly over the other, white shorts crisp against the vinyl cushion. A yellow one-piece showed at the hip, the collar of a pastel blouse slipping off one shoulder.

Even indoors, she kept her white wide-brimmed sun hat tilted low, the nylon tether of her red star-shaped sunglasses looped lazily around her neck.

She held a sweating can of Diet Coke in one hand, fingers wet with condensation, gaze soft and unreadable beneath the brim.

Larry nursed a Bloody Mary, stirring it lazily with a rubbery celery stalk, the rim of his glass dusted with Old Bay.

"Pace yourself, love," Colleen murmured, giving his forearm a light tap without taking her eyes off the water beyond the window.

Larry grinned and took a slower sip, unbothered, "First one doesn't count"

They'd built their little empire from a single roadside crab shack, picnic tables, paper-lined baskets, a chalkboard menu that changed with the catch.

Larry worked the kitchen, cracking jokes between orders, while Colleen ran the front like a general in flip-flops.

Over the years it grew, one location, then two, then more, until the business began to run itself and they could finally enjoy what it had bought them.

Larry leaned back now with the ease of a man who'd paid his dues. Portly, pink-cheeked, always grinning.

A soft-brimmed Panama hat shaded his face; a sun-faded Tommy Bahama shirt hung open at the collar. Flip-flops. Cargo shorts.

Bloody Mary within reach. Leisure fit him. He didn't take much seriously - except Colleen.

They'd met in the late '80s, when Larry bounced between handyman work and hauling crab traps for cash, and Colleen pulled double shifts at the front desk of the First Colony Inn in Nags Head.

It hadn't been love at first sight so much as rhythm. Shared sarcasm. Cheap beer. Neither of them good at faking a laugh, both of them drawn to the real thing.

That rhythm turned into a business - Kealy's Crab Shack - and then a life. The kind of partnership people noticed without always knowing why.

Colleen was the anchor; Larry the sail. Even now, decades in, the ease between them showed in the quiet glances, the easy jabs, the way they passed drinks without needing to speak.

Jack sat beside Colleen, sipping iced tea from a can, the straw bent at the top. He rocked with the boat's motion, one leg swinging off the bench, absent-minded and content.

Danny crouched in front of the fridge, pushing aside a six-pack of Busch and an old lemon to grab a Coke.

Footsteps approached from the deck. He glanced over his shoulder as Shel stepped back inside.

"Thought Tish was coming with you?" Danny said, straightening.

Tish, nineteen, pretty, sharp around the edges. A summer girl running hot on caffeine and impulse, splitting time between waitressing at Kealy's and chasing whatever felt fun. Danny had assumed she'd be at Shel's side for this trip.

Shel shook his head, "She bailed. Rough night. Said she needed to recover."

Larry perked up, "Tish? Our Tish? The waitress? A girl? A real girl?"

Colleen swatted his arm. Automatic. No heat behind it. Larry grinned.

Danny took his seat. The mood in the salon had lightened, voices low, laughter curling up in pockets. The kind of easy rhythm that came once the drinks were poured and the morning haze had worn off.

And then a shift, not loud, not sudden, but real. A subtle hush, like someone had turned down the volume without warning. Movement at the door caught in the corner of Danny's eye. Heads turned, voices trailed off.

A shadow stretched across the companionway, long and familiar. Danny looked up before anyone spoke.

He didn't need to guess.

"Hey, Mama!" Jack called out.

Ava stood in the doorway, one arm crossed, the other hanging loose at her side, fingers smudged with grease. There was a streak of dirt across her white linen blouse under her ribs, like she'd leaned into something she hadn't planned to.

Her hair was windblown, jaw set, eyes locked on him. Whatever talk had been bubbling in the room died off in an instant.

Danny felt his jaw tighten.

She hadn't come to chat. He could see it in her stance, rigid, simmering.

Whatever had happened before she walked in, she'd brought the weight of it with her.

"Got a minute?"

* * *

Danny followed her onto the back deck, keeping a few steps behind. The sun caught the edge of the railing, flashing off the water.

He kept his expression neutral, but his pulse had picked up.

"It won't start," Ava said, not looking at him.

He already knew what she meant, "The BMW?"

She looked down at the grease on her hands, then noticed the smudge across her shirt.

"Jesus," she muttered, annoyed. "It was fine on the way here. And yes, it has gas."

Danny let out a slow breath, forcing down the bite in his throat, "Well, I guess being on your own comes with perks like that."

Her eyes narrowed, "Why did I have to bring him?"

Danny blinked, "Jack?"

"Yeah. Why is it always me doing the early mornings? The gas. The mileage. You live like two blocks from the house."

He shifted, hands on the rail, "Because I was in New Bern."

She frowned, "What?"

"Last night. It's a three-hour drive, Ava. I took Shel down there, his mom just got diagnosed. Stage four pancreatic. He doesn't have a car, and he wanted to be there right after she got the news. I waited while they talked. By the time it was all said and done, it was one a.m., and we crashed at his cousin's place."

Ava said nothing, but he could see her wheels spinning.

"I was going to cancel this morning," he added. "I was wiped. But Shel said it might be good to get out, blow off steam, have some laughs. So, we drove straight here from New Bern. Didn't even go home first."

A long beat passed.

"You could've led with that," she said.

"You could've asked," he said quietly.

The silence between them thickened—familiar, layered, unsaid. Neither of them budged.

* * *

From inside, Shel kept an eye on them through the window. He couldn't hear the words, but the body language said enough, Ava's arms crossed tight, Danny stiff as a board, both of them locked in a familiar, silent standoff.

He glanced at Jack, who was watching too, his face tense, brow pinched enough to betray how much he hated seeing it.

That look, the kind kids wear when they've seen their parents argue before and already know how it ends.

Shel looked away, gave the kid a little more space than he

probably wanted. Some things you weren't supposed to witness twice.

* * *

Danny huffed a humorless laugh, "I told you not to buy the Beemer. Remember? But no, you had to have it, your image, right? I said sexy, but not reliable, didn't I?"

Ava's eyes narrowed, "Sure. Like you."

Danny's jaw tensed, "Whatever. Look, I'm going to tell you, no, suggest, what to do. If you call it mansplaining, I swear to God, I'm done. Capisce?"

Ava let out a sigh, "Fine. Go ahead."

Danny nodded, "Go back to the marina office. Tell them your car's dead. They'll know a mechanic. Call him. Get it towed-"

The salon door creaked open behind them.

Shel stepped onto the deck, Jack close at his side. The timing was too neat to be accidental.

"Hey, hey," Shel said lightly, too casually. "What's the word?"

Danny ran a hand down his face, "Car won't start."

Shel nodded, "Right. Well, hey, isn't there a mechanic….?"

"I'm aware," Ava cut in. "Plenty of mechanics. But I'm the one stuck sitting on my ass all day waiting for one."

Jack spoke up, tentative but hopeful, "Maybe you could rent a car?"

Danny's face lit up, "That's my boy! Rent a car."

Ava rubbed her temples, "Sure, bub. Solid idea. But then what? Drive home? And come all the way back when the car's fixed? And then back home? That's a lot of driving."

Shel threw up his hands, "Okay, okay, new idea. Tish couldn't make it. There's an open spot. So, get the Beemer towed… and come with us."

Danny exhaled sharply.

Jack's face changed at once, shoulders lifting, eyes brightening, the careful set of his mouth giving way to something open.

Danny saw how fast the hope came back, how badly Jack wanted this to feel normal.

"Yeah!" Jack beamed. "Family time!"

Shel grinned, "By the time we get back, the good Lord willing, the Beemer's fixed. Everyone wins."

Danny shot Shel a look.

Not everyone.

CHAPTER 12

The marina store smelled of sunscreen and stale beer, mixing with the faint, lingering musk of fish guts from the morning's bait deliveries.

Fluorescent lights buzzed faintly overhead, their glow casting everything in a dull yellow hue. The walls were lined with racks of lures, spools of fishing line, and stacks of magazines featuring grinning men holding up record-breaking catches.

At the counter, Charlie, the marina manager, sat wedged onto a stool too small for his broad frame. Fifty, balding, and built like a man who'd spent more time behind a desk than on the water, he used to run charters out of Ocracoke before a blown-out knee and a second divorce put him behind the counter.

Now he nursed a Styrofoam cup of bad coffee while his eyes stayed glued to the small TV perched on the counter cluttered with impulse-buy trinkets. The screen flickered with breaking news footage, the colors too bright, the audio slightly garbled by interference.

Ava walked past, sandals whispering against the dusty linoleum.

Charlie glanced at her, "You see this?"

She ignored him, barely giving the screen a glance as she made her way deeper into the store, past the racks of lures and tackle boxes, past the overflowing coolers packed with domestic beer and energy drinks.

The place had the look of a shop that hadn't changed in decades - worn shelves, faded price stickers, and a spinning wire rack crammed with postcards no one had bought in years.

* * *

On the television screen, Owen Dyer stood at the edge of the marina dock, shoulders hunched against the wind, his shirt plastered to his ribs. He faced the camera but didn't seem to see it. His eyes were red-rimmed, his jaw set hard, as if bracing against something unseen. The wind teased loose strands of hair across his face.

He didn't move to brush them away.

The chyron beneath him read:

SHARK EXPERT OWEN DYER SPEAKS AFTER DEADLY ENCOUNTER OFF OUTER BANKS.

Gone was the figure who had stood on the rail of Aquavantis, steady over the rising shark, issuing commands in a voice that cut through the storm.

The man on the dock looked stripped down to the bone, haunted, as though part of him was still out there on the platform, hearing the groan of steel and the slap of waves, watching the wrong kind of blood cloud the water.

His first words broke, "I mean…Christ."

He dropped his gaze, shook his head once, and tried again, "Give me a second."

When he looked up, his eyes had the distant focus of someone running footage in their mind.

"Johnny Cotton, our videographer, and my friend, succumbed to his injuries late last night. He passed away surrounded by people who loved him, after being bitten by the shark we were there to study."

The mic caught the groan of mooring lines, the slap of water against the pilings.

"Johnny had been with me from the start," Owen went on. "First one I ever trusted to stand that close on a platform. He didn't flinch when the weather turned or when the water boiled under us. He kept rolling, even when the spray hit his lens. He understood what we were trying to do out there."

His voice faltered on the last word.

"There's something in these waters," he said finally, quieter now.

He turned toward someone off-camera, sharp, reflexive, then back again.

"I used to think sharks were… misunderstood," he said. "That most of what we blamed on them was us."

He stopped. Swallowed.

"After today," he said, and shook his head once, "I don't know."

* * *

Ava passed a rack of thin T-shirts with faded, goofy slogans - *Bite Me, I Like Big Boats and I Cannot Lie, Reel Men Bait Their Own Hooks* - before stopping at the swimsuit section. The selection was sparse, clearly an afterthought in a store that catered more to fishermen than sunbathers.

Ava's fingers brushed over the fabric of a navy-blue one-piece, a practical choice. Sensible. Modest.

She hesitated.

Then she reached for something else, a white two-piece, simple and understated. Not modest, but not flashy, either. It felt like a choice she wouldn't have made a year ago. Maybe not even a month ago.

It seemed slightly out of step with the rest of the store, a quiet find in a place cluttered with kitschy souvenirs and weathered fishing gear. It came with a white cover-up, thin and a little cheap, with a drawstring tie at the waist and enough fabric to catch the breeze.

She took a breath, then slung it over her arm, turning for the register.

As she walked, a thought crept in, *What would Danny think if she showed up in this? Would he even notice? Would he care?*

The idea sent a strange mix of satisfaction and uncertainty through her, a reminder that some things between them were still unsettled, no matter how much she tried to push forward.

* * *

Behind the counter, Charlie barely looked up from the flickering TV.

"Cash or credit?"

"Credit."

She placed the white swimsuit and cover-up on the counter and slid her card across. The fabric looked out of place against the scuffed laminate, shrink-wrapped lures, and a half-empty cigar box that smelled like motor oil.

Charlie swiped it slowly, eyes already drifting back to the screen where Dana Whitmore, the local OBX News anchor, read from the teleprompter with practiced calm. Blonde, tight blazer, no emotion.

"…That was Owen Dyer, speaking earlier today from the docks in Morehead City," she said. "In the wake of yesterday's fatal shark incident, researchers are urging continued caution."

Charlie slid her card back.

"You headin' out today?" he asked, thumb tapping the register. "Might wanna keep them toes in the boat."

Ava tucked the card into her wallet, grabbed the suit, and gave him a tight-lipped smile, "I'll keep that in mind."

She pushed through the door.

The bell jingled overhead, light and out of place.

CHAPTER 13

Greg Turner steered his Jeep Wrangler through the quiet streets of downtown Hatteras, the village still shaking off the last brush with the storm.

Donnie sat strapped into his booster seat beside him—four years old, all knees and questions, his SpongeBob bathing suit still damp from the hotel pool.

Marie, Donnie's mom, was back in Nags Head, covering a shift she couldn't get out of. Greg had offered to take Donnie for the day. Just the two of them.

Hatteras stretched thin and exposed, a strip of land never quite at ease with the water pressing in on both sides. The island was little more than sand stitched together with sea oats and two-lane blacktop. Highway 12 threaded its way along the spine, bending where it had to, disappearing where storms had already claimed it once before.

Out one window, the Atlantic rolled and darkened as it fell away from shore. Out the other, the Sound lay flatter and more deceptive, water that looked harmless until it wasn't.

The town itself was little more than a clutch of buildings tucked behind the dunes - fishing charters, tackle shops, a gas station, a post office with irregular hours.

The Graveyard of the Atlantic Museum stood at the edge of town, a low-slung building filled with stories of shipwrecks and lost radio signals. The ferry terminal sat down the road, where boats crossed to Ocracoke on days the wind cooperated.

Pickup trucks outnumbered sedans. Locals knew each other by the shape of their boats and the sound of their dogs.

In summer, tourists came in droves, hauling kayaks and coolers and sand-caked kids.

In winter, the island exhaled, emptied out until only the year-rounders remained, watching weather fronts stack up offshore.

There was no hospital. No real police presence. When something bad happened, help came late, if at all. Bad storms didn't just knock out power, they cut the island off. Ferries stopped. The road vanished beneath the tide.

Isolation wasn't a feature; it was a fact. Gustav had come close, too close for comfort but it had veered enough to be called a near miss. Signs of the storm were everywhere. Shop windows were shuttered, some boarded up as a precaution. Sand dusted the sidewalks in uneven drifts, and palm fronds lay curled in gutters like discarded green flags. The air smelled of salt and wet wood, everything soaked but intact.

Greg and Donny passed the marina on the way out, a few slips stood empty, boats hauled inland or trailered the day before. Most were still there, rocking gently in their berths, lines drawn tight, hulls streaked with rain. One charter boat sat deeper than the rest, wide-beamed and scuffed, her transom low in the water like she'd taken the weather on the chin and stayed put.

You could feel it in the town, not panic, just the long exhale of people who knew it could've been worse.

He turned off Highway 12 and onto Pole Road, the sand-packed track that ran for two miles before dead-ending at the southwest point of Hatteras Island. The Jeep bumped along the rutted path, flanked by low brush and the occasional leaning pole that gave the road its name.

Greg had spent half his childhood out here, fishing with his father, watching the Atlantic slam into Pamlico Sound at the island's wild, windswept southern point.

Now he wanted to show it to his own son, let Donnie feel that same sense of scale and wonder. Something real. Something they could both carry.

They hadn't seen another vehicle since leaving town. Debris from the storm was scattered across the dunes, torn fencing, broken limbs, and seaweed twisted in the brush.

* * *

They reached the end of Pole Road a few minutes later, where the dunes thinned and the land gave way to sand and sky and not much else. Greg eased the Jeep onto a flat stretch near the sign, the same one that had stood since he was a boy, maybe longer.

The dunes here were worn low, wind-sheared and patchy, held together by salt-stiffened grass and scattered shells. Beyond them, the beach opened wide, flat and bleached, the sand packed hard from tide and tire, littered with driftwood, bait cups, and the occasional chunk of coral washed in from the bar.

The surf broke beyond the slope, not in neat rows but in ragged pulses, like it hadn't decided whether to come in or stay out. Foam crept up the beach in fingers, then vanished, leaving a shimmer of wet sand behind.

There were no umbrellas, no footprints, no signs of anything that hadn't come from wind or water.

Greg cut the engine and listened to it all, the hiss of the surf, the rustle of dune grass, the old Jeep ticking in the heat.

The post leaned slightly now, its wood sun-bleached and crusted with barnacles near the base. The lettering had faded to soft gray:

THIS IS WHERE
THE ATLANTIC OCEAN
MEETS PAMLICO SOUND

The weathered sign still stood at the edge of the beach, holding its ground while the water kept its distance. Beyond it, offshore, the surface changed, open ocean pushing in from one side, the Sound spreading flatter from the other, currents crossing where the land finally gave up its say.

"We're here," Greg said to Donnie.

Donnie craned his neck, peering through the windshield, "This it?"

Greg smiled, "This is it."

They climbed out. Greg popped the back of the Jeep, grabbing a towel, a water bottle, and the small nylon bag Donnie insisted on packing himself, mostly snacks and mismatched toys. The boy scrambled down barefoot, his sandals forgotten somewhere in the backseat, and planted himself in the sand with a grin.

Greg took a moment to breathe. The wind tugged at his shirt, and the air smelled like everything he remembered: sea spray, sun-warmed dunes, and the electric edge of the ocean, vast and unending.

A few hundred yards down, a lone fisherman cast into the surf, the rhythmic flick of his rod the only signs of life.

Greg slung the nylon bag over one shoulder and reached for his phone as Donnie wandered toward the sign, already ankle-deep in dry sand. The boy stopped at the base of the post, tilting his head to look up at the faded lettering. His curls bounced in the breeze, his SpongeBob trunks sagging far enough to make Greg smile.

"Alright, bud," Greg called. "Stand by the sign. Lemme grab a picture."

Donnie turned, squinting into the morning sun, "Like this?"

He jabbed a finger at the post itself.

Greg lowered the phone, shaking his head gently, "No, higher. Point at the sign. The letters. Not the post."

Donnie frowned, then lifted his arm, finger wobbling upward until it landed roughly in the right zone. His face lit up with a too-big grin, and Greg raised the phone.

He snapped a few quick shots, then a few more, adjusting his angle, backing up a step, catching the surf in the distance. Donnie's smile shifted from real to forced and back again as he fidgeted in place.

Greg scrolled through the photos, thumb flicking side to side. One had too much glare. Another had Donnie blinking. In the next, his arm was too low again. Greg sighed, tapped on the screen, adjusted the brightness - lost, for the moment, in the familiar compulsion to get it exactly right.

* * *

Behind him, the ocean whispered. Donnie took a step back from the sign. Then another.

He tore across the sand, the soft grains slipping under his feet, cool and wet near the edge where the ocean reached. He ran like he always did - like the world was made for running.

No hesitation.

No looking back.

The wind rushed past his ears, the surf roared ahead, and when he hit the foamy edge of the water, he let out a squeal that echoed down the empty shoreline. Salt stung his ankles. His SpongeBob trunks clung to his legs. He kicked at the surf, stomped through the swirls of white foam, laughing as each wave chased him and then pulled away.

He crouched down, fingers skimming the wet sand. Bubbles popped. Bits of seaweed twirled past. A shell, half-buried, glinted in the sun. Then something darker caught his eye.

Twenty yards offshore, a tall, triangular black fin sliced cleanly through the water, drifting from left to right in a slow, deliberate glide. Donnie squinted.

A light blinked from a device attached to the base of the fin, red, steady. On. Off. On again. The surf rolled, lifting and shifting, and for a moment he saw more than the fin.

He saw the creature's back, broad, grey, and scarred, moving beneath the surface. Then the water sloshed back down and it vanished.

He took a step forward. Then another. The cool water climbed to his calves, then his knees, suddenly, sharply, it was mid-thigh. His breath hitched, but he didn't turn back. His eyes stayed fixed on the spot where the fin had been.

A hand touched the top of his head.

Donnie jumped.

"Hey," Greg said, crouching beside him. "Don't wander off like that, bud. You scared me."

Donnie pointed toward the water, wide-eyed, "Tark!"

Greg looked, squinting into the bright waterline.

But the ocean was empty now. Restless waves and a shifting horizon.

"Tark," Donnie said again, more insistent.

Greg gave his shoulder a gentle squeeze, "Maybe. Let's stay close to shore, okay?"

Donnie didn't answer. He kept watching the water, waiting.

At four, his ability to create and track thoughts was rudimentary. But he knew what he saw.

Tark.

* * *

The current shifted.

Judy veered slightly, her broad head angling into the pull, muscles rippling in fluid sequence. Water pressed along her flanks, familiar and vast, the endless breath of the Atlantic. But now, something changed. A seam in the sea. She didn't know it as a line, but she felt it.

The salinity dropped.

The water grew heavier, thicker in her mouth. She tasted it with her gills, with the soft pressure across her skin, with the ancient sensors along her snout that read the ocean like a living map. Salt was memory. This was not that.

It was not wrong. Just new. *Different.*

Brackish.

She slowed. Not from caution. From curiosity, a primal pull born of lineage more than thought. She had followed something here.

Heat.

Vibration.

Instinct.

And now she was inside it, this strange, half-fresh sea.

The Sound.

Her lateral line fluttered with the turbulence, a language written in low pulses and pressure differentials. Shallows shifted beneath her.

The depth fell away, then rose again.

Beneath her, the bottom moved, not fast, but loose. Sandbars. Soft, yielding terrain.

She adjusted course.

Her dorsal fin, jagged and shortened from old violence, broke the surface for a breath, the tracker bolted to its base pulsing red in steady intervals, a signal stitched to flesh.

Judy felt no fear.

No doubt.

Only the expanding map inside her, rewritten with each flick of her tail.

The sea was changing.

She changed with it.

CHAPTER 14

The boat came off the line in 1996, the same year the DVD was launched and Dolly the sheep was cloned.

One of the last Hatteras Convertible's before the line was phased out - thirty-nine feet from pulpit to swim deck, with a hull meant to outlast mistakes.

Devildam wasn't built to turn heads.

She was built to endure. To hold her ground. Wide-beamed and all business. Her lines were sharp and traditional, the kind of design that didn't age so much as settle in. She didn't shine, didn't need to. She was made to take the hits and keep moving.

She spent her early years in Texas, christened Litigator's Dream by a Gulf Coast trial lawyer who kept her slipped and spotless but rarely took her out.

After a few years, a charter captain out of Galveston renamed her King's Ransom and ran her hard, tourists, tuna, the occasional booze cruise. She earned her rust. By the time Cap found her in Rockport, the shine was gone and salt had crept into the seams but she was upright and willing.

She wasn't fast. She wasn't sleek. But she had presence. That low, steady posture in the slip that said, "I've seen worse, and I'll see worse again."

Cap liked that.

He walked her slow, bow to stern. Felt the hull. Eyed the welds. The engines weren't pretty, but they turned over. She tracked straight and rode low. Built for open water. Meant to last.

He wired the money the next day.

The trip from Rockport to Hatteras took almost a month. Not because of breakdowns, though there were a few, but because Cap took it slow.

He hugged the coast, skipped across marinas and inlets like stepping stones. Morgan City. Pensacola. Fernandina. Charleston.

Then finally through Hatteras Inlet, weather-worn and sunburned but grinning like a man who'd found a second spine.

He named her Devildam. No christening. Just block black vinyl letters slapped on dry.

At first, she was his escape.

He fished alone or with old friends, early out, late in. He kept her clean, kept her honest. But after the divorce, the house felt hollow. The pension didn't stretch like he thought it would. So, he started offering trips, half day, full day, sometimes overnights if he liked the crew. Nothing fancy.

It helped. The money, sure. But, also the people. He liked seeing their eyes light up when the first fish hit. Liked the quiet on the ride out and the stories on the way back.

He didn't overhaul her. Kept her functional. One engine was replaced with a rebuilt Yanmar. The nav suite went from analog to something digital and secondhand. He reupholstered the salon cushions himself, cursing the staple gun and the arthritis creeping into his thumbs.

The biggest change came in 2018, around the same time he got the diagnosis.

Colon cancer.

Early, they said. Treatable. But the co-pays piled up, and the boat started slipping down the list. He took her out. Maintained her. But when things broke, he looked for cheaper ways to fix them. He hated it. But he had to.

That's when he swapped the battery system.

The old twins were dying, low charge, unreliable. He wanted something bigger, more stable. A house bank. Six AGM deep cycles mounted midship below deck. They would power the electronics, the bilge, lights, pumps, and the little fridge he kept stocked with bait and beer.

He hired a local guy out of Hatteras Village, Wesley Pike, a handyman with a welding rig in the bed of his truck and a cigarette always dangling from his lip. Not a marine outfitter, not by a long shot, but he worked cheap and didn't ask questions.

The rack was steel tubing, angle braces, and a plywood base. It looked solid enough.

Cap inspected it, tested it, bolted it to the stringers himself.

Good enough, he thought.

It had to be.

But salt doesn't forgive. It works slow, steady, absolute.

Rust spread through the welds. The plywood swelled and sagged.

He meant to fix it.

Meant to reinforce the braces, swap the base, rebolt the whole thing.

After the next trip.

After the next round.

After the weather cleared.

He never did.

Life is like that sometimes.

CHAPTER 15

Ava stood at the edge of the lot, watching as the tow truck driver crouched beside her BMW.

The mid-morning sun flashed off the metal hook as he looped the chains into place. Metal scraped against metal, sharp, grating, too loud against the quiet of the marina.

She winced. The car had been nothing but a headache since she bought it. Now it was being dragged off like some petty insult she couldn't quite shake. Another reminder that nothing in her life wanted to run clean.

She adjusted the cover-up draped over her white swimsuit, tugging at the hem. She'd changed in the marina's cramped bathroom a few minutes earlier, stuffing her grease-streaked travel clothes into her oversized purse like she didn't want to admit to herself why she was taking them off.

Like she should've been above caring what Danny thought, but wasn't. Not entirely.

Now, standing in the open, she could feel the driver's eyes track the line of her legs, her hips, the slight sway of fabric that didn't cover much. Not overt. Not rude. But noticed.

She wondered again if the suit was too much.

This isn't for him. Isn't for anyone, really.

It was about feeling different. Or at least, trying to.

She turned back to the truck as the driver slammed his door shut. "Appreciate it," she said.

He gave her a nod through the open window, "They'll call with the quote."

She offered a tight smile, then turned toward the dock, sandals slapping against the worn planks. Devildam swayed gently at the far end, the only boat with any life on it.

From the deck, Jack spotted her.

He waved both arms like a flag, grinning wide, "Mom! Over here!"

Ava raised her hand in return, shoulders relaxing enough to soften the edges of her face.

* * *

Danny sat on the gunwale, arms crossed over his chest, watching as Shel reached out to help Ava aboard. He didn't move. Didn't speak. Face unreadable.

Shel's eyes swept over her swimsuit and cover-up. He gave a low whistle.

Ava stopped mid-step and shot him a look, half warning, half smirk, "Seriously?"

Shel grinned, "I mean... damn. That suit cost what, twenty bucks? And yet, somehow, it works."

She rolled her eyes but didn't bother hiding the flicker of a grin, "Glad to have your approval, Shel."

Jack ran up to her, arms flung wide.

"The Kealy's are inside," he said. "They own all the crab places Dad works for."

Ava nodded, adjusting the hem of her cover-up as she stepped fully onto the deck. Danny finally unfolded his arms, exhaling through his nose like he was bracing for something.

She glanced his way, "Relax, crab king. I'm not here to ruin your day."

Shel grinned at the barb, all teeth and tanned charm. Danny knew he liked the way a little friction kept things lively.

It aggravated Danny more than he wanted to admit.

"Too late," Danny muttered, pushing to his feet.

He watched as Jack led her into the salon. The way she walked now, shoulders back, chin up, was different. More sure of herself. She fit in here, technically, but not really. Not in the way she used to.

The Ava he remembered had been softer at the edges, less
guarded. This version was crisp. Efficient. She usually dressed like
her calendar was color-coded and came with corporate perks.
Talked about bonuses. Milestones. Performance goals. He ran a
crab shack. She ran projections. They weren't even speaking the
same language anymore.

Danny lowered himself back onto the gunwale as Shel dropped
beside him with a dramatic sigh, legs stretching out like he was
settling in for the long haul.

Shel gave it a beat, then tilted his head, "You mad? You seem
mad."

Danny kept his eyes on the water, "Technically, I could fire you."

"Ever been fired from a crab shack? It's like sweet release."

Danny shook his head, the corners of his mouth twitching as he
suppressed a laugh.

Shel leaned against the railing, eyes on the marina, boats rocking
gently, ropes ticking against pilings, a few early tourists wandering
like they were posing for a travel brochure.

"What's the big deal?" he said with a shrug. "Tish bails, Ava
shows. Maybe it's fate. Dumb luck. Whatever. I invited Tish 'cause
I thought maybe you two would, y'know…"

He trailed off, let the silence hang long enough to make it weird,
then made the gesture. One hand formed a ring, the other jabbed
through it. Subtle as a sledgehammer.

"Real mature," Danny muttered.

"Always," Shel said, grinning.

Danny snorted, short and unwilling.

"She's twenty," he said. "And a coworker. I'm technically still
married. Not gonna happen. Now you've got me six hours on a
boat with someone doing her best to pretend this isn't awkward.
No more setups, okay?"

"Fair enough." Shel leaned back, still grinning. "But damn, she
makes that cheap suit look good."

Danny arched a brow, "I thought you were into fellas?"

"Depends which way the wind blows," Shel said.

Danny smirked and glanced back toward the cabin. Through the window, he could see Ava and Jack talking.

She tucked a strand of hair behind her ear, smiling down at their son. It was a good smile, warm, natural. It got to him sometimes.

"She changed," Danny said, more to himself than Shel. "Turned into someone polished. The right car, the right clothes, talking about bonuses and titles like they're oxygen. Me? I want to be present. In the moment. Know what I mean? I run a crab shack. It's not much, but it's honest."

He scratched at his jaw, "Jack's into all the stuff kids love now, YouTube, video games, dumb memes, and honestly, so am I. So, we do it together. We hang out. We get along. We laugh our asses off. But she thinks I..."

He made air quotes, "Lack drive."

He shook his head, "I've got drive. Same drive I had when we met."

Shel leaned back, watching him with something between amusement and sympathy, "Yeah? And how's that working out for you?"

CHAPTER 16

Inside the salon, the boat rocked gently beneath their feet, the walls creaking in rhythm with the shifting tide.

Jack sat on the starboard bench beside Larry, who lounged with his Bloody Mary in one hand and a look of mild curiosity aimed at the boy's phone.

Colleen sat on the other side of Larry, sipping her Diet Coke, while Ava had taken the spot next to her, legs crossed, fingers absently toying with the edge of her cover-up.

Near the galley, Kid moved around the small coffee station, tinkering with the stubborn percolator and muttering under his breath.

Outside, through the open door, Danny and Shel sat on the back deck, deep in conversation.

"I don't use Facebook," Larry said, watching Jack swipe and tap with mechanical ease.

Jack smirked without looking up, "Yeah. Facebook's for old people."

Larry raised an eyebrow, "Is that right?"

"Yep," Jack said, scrolling past a blur of pranks, dances, and stitched-together nonsense. "Snapchat and TikTok are where it's at now."

Larry squinted at the screen, trying to make sense of the flashing images, "Never heard of 'em."

Jack grinned, "Exactly."

* * *

Colleen and Ava sat shoulder to shoulder on the bench, half-listening as Larry and Jack traded jabs about social media. Larry's voice carried easily through the small salon, amused and unfiltered, while Jack grinned down at his phone, completely absorbed.

Ava smoothed her hands over the front of her cover-up, then cleared her throat.

"I don't think I've properly introduced myself," she said, offering a tentative smile. "I'm Ava North. Danny's wife. Jack's mom."

Colleen looked over, the corners of her mouth lifting in something kind and knowing, "Honey, I figured. Jack's got his daddy's eyes and your posture. Like he's ready to take over the world and roll his eyes while doing it."

Ava laughed, the tension in her shoulders easing a little, "It's been a while since I've been on one of these trips. Feels... different now."

Colleen nodded, catching the subtext, "Everything changes. When we first started out, it was me and Larry running one tiny crab shack, trying to keep our heads above water."

She smiled, "Literally and figuratively."

Ava tilted her head, "You started it together?"

"From scratch. A shack off the highway. We didn't know much, but we worked. Busted ass, as the kids say. Showed up every day, leaned on each other when it got rough."

She took a sip of her Diet Coke, "Built the whole thing on love, stubbornness, and caffeine. Lots of caffeine."

Ava could picture it clearly - long nights, fried seafood, laughter ringing through the screen door. Not glamorous, but real.

"Word got around," Colleen continued. "We opened a second spot. Then a third. Now it's a small chain. Nothing fancy, but folks know the name."

Ava nodded, genuinely impressed, "That's amazing."

Colleen shrugged, "Not sure it's amazing. But it's definitely something. Not what our kids wanted, though. They're grown now. Said they were done with the stink of crab and went their own way. Can't say I blame them."

"What do they do?"

"Our daughter married a real estate guy. Our son's in finance. Both solid. Both busy. But our granddaughter, Emma, she's our light. Stays with us every summer. Makes little movies on her phone. She's got an eye for it."

"She sounds incredible."

Ava's gaze drifted to Jack. He sat a few feet away, but already felt distant, pulled into some digital world she couldn't quite reach. Her chest ached. He was growing so fast. Every day a little taller, a little more opinionated. A little more his own person. But still her boy. Always her boy.

"It's wild," Ava said softly. "How they take over. How everything bends around them without you even realizing it. It's like... the best and worst drug in the world."

Colleen gave a knowing chuckle, the kind only time could earn, "Oh, honey. Truer words never spoken."

They heard the deck shoes first, steady footfalls descending from the wheelhouse. Then came the voice, full of grit and command.

"Morning, folks!"

Cap stepped into the salon, awake now, sharp-eyed, and fully in his element. Whatever grogginess the morning held for the rest of them didn't apply here, he was switched on, dialed in. The sea was calling, and he was ready to answer.

His sun-bleached Columbia shirt was buttoned to the chest, sleeves rolled to the elbow, the fabric sweat-ringed and crusted with salt. The vented shoulders sagged, and the chest pockets bulged with bits of line and clippings.

Tan shorts clung to his hips, wrinkled and sun-faded, and his bare ankles disappeared into worn deck shoes, no socks, just skin and salt. The captain's hat sat slightly crooked, like it had been knocked loose and forgotten. A silver chain glinted at his neck, the pendant hidden from view, tucked under the top button.

He glanced through the open cabin door and spotted movement on the back deck, then let out a sharp, two-fingered whistle.

"Come on in here, fellas!"

Danny and Shel stepped inside.

Cap turned to the others, flashing his crooked grin, "Mick Barton. Answer to Mick. Micky. Cap Mick. Friends call me Cap."

He scanned the room, "Where's Kid? KID!"

Kid raised a hand from where he stood by the coffee station.

"There he is. That's Kid. He'll make sure you're fed, caffeinated, and generally not dead."

Kid gave a loose half-salute, his usual grin already in place.

Cap moved through the room, shaking hands, sizing people up with quick reads, "Y'all ready to make some enemies out there? We're gonna tangle with giants today, I can feel it."

He checked his watch, already turning back toward the stairs, "Give me five minutes. Need to ping the weather, run the fuel numbers, and double-check the sonar. Then we push off. Kid, knock out the safety check, if ya' will."

* * *

Kid ran the guests through the safety check - life jackets, fire extinguisher, radio - then headed for the back deck to do a final gear check.

Shel trailed, lighting a cigarette with a flick and shielding the flame from the wind. The salt air tasted like rust and possibility. He leaned against the rail, watching as Kid crouched near the rods, fingers moving fast, checking lines, tweaking drag, securing gear like it was second nature.

"Is Kid your real name?" Shel asked, already guessing the answer.

Kid smirked without looking up, "Nah. Cap calls all his deckhands that. Easier than remembering names, I guess. I'm André. Just passing through. Here for the summer, school's calling."

"Lemme guess," Shel said. "Marine biology."

"Studio art," Kid replied, snapping a clasp shut.

He straightened, tossing Shel a look like he expected to be judged.

Shel raised his eyebrows, "No shit. I'm visual arts."

Kid wiped his hands on a rag, "My parents are torn between being terrified and proud. They say, 'Follow your passion,' but I think they're probably picturing me broke and couch-surfing by twenty-five."

Shel tapped ash into the breeze, "That's just how parents love you, half belief, half panic. I say keep going. Blaze a path."

Kid shrugged, "At least they didn't push me to finance. I'll take broke and happy over rich and dead inside."

Shel nodded, looking out over the water, "I thought about transferring. Maybe New York. Big scene. Big weird. Big risk."

"Yeah? I dig it." Kid said. "Big city dreams and neon paint."

"Yeah," Shel said. "And maybe someplace where I don't have to explain myself every five minutes."

Kid let that sit, "I get that."

The cabin door creaked open and Jack spilled out, practically buzzing. Shel flicked the cigarette into the wind and straightened, like a guy caught doing something he told someone else not to.

Kid brightened, "What's up, little man? Ready to catch the big one?"

Jack nodded, eyes wide, "Think I might get a swordfish?"

Kid laughed, grabbing a clean t-shirt from the rail and tugging it over his head.

"Bold. I like it."

He ruffled Jack's hair, "Tell you what, if you catch a swordfish, I'll clean it myself and let you take the picture."

Jack grinned, "You're on!"

Shel smiled, watching the kid beam. For a moment, the hum of the engines, the soft creak of the dock lines, and Jack's excitement all seemed to settle into something that almost felt like peace.

Kid smoothed his shirt into place and nodded toward the wheelhouse.

"Cap's got that look today," he said. "When he gets quiet like that, it means he's locked in. We're gonna find the big fish."

Shel followed his gaze. Through the glass, Cap stood motionless at the helm, eyes fixed on the instruments and the water beyond.

Kid smirked. "Trust me. We always find the big ones."

* * *

Larry leaned back on the starboard bench seat, vinyl creaking under his weight. Colleen was next to him, legs crossed, her Diet Coke balanced on one knee. Across the salon, Ava and Danny were at the table, seated opposite each other, bodies pitched slightly forward, their conversation low but not quite low enough.

The small space made it impossible not to listen.

"I talked to the lawyer," Ava said. "She's got a slot next Thursday."

Danny shifted in his seat, "I can't take off in the middle of the week. I've got two new hires starting. We're already short."

Ava didn't answer right away. She stared at him, her expression unreadable. Larry could feel the silence draw tight, stretched thin between them.

He took another slow sip of his Bloody Mary and averted his gaze. The drink was warm now, but the rim had that sharp Old Bay bite he liked.

Next to him, Colleen tilted her sunhat to deflect the light and maybe some of the tension from across the table.

"They're trying to whisper," he muttered under his breath.

"They're failing," Colleen replied, eyes fixed on Ava's posture. "She's dressing for someone."

Larry arched an eyebrow, "You used to look like that."

"Used to?" Colleen murmured. "I think she's dressing for you. You're obviously the alpha male."

Larry snorted, "For sure. She took one look at the man boobs and pelt of gray chest hair and thought, *I gotta get me some of that.*"

Colleen gave his knee a light tap, "Rawr."

He smirked. They didn't need to say much. A look, a tone, enough to tell how the hand was playing out. This hand was tense, quiet, packed with unspoken history.

Across the salon, Ava caught Colleen watching and pointed at her hat, "I like your hat."

Colleen straightened it with a pleased smile, "Thanks, dear. Keeps the sun off my shoulders."

Larry didn't say anything. He didn't need to. He leaned back, glass in hand, and let the hum of conversation wash over him. The boat hadn't even left the slip, but the air was already thick with weather, the kind you couldn't see coming on radar.

As Kid, Shel, and Jack stepped in from the back deck, faces lit with energy and sea air, Cap descended from the wheelhouse, slow and steady.

He had a folded printout in one hand, tapping it absently against his palm.

His expression gave it away before he said a word, something less than good news.

Larry clocked the shift immediately. Cap exhaled through his nose like a man bracing for impact.

"Alright, folks," Cap said, voice clear but calm. "Gather up a sec."

The room quieted.

"Storm's left the ocean in a bad mood," he said. "Still churned up from last night. Whitecaps, rough water, gusty on the edge. I could take you out there, but unless you've got a thing for vomiting over the rails, it's not worth it. We can reschedule, or, if she settles down by noon, head out for a half-day."

Jack's face fell, "But I wanted to catch a swordfish."

Before anyone could answer, Kid scratched his jaw.

"What about The Sound?" he asked. "Remember the red drum we pulled off Swan Quarter two weeks back? That was after a storm, too."

Cap raised an eyebrow, considering, "Ayuh, we did."

He looked to the window, where Pamlico stretched wide and deceptively peaceful.

"She's a whole different creature, brackish, shallow, moves fast underneath. You get red drum, flounder, maybe a tarpon if we're lucky. Not as flashy as the ocean, but she can surprise you."

Shel turned to Danny, "I mean, we're here."

Danny rubbed his jaw, clearly doing the mental math, "It's a chunk of change."

Larry took a sip of his Bloody Mary and shrugged, "You guys are the superstars. Your reward. You want the Sound? We do the Sound."

Jack turned his big eyes on his father, "Please, Dad? We came all this way."

Danny hesitated for a breath, then nodded, "Yeah. Let's do it."

Cap gave a short nod, decision made.

"Alright," he said, already turning back for the stairs to the wheelhouse. "Give me another five minutes to re-rig and adjust the plan. We'll make it work."

A few heads nodded.

Someone said, "Sounds good," low and easy.

Even Ava let her arms drop to her sides, some of the tightness easing out of her shoulders.

Larry caught the shift in the room. The mood had lightened, not excitement exactly, but something better.

Curiosity.

It wasn't how Larry had pictured the morning going.

Still.

The trip was on.

CHAPTER 17

Devildam rumbled out of her berth, twin diesels biting the water as she slid past the other boats in the marina.

Mid-morning light glinted off polished hulls as Cap guided her down the row, dockworkers offering lazy waves. Gulls lifted from the pilings and swung in behind the stern, sharp-eyed and crying as the wake stirred scraps from the water.

Then she was clear of the docks, turning west toward the open spread of Pamlico Sound.

* * *

Devildam's wheelhouse sat perched above the salon, reached by a narrow staircase rising through the forward bulkhead. At the back of the space, beside the top of the stairs, a steel-framed door opened onto the walkaround, a tight ledge bolted to the superstructure.

A low pony wall separated the stairwell from the door, plain but essential, keeping anyone from stepping backward into open air on their way out.

The wheelhouse itself was compact and purposeful, built for use rather than comfort and worn down by years of salt and sun. Wood-paneled walls held a scatter of nautical charts and expired fishing licenses, along with a faded photograph of a younger Cap standing beside a massive marlin, proof of a time when the work had felt different, or at least easier to pose for.

Overhead, navigation instruments hummed softly, GPS, radar, depth finder, VHF radio, its mic hanging from a metal clip, ready to crackle to life. The gear crowded the space without overwhelming it, each piece exactly where Cap expected it to be.

At the center sat Cap, relaxed but fully in command, leaning into the worn captain's chair, its cracked red vinyl molded to him after years at sea. One elbow rested on the arm, fingers tapping lightly against the wheel while his other hand adjusted the throttle without looking.

He belonged here.

The boat answered to him in small ways, in the timing of his movements, in how he anticipated the water before it made itself known.

Power chords rolled from the CD player built into the console, Born to Run humming through the wheelhouse. The music settled into the space like another instrument. Cap's eyes followed their familiar circuit, chart to water, water to instruments, holding the Sound steady ahead, the shoreline's shape, the quiet confirmations of the gear mounted above the glass.

Mounted overhead, just forward of the helm, a sawed-off Remington 870 rode in a welded stainless bracket, grip down, muzzle forward, safety on. Easy to reach. Not for show.

Cap had bolted it there years back, tied directly into the steel framing above the console. A habit born of too many rough nights and too many strangers aboard. He trusted the sea, mostly. It was people who made him nervous.

Buoys marked the water ahead, red and green, rocking with the tide, threading a safe line through shallows that would ground an inattentive captain. Beyond them, marsh grass shifted along distant sandbars. Pelicans and terns drifted near the markers, dipping for breakfast. To starboard, a scatter of weathered pilings broke the surface, the last trace of a dock the Sound had reclaimed.

Cap had run this stretch more times than he could count.

The stairs creaked behind him, sharp against the steady hum of the engines. Cap didn't look up, but he felt the change in weight and rhythm as someone climbed.

A small head appeared at the top of the stairwell, eyes wide, feet stopping short.

Cap caught it in his peripheral vision and reached out, turning Springsteen down with a flick of his fingers. The gravel in the Boss's voice fell away, leaving the low thrum of diesel and the soft creak of the hull working beneath them.

"Come on up, Bub," Cap said without turning. "Grab the chair."

Jack hesitated, one hand gripping the rail, then climbed the last few steps into the wheelhouse. The light hit him full, and he blinked, taking in the sprawl of dials, gauges, and the wide, weather-scuffed windshield.

Cap stood and patted the thick cushion of the captain's chair. It creaked a little under his palm.

"Sit her right there. What was the name again, mate?"

"Jack," the boy said, climbing into the seat, legs dangling slightly above the deck.

Cap gave a satisfied nod, "All right then. Captain Jack. Like in them movies."

Jack's face lit up, "Pirates of the Caribbean."

Cap snapped his fingers, "That's the one. You ever take the helm before, Captain Jack?"

Jack shook his head quickly, but the grin on his face said he'd thought about it.

Cap leaned in, dropped his voice to a low whisper, "That makes two of us."

Jack blinked, processing, then frowned slightly.

Cap let it hang a second longer before breaking into a raspy laugh.

He clapped Jack gently on the back, "I'm messin' with you. Don't you worry. I've done my fair share of steering."

Jack exhaled, shoulders dropping as he settled into the chair. The vinyl was cracked and warm, the foam inside molded by years of storms and sweat.

Cap turned his attention back to the helm and pointed to the wheel, "Go on. Give her a little nudge to starboard. That's to the right."

Jack reached out, both hands on the wooden wheel, turning it a bit. The resistance was light but real - connected. The boat shifted in response, adjusting course.

"There you go," Cap said. "Smooth. No jerking. You're a

natural."

Jack focused on the horizon, then pointed toward a set of red markers bobbing in the distance, "What are those?"

Cap followed his line of sight.

"Channel markers. Red's on your starboard side when you're coming back in, green's to port. Easy way to remember it? 'Red, right, returning.' Means when you're inbound, heading home, keep the red on your right."

Jack nodded, chewing on that.

"Is the Sound the same as a bay?"

Cap tilted his head, "Close enough. But a sound's usually bigger, wider. Deeper in spots. Pamlico's almost the size of Delaware. Not quite ocean, not quite river. Brackish water, half salt, half fresh. Even the Sound doesn't know what it is some days."

Jack looked out at the water, then down at the map spread across the chart table. Contour lines twisted like fingerprints, depth markers and hazard zones scattered across the page like a code he couldn't crack.

"Where are we going?"

Cap tapped a blank stretch of water near the middle of the chart, "Right about there. Not much on the map, but the bottom's soft and the current pulls good bait. Where we're going's not marked, Captain Jack. True places never are."

He pulled off his cap and ran a hand through the thin hair that clung stubbornly to his scalp. He was supposed to lose it during chemo. That's what the doctors said. But here it was, still hanging on. Like him. Not what it used to be, but enough.

Jack watched him for a second, quiet, curious, like he was trying to figure something out. Cap could feel the boy studying him, probably wondering about the hair, or the lines on his face. Most kids did. They didn't understand chemo or remission, not really. Just sick or not.

And Cap didn't look sick. Not really. Not anymore.

Jack turned back toward the windshield, "Think we'll see a swordfish?"

Cap rocked his head side to side, thoughtful, "I gotta be honest, Captain Jack. I've never seen a swordfish in the Sound. Not once." He smiled. "But I've seen plenty of marlin. Close enough, right?"

Jack nodded. It was.

* * *

Devildam cruised between the channel markers, her wake curling out in twin frothy trails. The water here was calmer than the Atlantic but unsettled, stirred up from last night's storm. Swells rocked beneath her hull in slow, irregular pulses, the kind that didn't look like much but would wear you out over time.

In the wheelhouse, Cap gave her a touch more throttle. The engines responded with a deeper growl, the vibration rising through the deck as the boat sliced across the open Sound. Foam spiraled off the stern, a white ribbon trailing into the haze.

Devildam wasn't built for speed. She rode low and steady, a deep-V bruiser that cut clean through chop that sent lighter boats scrambling.

These days she topped out around fifteen knots, less when she was loaded, but Cap liked her that way. He didn't need fast. He needed a boat that held its ground when the water turned ugly.

* * *

Danny sat on one of the built-in benches in the salon, elbows on his knees, eyes closed. The low thrum of the engines pulsed up through the deck, steady, familiar. A sound he could sink into.

He wasn't sleeping. He was letting the hum fill the space where conversation might've gone.

He kept thinking about the night before, waiting in the living room while Shel and his mom talked in the kitchen. He'd heard fragments. Words like aggressive and advanced, followed by a silence that said more than any full sentence could.

Every so often, Shel's voice would come through, calm,

92

measured, but Danny could hear the effort it took to keep it that way.

What stuck with him wasn't the diagnosis. It was the shift he knew was coming. The way the news rippled. Bent everything around it. Shel's family was headed into uncharted territory now, and not necessarily good territory.

The kind where roles change overnight.

Where resentment creeps in.

Where people drift or collapse.

And yet, somehow, Shel managed to smile this morning. He moved through the day like the same kid, bright, steady, cracking jokes. Danny didn't know how he did it.

He hoped it wasn't the kind of strength that cracked from the inside.

* * *

On the back deck, Larry leaned on the starboard railing with Colleen beside him. Her arm hooked lightly through his as she sipped her Diet Coke, pointing toward the distant marsh where a group of white egrets took flight.

Larry raised his phone and snapped a few photos, not checking them before slipping the phone back into his pocket.

Shel hung off the port side, elbows on the rail, sunglasses low as he scanned the water with a bored but curious look, half watching for fish, half watching for the unexpected.

Near the transom, Kid tightened a rod holder, the stainless fitting clicking into place. He moved by instinct, securing a lanyard, checking gear, eyes sweeping the deck and water in a quiet inventory. With his tasks done, he disappeared into the salon to prep drinks for the guests.

Ava stood near the ladder, one hand on the rail that led up to the walkaround, her back to the salon. She kept to the lee of the wall, where the wind broke a little.

Spray lifted off the wake and cooled her calves. Her cover-up tugged and settled. Behind her sunglasses, she gave nothing away, facing the horizon as if it had asked her a question first.

The salon door creaked open, and Jack stepped out, blinking in the sunlight. He looked around until he spotted her, then stepped over.

"Everything good?" Ava asked, pushing her sunglasses down enough to meet his eyes.

Jack nodded, smiling wide, "Cap said I could steer later."

Ava smiled back, small, but honest, "That's a big job."

"I'm ready," he said.

And the way he stood, feet planted and shoulders squared, she believed him.

For now, at least.

The salon door swung open again, and Kid stepped reappeared, a pitcher of Bloody Marys in one hand, a pitcher of mimosas in the other. He grinned like he was about to deliver communion.

"Alright, y'all," he called. "Breakfast of champions. Let's get this party started."

* * *

In the wheelhouse, Cap eased the throttle past the notch that held her at ten knots. He felt the hum rise beneath his fingers, the vibration moving up through the console and into his bones.

Devildam responded instantly, surging forward with quiet power, like she'd been waiting on his hand to give her the go. Out here, behind the wheel, everything still made sense.

This was his space, steel, glass, gauges he could read at a glance. A place where effort translated into motion, where decisions had weight but never wavered. The sea didn't sugarcoat anything. It demanded respect, and in return, it offered truth. Not the kind you wanted, always. But the kind that didn't flinch.

He scanned the horizon, the thin line between sky and water, and exhaled slow through his nose. There were no IV drips out here. No sterile rooms. No doctors couching bad news in soft language.

Only tide and weather, current and hull, and the knowledge that if he held the wheel steady, she'd go where he told her.

It wasn't freedom exactly. But it was something close. A version of control he could count on.

The boat cut cleanly through the water, foam peeling off in white ribbons. Wind buffeted the wheelhouse windows, and the air smelled clean and briny, no antiseptic, no recycled ventilation.

Cap let his hand rest on the throttle, feeling every vibration like a heartbeat.

For the first time that morning, a quiet smile tugged at the corner of his mouth.

This was his rhythm, his element.

The one place that didn't ask him to be brave or sick or strong. Just capable.

This was home.

CHAPTER 18

Thirty minutes later, Devildam drifted to a stop near a weathered red buoy, its paint chipped and rust-streaked, bobbing lazily in the gentle roll of the Sound.

The current swirled around it in lazy spirals, tugging at a clump of floating seagrass caught on its base. Barnacles clung to the metal like armor, crusted and sharp. A gull screeched overhead, banking wide as the engines idled to silence.

Beneath the surface, the water was deceptively clear, sunlight piercing through to reveal rippling sand and eelgrass, but Cap knew better. The bottom here never stayed the same. One tide could erase a ridge. Another might create something new.

He stepped out onto the walkaround from the wheelhouse, hat low over his brow, expression focused. From there he took a long look at the shoal ahead, a sandbar maybe twenty yards out, barely submerged, its edges traced by the lazy curl of small breaking waves.

"Over the side, Kid," he said, voice calm but certain. "That shoal's crawlin' with 'em."

Kid didn't hesitate. He snatched the long-handled net from the rack and launched it toward the shoal in a smooth, spear-like motion, the aluminum handle flashing once in the sun before it hit the water. Then he peeled off his shirt and tossed it to the deck, muscles taut beneath his dark skin. In one fluid motion, he stepped onto the gunwale, and dove into the Sound.

The splash echoed off the hull, and a fan of ripples spread outward as Kid cut through the surface, disappearing for a beat before his head broke the water again. His strokes were smooth and powerful, his body slicing cleanly through the Sound with the economy of someone born into saltwater.

Cap descended the ladder from the walkaround, shoes thudding softly on the deck. He moved to the rail without a word as the others gathered behind him. Shel leaned in, hands braced on the metal rail. Jack squinted into the glare, trying to see what Cap saw.

Ava stood a little apart, arms folded, her gaze flickering, watching Kid's progress with a mix of curiosity and caution.

* * *

From the water, the shoal revealed itself, a pale rise just under the surface, its outline flickering as the light shifted. It looked as if it might vanish if he lost the angle. A low hump of sand under a skin of moving water, its edges falling away into darker patches where the bottom dropped off, and whatever waited there.

Kid reached the edge, touched bottom, and rose to his feet in waist-high water. The net lay a few feet away, half-submerged and rocking gently in the shallows.

He waded over, grabbed the handle, and lifted it with a practiced motion, water streaming from the mesh. The sand shifted under his heels, uneven, soft.

Fish scattered at his arrival, small, bright-bodied things flashing silver as they darted through the eelgrass, silt kicking up behind them. A horseshoe crab trudged along the bottom, its domed shell furrowed with scars, leaving a fine, wavering track through the muck.

He glanced back toward Devildam, where the others watched from the deck. Cap had stepped up to the rail, one hand braced on the edge, squinting into the glare.

Not at him, past him.

Kid turned to follow his gaze.

Something about the water beyond the shoal looked... *wrong*.

Not dramatic. Just off. The current curled in a slow, wide arc where it should've run straight. A darker patch lingered beyond reach, unmoving. He squinted, trying to track it.

The silence pressed in, no gulls, no chatter from the boat. Even the net felt heavier in his hand.

Kid shifted his footing. He wasn't nervous, not really. He'd grown up in water like this. But the quiet was starting to feel personal.

"Incoming!" Cap's voice cut across the water.

A white plastic five-gallon bucket flew from the boat, sun-flashed and spinning. Kid caught it mid-air without looking, adjusting his grip by feel. Years of muscle memory did the rest.

He turned back toward the deeper water, bucket in hand, but the darker patch was gone.

Or maybe deeper.

He stood there a moment longer, searching the surface. Nothing moved. Nothing called.

He couldn't quite shake the feeling that something had seen him first.

* * *

The guests leaned over the rail, intrigued, squinting into the sunlight as they watched Kid move through the water. He waded slow and deliberate across the shoal, net in hand, pausing now and then to jab quick and low into the sand.

Whatever he was doing, it wasn't random. There was rhythm to it. Precision. But no one on board seemed entirely sure what they were seeing.

"Is he… fishing?" Shel muttered.

Cap crouched beside Jack, lowering his voice enough to make it feel like a secret.

"Say, Captain Jack," he said, nudging him gently with an elbow. "Know the best kind of bait?"

Jack shook his head, eyes wide and fixed on Kid's net as he brought it up again, this time with something pale and flickering inside. A crab, maybe. Quick-legged and half-invisible in the light.

"Live bait," Cap said, flashing a grin and a wink. "Always better when it doesn't know it's about to be lunch."

Jack blinked, "That's messed up."

"That's fishing," Cap said. "Wait till you see what we do with it."

The water lapped around Kid's thighs, warm and shallow, broken by small ripples as he moved. Net in one hand, the white bucket in the other, he took slow, measured steps. The shoal shifted underfoot, soft sand giving way to hard-packed ridges, eelgrass brushing his calves. Sunlight lit the skin of the water; below it, everything dissolved into shimmer and shadow.

A fiddler crab broke from a knot of drifted seaweed, small bodied, long-legged, one claw absurdly oversized. It moved sideways in quick, uneven bursts, the raised claw held high as it skittered for cover. Its mottled shell caught the light in flashes of dust and clay, the colors of mudflats and tide pools.

It vanished beneath a thin skim of sand.

Too slow.

Kid dipped the net fast and flat, the motion clean and practiced. Water hissed across the rim as he lifted, guiding the crab into the deepest pocket of mesh. Mud-brown shell. Legs kicking. The big claw snapping once, reflexive.

He tipped the net over the bucket and let it drop. Click-clack. Plastic rang. Legs scrabbled for purchase.

A minute later, another followed, lighter this time, a quick tick and scrape as its claws raked the sides, already testing for a way out.

He scanned the water again, eyes trained for the signs, the hint of motion, a twitch in the sand, the wrong shape at the right time. He saw one pause mid-step, then vanish in a blur.

The rhythm took hold - net, scoop, tilt, drop. The crabs went in one by one, their collective skittering growing louder inside the bucket. A soft, constant whisper of legs on plastic.

He liked this part. The simplicity of it. The rhythm. One hand, one tool, one result. No voices. No explanations. Just sun and water and the satisfying ka-clack of something caught before it could get away.

* * *

Jack leaned against the rail, eyes following Kid as he moved along the shoal, net in one hand, bucket in the other, scooping up the twitchy little crabs with a precision that didn't seem taught so much as inherited. It was quiet work, oddly satisfying to watch.

Something out past the edge of the shallows caught Jack's eye, a float bobbing a few yards off, squat and round, its faded orange and white bands dulled by sea spray.

It moved differently than the buoy beside the boat. Lower. Softer. The rope beneath it stretched taut, disappearing into the dark like it had somewhere to be.

Cap followed the boy's gaze.

"Lobster trap," he said. "Marker tells you where the gear's sitting."

Jack leaned out a little farther, squinting. The rope pulsed, slow and shallow, like something was shifting below. Something alive.

Cap let the silence hang, the wind filling the space where more words could've gone.

The float bobbed gently in the current, anchored to a trap that looked undisturbed, though there was no real way to know. For all Jack could tell, it had sat quiet all night.

Still, something about it felt spent. Like whatever should have been inside was already gone.

"Jesus!"

Every head snapped toward the shoal. Kid jerked upright, water flying off him, eyes wide. He stumbled backward, one foot catching a hidden ridge of sand. The bucket in his hand rocked wildly, fiddler crabs scrabbling against the plastic with a sound like dry leaves in a gutter.

He kept it upright, barely, but fell hard, landing in a splash that sent water fanning out in all directions.

He came up fast, coughing, net in one hand, bucket in the other. His head whipped toward the boat.

"Something bumped me," he shouted. "Hard."

Cap was already at the stern, eyes scanning the waterline, "You bit?"

"No," Kid called, voice shaky. He turned, pointing behind him. "Shark. Small one. But it's dead."

The shape bobbed beyond the edge of the shoal, gray, torpedo-sleek, limp in the water.

Cap reached for the coil of line at his feet, "Heads up!"

The rope snaked through the air in a clean arc. Kid dropped the net and snatched it with his free hand. No hesitation, he worked fast, looping the end around the shark's tail with three quick turns and a jerk to cinch it tight.

"You got it?"

"Yeah. Go," Kid replied.

Cap braced against the rail and hauled. The line went taut, water sliding off the rope in glinting rivulets. The shark's body dragged through the shallows, turning slightly with the pull.

Kid didn't wait to watch. He slid the net's safety loop over his wrist and tightened it, then grabbed the crab bucket in his free hand.

Wading out a few steps, he kicked off into deeper water, swimming on his side with one arm held high to keep the bucket clear. The net dragged behind, tethered to his wrist. He used his free hand and steady kicks to keep afloat, angling toward the swim ledge on the back of Devildam as the current pulled him wide.

Onboard, the others watched Cap haul in the shark.

Jack's voice broke it, "That's a shark. That's a real shark."

Cap grunted as he hauled the carcass aboard, "Used to be."

The dead shark thudded against the hull, then came over the rail, landing on the deck belly-down with a wet slap.

Kid reached the swim ledge a moment later, a slick strip of fiberglass jutting out above the waterline, narrow as a church pew and lined with cleats and an algae-streaked grab rail. He hauled himself up, the bucket still wobbling in his grip, then stepped through the transom door onto the back deck.

Cap handed him the bucket lid. Kid snapped it on, set the bucket down, and nudged it with his foot. It slid past the shark and into the corner, where it bumped once and stayed put.

The juvenile great white already showing signs of decay. The wound ahead of its dorsal had widened slightly in the hours since the fatal blow, jagged, raw-edged, the flesh around it curling back in pale, softened layers.

Bits of seaweed clung to the torn cartilage, and a faint greenish film had begun to spread along the gills. The eyes, once sharp and glassy, had clouded over to a dull, lifeless gray. A thin trickle of fluid leaked from its mouth, pooling against the planks and mixing with the smell of salt and slow rot.

Kid used his foot to tip it onto its side. The mouth sagged open, pale pink and slack, gums crowded with serrated teeth, some fully formed, others still set beneath the surface. They caught the sun and flashed wetly, all of them made for the same work.

None of it mattered now.

Ava folded her arms across her chest, a flicker of unease tightening her face as she stared at the carcass.

Beside her, Larry gave a low whistle, his usual swagger dulled as he shook his head. Colleen wrinkled her nose, her oversized star-shaped sunglasses slipping low, but she didn't look away.

Even Shel, who rarely flinched at anything, edged back half a step and muttered, "Damn. That's gnarly."

Cap wiped his hands on a rag, "Relax, folks. This one's bitin' days are over."

Colleen pushed her sunglasses into place and peered down at the small shark, "Is that a great white?"

"Ayuh," Cap confirmed. "Juvenile. Looks like he tangled with a boat prop and lost. Cut his spine, I'd wager."

Danny shook his head at the loss, "Me and Jack saw that on one of those shark shows. The sharks bite at the propellers. Doesn't seem smart."

Cap looked at the motionless body on the deck, "Maybe we're not supposed to understand. Not all of it."

Jack crouched down, curiosity outweighing caution. As he leaned closer, the sour, briny stench hit him, thick and clinging, like something left too long in the sun.

He recoiled slightly, covering his nose with the crook of his arm. "Ugh. Why does it smell like that?"

Cap kept his eyes on the carcass, "Death sets in quick. Saltwater slows it down some, but it don't stop it. Organs go first. Then the gills. Everything else starts unthreadin'."

Jack nodded, swallowing hard, but stayed where he was. His fingers hovered above the serrated teeth, his breath shallow as he traced the jagged curve with his eyes. He wasn't repulsed, he was fascinated, the sharp edges, the cavernous mouth, the raw efficiency of it all.

He tried to picture it days ago, moving under the waves, fast, clean, cutting through the water like it knew exactly where to go. Everything about it looked meant for that kind of motion.

Now it was just a shape. Teeth. Lines. The suggestion of danger without any of the force behind it. Whatever made it move was gone.

The thought unsettled him. In a way he couldn't quite name, it felt like what happened when something strong failed, when noise dropped to nothing, when motion stopped and didn't start again.

Ava took a step forward, voice sharp, "Careful….."

She looked at the others, scanning their faces, "Did none of you see the news this morning? A man died, some kind of shark attack. Not far from here. Out in the Atlantic."

Jack didn't react. He stayed crouched, inches from the carcass, studying its mouth like it was a museum exhibit.

Danny stood a few feet away, arms crossed, gaze on the dead shark.

"Whatever that was," he said, nodding toward the carcass, "It's not this."

Ava didn't answer, but her eyes lingered on the shark.

Larry, ever the showman, grinned, "Imagine them chompers on the wall? What a conversation piece. I gotta have 'em. How about in your restaurant, Danny?"

Danny stared down at the shark stretched across the deck, its weight settling now, making it all look a little misshapen. The skin had dulled, the gills collapsed in on themselves. But the head held its shape, wide, solid, the jawline unmistakable even at rest.

Jack bet his dad had never seen a mouth like that outside of TV. All that engineering for a single purpose. Rows of teeth layered like intention, everyone curved inward, built to hold on.

* * *

Danny tried to picture it: the grin fixed in bone, mounted clean and white on cedar, a small brass plate beneath. People would ask. He'd give them some version of how they came across it.

But the image felt wrong.

Decorative.

Empty.

The shark had already been dead when they hauled it up. No struggle. No risk. No hunt. Just Cap lifting it over the rail and the heavy sound of its body hitting the deck. Nothing earned. Nothing tested.

And still, he found himself wondering what it would be like to keep it. Not as a trophy. As something else. A marker at the edge of a chapter. Proof that even clean breaks left something behind.

The divorce wasn't final. No papers signed. No bags gone for good. Just the slow, invisible shift, the distance growing between words, meals, days. He hadn't wanted a fight. Hadn't wanted to lose. Yet here he was, standing over something he hadn't chosen, trying to decide what was worth carrying forward.

"Yeah," he said. "I'll take it."

Cap smirked, "You're the guest. Kid?"

Kid turned toward the cabin wall, where a machete rode in a metal bracket, its blade nicked and dulled from years of use. He slid it free in one smooth motion, tested the grip, and stepped toward the dead shark.

* * *

With a grunt, Kid gripped the decapitated shark by its tail. The body was cold and slick, the kind that clung to your palms no matter how hard you wiped. It was heavier than it looked, dense, stubborn, all of its weight refusing to go where you told it.

The strain pulled something loose in his memory. Cap earlier that summer, hauling a fouled anchor by hand when the winch jammed, no leverage, no help. Just Cap leaning back, boots braced, shoulders set, dragging iron and chain out of the Sound inch by inch. Kid had stood there then, surprised by how much force the old man could still put through his frame.

He took a breath now, tightened through his shoulders and back, and lifted. The shark came up in one clean motion, swung over the gunwale, cleared the rail by inches. From the torn neck, a rope of congealed blood spilled free, stippling the deck before trailing behind the body like ink in water.

It hit the Sound with a dull, meaty splash and disappeared.

A bloom of red unfurled beneath the surface, thick and clouded, swirling through the shallows like smoke in the wind. The current grabbed it fast, stretching it thin, tearing it into ribbons that faded as they drifted.

Jack leaned closer to the rail. Ava didn't. Nobody spoke.

The carcass bobbed to the surface, rising in a slow, awkward roll. The chop caught it sideways, turning the body until its pale underbelly flashed in the sun.

Gases from the decay had built up under the skin, giving it a swollen, unnatural buoyancy. It didn't float like something alive, it drifted, slack and swollen, spinning lazily with the tide.

Above, a gull appeared. And then another. They shrieked, sharp, urgent.

* * *

Kid knotted the top of a clear plastic bag, the severed shark's head bulging inside, misshapen by the press of cartilage and muscle. Its snout pushed against the film, distorting the shape into something grotesque, half-formed, wrong. A dark smear pooled at the bottom, leaking slowly from the ragged wound where the spine had been cut.

Through the plastic, its black eyes stared outward, glassy, vacant, and far too intact for something so violently ended.

He handed it off to Danny, who took it with both hands and a perplexed look on his face, like he was holding a prize watermelon at a county fair.

Colleen recoiled, her lips curling into something halfway between disbelief and revulsion. "That is straight-up disgusting."

"How many crabs you figure you've sent to their boiling death, hon'?" Larry asked Colleen with a grin on his face. "If anyone's the monster here, it's you."

She sighed, "That's a valid point."

Ava turned away, arms crossed over her stomach, her body language pulled in tight like she was bracing for a hit or holding something down.

Even Shel winced.

"Man," he muttered, shaking his head. "That's a little too real for me."

Danny popped the cooler lid and dropped the bagged head inside. It landed with a heavy thunk against a bed of ice, the bag crinkling as it settled. He wiped his hands on his shorts and then headed into the salon, like a criminal fleeing the scene.

Kid grabbed the push broom from where it rested against the rail and swept the deck, working blood and scales toward the scuppers with the calm efficiency of someone who'd done worse with less. The bristles slapped wetly against the planks, scrape, drag, repeat, the rhythm steady and detached.

* * *

At the helm, Cap eased the throttles forward, the twin diesels answering with a low, throaty growl. Vibration spread through the deck as Devildam began to move, slow at first, then finding her stride. The chop against her hull deepened into a steady rhythm as she cut ahead, bow lifting slightly with each surge.

He kept one hand on the wheel and glanced over his shoulder. His guests were clustered on the back deck, scattered between the rail and the ratty beach chairs they'd claimed earlier, sun-faded things with sagging arms and rust-bitten joints.

Some sat, drinks forgotten in their laps; others stood off to the side, arms crossed, eyes drawn back to the cooler with the shark head. No one stood close. They gave that part of the deck a wide berth, instinctively avoiding the dark slick where shark blood traced the planks.

The mood had changed. Not silent, but subdued. The laughter had drained out of the group like water from a cracked hull. It would return later, probably, smoothed over by drinks and distance. But Cap had seen this before. The image would stick with a few of them longer than they'd admit. It always did, when the blood was real.

The land lovers never seemed to get it. They liked things clean. Sanitized. Death behind glass, behind curtains, zipped up in tidy bags and buried in straight rows. Out here, death didn't hide. It came fast.

Bloody.

Honest.

The shark was already dead, sure. But it meant something to see it carved like that. Exposed.

Cap turned back to the helm, adjusted course by touch. He exhaled slowly, watching the Sound widen in front of him.

Maybe Kid had gone a little overboard with the machete. Too much muscle, not enough finesse. Cap had seen it in his face, a flicker of something more than instinct. A performance. Like he was trying to hack his way through more than cartilage. Trying to sever something that didn't want to let go.

Hell, they were all carrying something out here. Loss, mostly. Not always loud. Not always fresh. Sometimes it came years after the paperwork was signed, after the final slam of the door.

Cap steadied the throttle, his palm pressed flat to the lever like he was taking a pulse. Out here, he could feel every beat of the boat, every subtle shift in wind and water. It wasn't control over the sea, not really. That was a myth people liked to tell themselves. But it was something. A kind of order. A rhythm. A conversation between man and machine.

He adjusted course a few degrees, eyes narrowing against the light where the sun danced off the water like sparks off steel. Their destination wasn't marked, but he knew it by feel, a subtle slack in the current, a softness in the air. The kind of place you couldn't plot on a chart. The kind of place you only found if you'd lost something first.

With a quiet nod, he pushed Devildam toward it.

Sometimes, the big ones waited there.

And sometimes, they didn't.

* * *

A thick, steady trickle of blood seeped from Devildam's scupper on the starboard aft quarter, winding down the hull in deep crimson rivulets. The motion of the water smeared it into irregular streaks across the white fiberglass, like an artist's careless brushstrokes.

As the boat picked up speed, the blood spiraled into the wake, unraveling into long, swirling tendrils before dissolving into the Sound.

Beneath the surface, the murky stain drifted in slow, curling wisps, a whisper of violence in the otherwise placid water.

CHAPTER 19

The cry of gulls pierced the air, sharp, insistent, echoing across the wind-chopped surface of Pamlico Sound.

Their wings flapped in chaotic bursts as they wheeled and dipped over the floating, headless corpse of the juvenile great white. The small body bobbed awkwardly in the swell, rolling side to side as if the tide itself were toying with it, tugging it back, then letting it go.

Feathers flashed white and gray as the gulls descended in a screeching frenzy, their beaks stabbing at soft tissue, slipping on wet cartilage. One latched onto the jagged wound near the dorsal, jerking back a strip of flesh and releasing a slow spiral of fresh blood that curled and diffused into the surrounding blue like red smoke.

Then - a shadow.

Judy.

She came from below, a mass of muscle and intent, twenty-one feet of prehistoric grace. Her dark form rose silently through the layers of brackish green, blending with the lightless contours of the deeper channel.

For a moment, she was nothing, then everything. The silver flash of her underside caught a shaft of light as she tilted, revealing the ghostly curve of her jaw, the scars along her flank, the steady, inhuman calm in her approach.

The gulls faltered mid-feast, sensing the change, their cries rising in a new register, urgent now, not possessive but afraid.

* * *

The signal shifted.

It wasn't the blood she had tracked that from a distance. Nor the meat, rich with oils. It was something beneath, quieter but absolute.

Decay.

Cell death.

The chemical unraveling that marked a body as spent.

Judy slowed. One slow sweep of the caudal fin. Then another. Pressure gradients wrapped her body, informing her of nearby mass, temperature, vibration.

She circled down.

The shape above was known, its dimensions familiar, even kin-like. But the charge was gone. No tremor of life. No flicker of current along the lateral line. No electromagnetic field.

She had come near enough to strike. Near enough to open it and feed. But the water told her: not this. Not now.

Her body flexed, redirecting with precision. She peeled away from the carcass without urgency or hesitation, slipping into deeper water. Not avoidance. Not retreat. Simply done. The equation shifted.

A final flick of her tail sent a pulse through the shallows. The force fractured upward, broke the surface, and splashed hard into the gulls above.

Wings flapped in confusion. Screeches rose. Spray soaked feathers. One bird spiraled down and struggled to lift again. Judy did not look back.

She cut a wide arc, sensors recalibrating. The carcass was behind her now, useless, silent, already being broken down by the sea. Nothing in her lingered.

Ahead: vibration. Low, rhythmic. Twin signatures, pulsing through the column like drumbeats. Foreign. Constant. Calling.

She turned toward it.

The water deepened, light above, compression below. Blue shaded into green, then darkened into something near-black.

Around her, turbulence faded into a smoother flow.

Salinity.

Temperature.

Motion.

She adjusted course without thought.

CHAPTER 20

At the helm, Cap eased the throttle up to twelve knots.

Devildam responded like she always did, sure-footed and smooth, slicing clean lines through the Sound. The vibration through the wheel was steady, balanced, like a heart beating in sync with his own.

Springsteen played low on the wheelhouse stereo, a thread of sound beneath the hum of engines and the slap of water against hull. That old thrum of defiance and motion. A song built for open roads and long wakes - for men who needed to keep moving because stillness made the ghosts too loud.

Cap didn't sing along. He listened, hands on the wheel, gaze fixed on the horizon, the sun catching the edges of the spray like a flare of memory. There'd been a time when he thought he'd outrun all this, cancer, regret, everything left unsaid. Now he was grateful to stay a step ahead of it.

Cap had the side windows cranked all the way open, and the wind tore through the wheelhouse, warm and briny, whipping at scattered charts and rustling the old CD cases stacked by the console. His sun-bleached sleeves were rolled high, his cap tossed on the dash, leaving thin silver strands to dance wild in the gusts. He didn't mind.

It felt good.

Free.

From his shirt pocket, he pulled a crinkled plastic baggie.

With a flick of his calloused fingers, he tipped ten pills into his palm, a mix of painkillers, chemo meds, and whatever else they told him to take to keep his body moving. No ceremony, no hesitation. He tossed them all back and reached for the half-empty Budweiser sweating in the cupholder.

A long swig chased them down, the bite of beer cutting through the chalky bitterness. He rolled the bottle in his fingers, watching the condensation drip down the label, then set it aside.

He reached for the throttle again, not to adjust it, to feel it.

Solid.

Responsive.

Alive.

* * *

The shoal wasn't there yesterday.

The hurricane had carved it overnight, dragging sand and sediment from the floor of the Sound and dumping it here, a hidden rise built by chaos. Currents funneled the storm's fury into this shallow stretch, piling up grit, shells, and shattered stone in a ridge just beneath the surface.

It looked like nothing. A soft bump beneath the waterline. But it hid teeth, jagged rocks, sunken debris, the kind of sudden terrain that could gut a hull in seconds.

The storm had passed, the skies gone quiet, but the Sound wasn't done. The trap was masked not just by depth, but by the bright shimmer of sun on the surface, each ripple scattering light in a way that erased the shadow beneath.

It had built a snare - and waited.

* * *

Devildam struck.

Not with the violence of speed, she wasn't fast anymore, but with the full weight of her certainty. A boat doing ten knots carries the momentum of trust, of repetition, of years spent knowing where the water ends and the danger begins.

But the bottom had shifted, and no one saw it.

The impact came with a sound that wasn't metal or water or anything the human body could properly categorize.

It was ending.

Sudden.

Unforgiving.

The keel took the blow first, then the entire hull stiffened like a spine jarred in a fall.

Cap was mid-inhale when it hit, no time to exhale.

The boat stopped dead and threw him forward. The console surged up and slammed into his ribs, hard plastic biting as the air burst from his lungs in a single grunt. His knees folded and he crashed back into the chair, stunned.

The half-drunk beer leapt from its ledge and shattered against the console, foam and brown glass spraying everywhere. For a second there was only the bright wash of pain behind his eyes and the loose charts lifting free, scraps of paper fluttering through the wheelhouse like ghosts.

Then came the groan, low and structural. The sound of things yielding. Bolts twisting in their beds. Water finding places it wasn't supposed to go.

Cap stayed hunched in the chair, one hand clamped to his ribs, waiting for air that wouldn't come. For a heartbeat he didn't know what had happened, only that the boat had stopped where it shouldn't have.

His other hand found the throttles by habit and pulled them back, killing the engines before his head caught up.

Somewhere below, something shifted, a muffled knock, a change in pitch, a weight gone wrong.

* * *

On the back deck, chairs flipped. The cooler shot across the fiberglass and slammed into the bulkhead, the lid popped, the shark head inside thudding once, grotesque and heavy, eyes rolling behind clear plastic.

The crab bucket tipped hard, its lid snapping loose as it bounced into the bulkhead with a hollow clang.

Someone shouted - Larry maybe, or Shel - a syllable, cut off.

Kid had unwrapped a sandwich, holding the wax paper in one hand, when the boat lurched. He hit the deck hard, palms down, sliding across the fiberglass. The sandwich went with him, and when he caught himself, his hand landed squarely on it. It flattened under his palm, forgotten.

Danny slammed sideways as the deck jolted, his shoulder crashing into the salon wall. The shock hit like a sucker punch, no warning, no time to brace. He caught himself with one hand on the bulkhead, muscles tight, knees bent, waiting to see if the boat would list again. The impact rang through his bones, a hollow thud in his ribs and a spike of adrenaline in his chest.

Ava stumbled as a folding chair crashed into her shin, her palm slamming the rail for balance. Her sunglasses dropped, caught mid-fall by their tether, swinging.

Her first thought was Jack, *Where the hell….?*

The bathroom. Below deck.

* * *

Inside the salon, Larry groaned, face pale, hand clutching his side.

Colleen steadied herself, one arm across the table, her spilled Diet Coke pooling across the surface of the galley table in a slow, arterial smear.

Shel stood crooked at the bulkhead, one shoe off, a look of disbelief settling into the lines around his mouth.

And then came the fall.

The stern, lifted by momentum, dropped hard.

It hit with a wet, hollow boom that rang through the ribs of the boat. Water exploded outward from the transom and over the rails, blown into white spray.

What came back aboard was scraps and aftermath, cold splash at the ankles, the remains of Kid's sandwich, streaks of shark blood, beer rinsed thin and gone.

* * *

When Devildam grounded, her momentum bled out in an instant but the dinghy didn't know that yet. It kept coming, surging forward on its own inertia as the painter snapped tight between them, drawn straight and humming like a nerve.

The stern dropped, and the line yanked the dinghy's bow down hard. Water climbed its nose, slapping over the gunwale as the little boat pitched forward, nearly pulled under before the tension finally spent itself.

The painter dipped low, sucked into the still-spinning props. It coiled fast, wrapping tight with a dry, choking snap. The dinghy slammed into the transom and bounced once, then wedged hard against the stern, fiberglass grinding against fiberglass, a long shuddering scrape that set teeth on edge.

Devildam wheezed once.

Then gave up her breath.

* * *

Cap didn't move. Not yet.

He felt more than heard the bilge pumps kick on, a faint vibration through the deck, rhythmic and distant, like a heartbeat under the floorboards. Automatic, reliable.

For now.

He could feel her beneath him, the old boat. The creak in her knees. The splinters working loose in her joints. He'd kept her afloat longer than he had any right to. Patched over stress fractures. Reinforced tired welds. Pretended she was something she wasn't.

But she'd met a truth she couldn't outrun. And now the sea was almost certainly inside her.

His ears rang. His ribs ached.

His eyes cracked open. Something was off.

He was in the helm chair, slumped hard over the wheel, ribs throbbing where he'd hit. Light stabbed in from the front windows, too bright. Shadows pooled beneath the consoles like oil.

A high, metallic ringing filled his skull, shrill and unrelenting.

Every breath scraped like gravel through his chest.

Movement. Pressure on his ankle.

"Cap?"

It came through fuzz, distorted and far away.

"Cap, can you hear me? C'mon, man, wake up."

Cap stirred, flinched. Blinked hard. A shape took form beyond the pony wall, Kid, crouched on the steps below the helm, one hand clamped around Cap's ankle, the other braced against the frame. His face was tight with worry.

Cap pushed himself upright with a grunt, one hand gripping the wheel, the other finding the edge of the dash. The ringing ebbed, slowly giving way to the creak of the hull and the distant slap of water.

He coughed, sharp, dry. Pain lit up across his ribs. His mouth tasted of metal and bile.

"What the hell…" he rasped.

Kid let out a shaky breath, relief breaking across his face, "We hit. Grounded. Hard."

Cap groaned, dragging his hand down his face. It came away damp, sweat, salt, maybe blood. Hard to tell. Everything hurt in a low, buzzing way, like a deep bruise hadn't settled yet.

"Ah, Christ on a cracker," he muttered.

His ribs ached with every breath. His mouth was dry. The wheel under his hands felt wrong, still, like a dead thing. No give. No vibration. No promise of motion.

He glanced toward the windows, at the stunned silence on the back deck. Nobody was shouting. That could mean they were fine. Or it could mean they were in shock.

A chill crept down his spine.

Did I get someone hurt?

The thought clawed through him with more force than the collision. His mind flashed to Jack, small and wide-eyed. Ava, tense and barely forgiving. Shel, with that lazy posture that would've offered no protection. Larry, proud and loud, not a seatbelt in sight.

They were all out there. Trusting him.

He squeezed the wheel harder, knuckles whitening. His own pain didn't matter, not the throb in his ribs, not the sting in his shoulder where something had yanked hard. What mattered was the people on his boat. And whether he'd failed them.

He was supposed to know these waters. Every shoal. Every trick of the tide.

He'd run this route a hundred times, hell, maybe more. No radar blip, no swell to tip him off, just ten damn knots and a false sense of familiarity.

And now?

Now he looked like a fool, a captain who'd run his own boat aground during a full charter.

He didn't care about the embarrassment. But they would. They'd whisper about it. Post about it. Maybe someone had even filmed it, the jolt, the shout, the chaos that followed. People didn't experience moments anymore; they documented them.

His name would be on it.

Cap screwed the pooch.

Devildam ate dirt.

Never going back on that boat again.

He gritted his teeth, forced himself upright. Whatever pride was bleeding out of him could wait. He needed to know.

He turned to Kid, voice low but firm, "Anyone hurt?"

CHAPTER 21

Jack had been about to visit Cap in the wheelhouse when the urge to pee hit.

He ducked into the cramped head at the bottom of the stairs, squeezing into the narrow space between the toilet and the mildewed sink, one hand on the wall for balance. The air stank of disinfectant, salt, and old urine trapped in the pores of the fiberglass.

That's when the boat hit.

One violent jolt, like they'd struck something alive. The world pitched sideways. Jack slammed shoulder-first into the bulkhead, his forehead bouncing off the mirror. A sharp, metallic thud reverberated through the hull.

Then, stillness.

No more forward motion. The engines had gone quiet. Only the groan of the hull and the slap of unsettled water remained.

He let out a low, shaky, "Holy shit," and stepped into the passageway, heart hammering.

The narrow stairs rose ahead, steep, half-lit. He climbed fast, one hand brushing the wall for balance.

The salon was a mess, coolers tipped, empty cans rolling. But everyone was upright. Larry hunched at the table, one arm across his ribs. Colleen pushed her sunglasses into place and Shel retrieved his cigarette from the deck, looking dazed.

No one was screaming.

No blood.

No panic.

Only shock.

Ava crouched beside Jack near the salon steps, her hand tight on his arm.

"Are you okay?" she asked, her voice thin with fear, sharper than she meant.

Jack nodded, blinking, "Yeah… I think."

She scanned him, shoulders, knees, face, like she didn't quite believe it.

"What the hell was that?" she asked Larry.

He looked over, brushing spilled Bloody Mary from his shorts, and shrugged: *don't know.*

"I want to see," Jack said, already moving toward the door.

"Jack, wait."

But he was gone, weaving through the clutter, heading for the deck with wide eyes and fast steps. Ava rose slowly, her jaw set, the sting of fear shifting toward anger.

Jack stepped onto the side deck and moved forward along the gunwale. He walked with his arms out for balance, slipping into the rhythm without thinking, years of backyard fences, jungle gyms, and American Ninja Warrior reruns guiding his feet.

His mother's voice echoed faintly in his head: *Watch your footing, Jackie.*

At the bow, he gripped the rail and looked out.

Devildam had stopped dead, her nose buried in a submerged shoal, nothing above the surface, a murky blur beneath the water. The silt was settling, curling in slow clouds around the pale mound below.

Jack watched the patterns drift and fold, and for a moment it reminded him of the mornings his mom would ask him to add cream to her coffee, the way it would billow out in pale ribbons before dissolving. He could make out the shape of the shoal, vague and uneven, like the ghost of land not meant to exist.

No buoys.

No markers.

No warning.

A hidden island of sand and grit sculpted by the storm and waiting in silence to wreck something else.

He looked back toward the wheelhouse.

Through the angled glass, Jack could see Cap slumped in the helm chair, one hand gripping the wheel like it might steady him.

His eyes were open, staring past the consoles, but unfocused, like
he was replaying the moment, trying to figure out what had gone
wrong.

Kid stood beside him, one hand braced on the pony wall, the
other half-raised as if unsure whether to help or back off. His
mouth moved in quick, low bursts, talking, maybe checking for
injuries but Cap didn't answer. Didn't nod. Didn't blink.

From this distance, Jack couldn't hear the words. But he could
see the look on Cap's face. The tightness around his mouth. The
furrow between his brows. The way his whole body seemed smaller
somehow, like the hit had taken more than the boat's momentum.

Jack scanned the Sound.

Empty. In every direction.

No boats.

No shoreline.

Water stretched out to the horizon, rippling under a sharp wind
that hadn't been there a moment ago. Overhead, the sky had
turned brittle blue, high and endless, like it was watching without
offering anything back.

The only sounds were the low hiss of waves against the hull and
the slow tick of something dripping from the rail.

* * *

The air hung heavy.

Danny could feel it, that strange stillness after motion, the low
buzz of adrenaline slipping away, leaving everything dull and raw.

The back deck had been put back in order, roughly, coolers
shoved into corners, rods re-racked, loose crabs wrangled and the
bucket sealed again. Everything looked in order, more or less. But
no one moved like it was.

The guests sat scattered, some on the side benches, some
slumped into the sun-bleached beach chairs, reset after the crash. A
few straddled the rails, elbows on knees, eyes on the water.

Shel held an ice pack to his brow, grimacing with each throb, his mouth drawn tight beneath the bruising. He worked his jaw side to side, slow and careful, like something wasn't lining up right.

Ava rolled her shoulder slowly, the skin red and tender where she'd caught the bulkhead wall. Larry looked hollowed out, his usual bluster dulled by the heat. Sweat gleamed down the side of his neck as he exhaled hard and wiped it away with the back of his hand.

Jack reappeared from the bow, flushed, eyes too wide, the corners of his mouth twitching like he hadn't quite figured out how to make his face settle.

Cap and Kid stepped out from the salon a beat later, the door creaking behind them. Both moved slowly, scanning the deck past the scuffs and dents, as if the obvious damage wasn't what worried them most.

Cap's jaw was set tight, but when he spoke, his voice was steady.

"Anyone bleeding? No? Good. My profound and sincere apologies, but it appears we're grounded."

Jack, standing near the port rail, pointed forward, "You can see it. I was up front. It's like a little submerged island."

Danny crossed his arms. The pressure in his jaw climbed as he stared at Cap.

Unbelievable, he thought. *We were supposed to be in good hands. The old man had claimed to know these waters like his own backyard and now this? Grounded in broad daylight like amateurs.*

Danny could already feel the day unraveling in his chest, a slow twist of heat rising up the back of his neck.

"I thought these things were marked?" he said tightly.

Cap looked back at him, no excuses, no defense. Plainspoken and calm.

"Ayuh. Almost always."

Kid crouched, gathering a half-crushed beer can and bits of his smashed sandwich. Danny watched him move, busy hands, eyes that wouldn't quite meet anyone else's. Doing anything to avoid making it worse for Cap.

Cap continued, voice low but clear, "I don't know why it wasn't marked. Fifty times I've been this way, and fifty times had safe passage. My guess is that hurricane, Gustav, played hell with the currents. Stirred things up. Not the first time. Won't be the last."

"And in case you're wonderin'?" he said, directing his gaze to Ava as if he could read her mind, "Devildam does have radar, depth finder, and GPS chartplotter. None of them woulda helped. What woulda helped was forward lookin' sonar. And she don't have one of those."

Ava started to respond, "Yeah, but if…"

Cap raised a hand, not emphatic, not angry. But final.

"Miss? Respectfully. Whatever you're about to say most likely won't help. We're grounded. Past tense. How about a sec to catch my breath?"

She froze mid-sentence, then gave a single, quiet nod.

Cap paused, then turned to Kid, "Hop in. Take a gander. Check her hull. I'll check below deck. Make sure we're good."

Then, to the group, "You folks sit tight. Help yourself to a drink. With a little luck, we'll put this nasty business behind us and be free in a jiff."

Danny watched him go, saying nothing, thoughts storming behind his eyes.

* * *

Kid moved carefully along the starboard rail, a bright orange probe pole gripped in both hands. At the bow, he eased it over the side and let it drop. The tip struck bottom almost immediately, barely two feet of water beneath the hull. They were lodged hard into the sandbar.

He worked his way aft along the gunwale, stopping every few feet to test again. Three feet. Then five. The slope fell away fast. By midship, the hull was already lifting, floating more freely with each shallow roll.

At the stern, he unlatched the transom door, slipped off his shoes, and stepped through. He eased barefoot onto the swim ledge and let the probe sink, past seven feet, then eight, before it touched bottom.

That was the break. The edge of it.

He moved to the back deck and swung the transom door shut behind him, the latch clicking into place. Then he made his way forward, walking the length of the rail toward the bow. The Sound was quiet now, the boat shifting gently against the shoal, unsure whether to settle or break free.

He moved with effortless grace, like his body already knew the math. At the bow, he gripped the rail, swung a leg over, and dropped feet-first into the shallows below.

He landed steady, knees flexed, the sand shifting beneath his heels. The cool water wrapped around his calves, biting gently at sun-warmed skin. A shiver ran up his back.

He stepped forward, probe pole in hand, and drove it into the seabed directly in front of the bow, marking the depth, taking the measure of how hard they were stuck.

He adjusted his dive goggles, took a breath, and slipped beneath the surface.

* * *

Beneath the water, everything shifted. Sound vanished, drowned beneath pressure and a hush thick as velvet. Sunlight filtered down in wavering beams, fractured by the rippling surface, casting golden ribbons across the ridged sand.

The silt hadn't fully settled, clouds of it curled and drifted like smoke, stirred by the hurricane and the hull alike.

Kid reached out and ran his hand along Devildam's underside. Where the hull met the shoal, the temperature dropped, sun-warmed fiberglass giving way to cold sand packed tight by the storm. He pressed gently and felt resistance. Firm. Locked in. Not good.

He kicked off lightly, drifting along toward the stern, each slow movement sending eddies through the sand. The slope beneath him fell away sharply, the known edge of the shoal dropping into a sudden blue-green void. The edge was abrupt, like the floor of the Sound had been bitten off.

Below that - nothing.

Twenty feet of deepening blue, the bottom swallowed in shadows. No sound, no shape, only pressure and a growing sense that something was watching. The water felt thicker here. Older. Like it remembered storms, wrecks, things dragged into it and never returned.

Kid hovered at the drop-off, suspended. Alone in a silent cathedral of light and shadow.

He felt small.

Exposed.

Devildam was close but in that moment, she could've been a mile away. And whatever else was out there… it didn't feel far at all.

* * *

Cap crouched near the center of the salon and hooked his fingers through the flush-mounted deck ring. With a grunt, he pulled open the engine hatch. The hinges moaned as warm, rank air rolled out. Diesel fumes, old bilge water, and the sharp sting of battery acid carried up like breath from a sick body.

He squinted into the dark below, reached blindly along the underside of the hatch frame, fingers brushing metal and wiring. There. The switch.

Click.

A dome light blinked to life with a faint delay, casting a weak amber glow across the engine compartment, enough to show what he didn't want to see.

The water had claimed territory.

"Damn. Damn. Damn," he muttered.

Pooling silently in the bilge beneath the batteries.

The compartment was tight, four feet deep, maybe three feet wide in the middle, flaring a little near the stern. A man could wedge himself inside, but only if he was willing to crawl and knock elbows against the stringers, the thick ribs of the hull that braced the floor above.

The fiberglass walls were streaked and sweating. A sagging layer of soundproofing clung to the overhead, discolored from years of oil mist and condensation.

The twin diesels sat low on their mounts, port and starboard, dark and unmoving. Between them ran a narrow access trench, eighteen inches across, lined with rust-speckled pipe runs and bundled wiring.

Midship, suspended on a rickety welded steel frame bolted to the stringers, was the battery rack, black-painted, boxy, knocked slightly out of square by years of vibration and torque. The pressure-treated plywood beneath the batteries bowed under their weight.

The six AGM batteries were arranged in two rows, three on the bottom, three on top. Thick, color-coded cables ran from terminal to terminal, bundled with zip ties, feeding into fused blocks mounted on the forward bulkhead. The setup had worked for years. But now it looked like a countdown. The stress of the sudden stop had been too much for one of its legs, and it had collapsed inward.

Cap shifted, leaning farther over the hatch lip to get a better look.

The bilge was the lowest part of the compartment, a narrow trough molded into the fiberglass to catch whatever water made it past the seals. Normally, it was dry, or close. A cup or two, maybe, from condensation or the shaft seal. That's what the bilge pump was for, float switch kicks on, out it goes.

Automatic. Routine.

But this wasn't routine.

Three inches of dark water shimmered in the bottom, rippling with every slight tremor of the boat. The plywood shelf sagged further under the weight, already starting to swell.

One of the bottom-row batteries hovered barely a finger's width above the waterline.

A few more hours, and it wouldn't.

Cap exhaled through his nose, slow.

Could be nothing. Could be water from the impact, sloshed in from the shaft tunnel. He wanted to believe that. But his gut told him different.

Something was coming in. Slow, steady. Not a spill, not a splash, a presence. A leak with intent. And the bilge pump hadn't caught up.

Not yet.

The midship bilge pump kicked on with a sluggish wheeze. Cap heard the sputtering rattle of water forced through the discharge line, uneven, strained. The motor kept running, but the rhythm was off.

No urgency.

No strength.

Only survival.

Devildam had three bilge pumps: forward, midship, and aft, each wired direct to the battery bank. Float switches triggered them automatically. Manual overrides were available, but they wouldn't matter if the power died. The midship pump was the most important, sitting in the lowest sump, right beneath the battery rack. And right now, it was the only thing keeping her afloat.

He stared at the waterline.

It hadn't climbed in the last minute. That was something. The pump might be holding pace. Maybe.

But if there was a leak…

And the leak got worse…

If the pump motor overheated…

If a few more inches crept up and kissed the exposed battery terminals…

She'd go dark.

In an instant.

Cap rested one hand on the hatch frame, the other pressed flat against the deck. He felt the vibration of the boat's bones.

Faint, but steady.

"C'mon, girl. You've taken worse," he whispered. "Hold it together. Just a little longer."

He sat back on his heels and sighed. The faint gurgle of the bilge pump echoed through the stillness like the tick of a fading clock.

* * *

Kid surfaced beside Devildam's transom, hands grasping the swim ledge, breath catching in his throat. The boat loomed above, thirty-nine feet of fiberglass riding low in the shallows, like something spent but holding on.

He grabbed a breath and slipped beneath the surface, facing the bow. A ripple of unease passed through him. Behind him, the Sound stretched wide and heavy. No hull. No frame. Just the heavy open water, and the slow, unwelcome awareness of being exposed.

Light filtered through the green haze above, casting shifting patterns across the hull. Devildam's twin props sat below the stern, mounted on separate shafts that extended aft at a slight downward angle from the inboard diesels.

Each shaft was supported by a bronze strut bolted to the hull, with a rudder mounted aft, one on each side. The layout was tight. Industrial. Everything exposed. Everything vulnerable.

The port prop was clear.

But the starboard shaft was a mess.

The dinghy's painter had wrapped around the shaft and blades like a winch, cinched tight and jammed between one of the blades and the rudder post. The line was swollen with water, fibrous, slick with sand, looped tight, like it had been pulled by panic and torque. The blade couldn't spin. The rudder couldn't move. Not until the rope came off.

Kid eased closer, careful not to kick up silt. He reached out and began working the line. One strand pulled free. Then another. But it was slow, stubborn work, every inch gained exposing three more turns beneath it.

The line had doubled back on itself, twisted into tight figure-eights, pulled into the shaft seal and knotted along the leading edge of the propeller.

His breath tightened in his chest. He ignored it.

Focus. Untie. Yank.

Then, a change in pressure.

Not sound or touch, but a shift in the water around him, subtle and unmistakable.

Something was near.

Something big.

Something dangerous.

He twisted at the waist, slow and fluid, and looked into the open Sound. Green. Light. The endless drift of particles through space. But the feeling didn't fade.

He turned back to the shaft and gave the rope one last pull—but it barely budged.

Not happening.

Not like this.

* * *

Kid burst through the surface with a sharp gasp, grabbing the swim ledge rail. Danny was already there, crouched low, eyes scanning his face.

"What'd you see?" he asked, voice tight.

Kid wiped water from his eyes, breathing hard, "It's a mess. Painter's wrapped tight, shaft and rudder both."

He paused, catching his breath.

"We're gonna need something to cut," he said finally. "And a lot of time."

* * *

Cap ducked into the narrow storage hall next to the stairs. It was cramped, barely shoulder-width, typical of boats like Devildam, where every inch of space got used, hidden, or repurposed.

The old gear locker sat behind a warped teak panel. The door stuck, always had, so he gave it a hard tug and caught the latch with his boot as it swung wide.

Inside was the usual mess: salt-stiffened life jackets, an old chafe guard, coils of line tangled with flares and spiderwebs of forgotten zip ties.

The smell hit him immediately, fiberglass dust, diesel residue, and damp canvas. He reached in, rummaging past a rusted gaff and a half-empty bottle of marine degreaser, until his fingers found what he was looking for.

A red plastic warning cone, knee-high, scuffed and sun-faded from years of UV, sat wedged against the bulkhead. Tucked behind it, crammed in sideways, was a hand-operated bilge pump. The body was compact and utilitarian, a diaphragm unit with a long steel handle folded flat along its frame. The rubber bellows had gone soft with age but hadn't split. It would still pull.

A length of heavy hose was coiled tight and zip-tied to the pump's side, its surface chalked and stiff but uncracked. Old gear. Not elegant. Not fast. But built for the kind of day when power didn't matter and muscle did.

Cap hauled both out, shook off a few flecks of dried salt, and stepped back into the salon.

He crossed the deck, stepping carefully around a loose cooler lid and the scattered remains of a tackle kit, and stopped at the open engine hatch, gaping midship.

He set the cone upright beside the hatch, bright red against the dull beige of the carpet, a quiet warning in a space where nobody else was looking. It wasn't for the others. It was for him.

A marker.

A reminder.

Don't forget what's beneath your feet.

He laid the manual bilge pump down beside the hatch. He didn't test it. No point. It was a last-ditch tool, a manual backup if everything else failed.

Just in case.

Cap stood there for a moment, palm resting lightly on the edge of the cone, listening. The boat creaked, distant and tired. The built-in bilge pump clicked on every few minutes, but the rhythm was lagging. Losing ground.

* * *

Kid slogged through the shallows, each step sinking into the soft, shifting sand. Water streamed from his shorts as he reached the hull near the bow and planted both hands against it, steadying himself.

He braced his feet, squared his shoulders, and shoved with everything he had. Muscles in his arms and legs tightened and burned, the effort making his breath come in short, controlled bursts.

Devildam barely shuddered. Gritting his teeth, he adjusted his stance, shifting his weight lower for more leverage. He pushed again, harder this time, his feet digging into the shifting seabed.

Nothing. The boat didn't budge. Not one inch.

He pressed his forehead against the hull for a moment, catching his breath, then slapped the fiberglass in frustration.

Damn, she was heavy.

With a sigh, Kid grabbed the rail and hauled himself aboard, arms trembling from exertion.

CHAPTER 22

In the salon, Cap heard Kid haul himself up over the bow rail, the wet slap of bare feet on fiberglass followed by a sharp exhale.

He turned as Kid passed the side windows and hopped down onto the deck, water sheeting off him, hair dripping into his eyes. The boy looked pissed, jaw set, eyes flat, but not panicked. That was good.

Cap headed for the back deck, moving stiffly. His ribs throbbed from the earlier jolt against the wheel, but he kept his face unreadable. No use showing wear.

Two faded life preservers, each stenciled DEVILDAM in flaking black letters, were tucked under one arm. He tossed them to the deck without a word, another just-in-case, same as the manual bilge pump, same as the warning cone by the hatch.

He wasn't expecting to need them. But he'd been wrong before.

Kid caught his eye and said it straight.

"Stuck like a duck, Cap. Starboard prop's wrapped tight with the painter. Shaft's frozen. Rudder too."

Cap gave a small nod. He figured as much, but it landed heavier than he liked. He could tell by the way the dinghy was butted against the stern that the painter had gone foul. He glanced down at his old Submariner, the one he'd worn through hurricanes and hospital visits. The bezel was scratched, the band loose, but it kept time. He tapped the face once, doing the math.

Three hours, maybe, before the tide would lift them. If the tide would lift them. The waterline in the bilge hadn't moved much. That was the good news.

The bad news was, if it did, if it climbed a few inches more and kissed those lower batteries, they'd be dead in the water.

He wasn't about to say that.

"Alright," he said aloud. "Smidge of water below. Might not be anything."

Danny stepped forward, arms crossed tight, an edge in his voice, "So what's the story?"

Cap met his eyes and spoke in the same easy drawl he used on green deckhands and angry project managers.

"The story is, sir, we're stuck. Might have a little leak. Nothin' dramatic. So, we've got two choices. One, we sit tight and wait for the tide to lift us. That'll take, what, three hours?"

He glanced at the watch again, buying a beat, "Give or take."

He gestured toward the rail, where the water lapped gently against the hull.

"Option two, we hop over the side, give Devildam the ol' heave-ho. With most of the weight off the deck, no offense, Mr. Kealy…"

That got a few chuckles. Even Larry cracked a grin, shaking his head.

Cap continued, voice steady, "And a little muscle from our young studs here, we might pop her loose in five minutes. Push her back a few feet, get into deeper water. She's not stuck bad, just grounded soft."

"Can you back out?" Jack asked.

"We would, Cap'n Jack, but one prop is bound good. We need both. We try to back up with one prop, we'll yaw. We don't know what the shoal is made of. We find a rock or piece of old rebar, could tear the hull wide open."

Jack nodded.

He didn't mention the pump cycling every thirty seconds. Didn't mention the plywood under the batteries going spongey. Didn't mention the manual bilge he'd staged by the hatch.

Just in case.

"And why not untangle the rope first, the painter, and use both engines to back out?" Danny asked.

Cap forced a smile. *Patience,* he thought.

He'd done this dance before. Not this boat, not this shoal, but the same story. Too many times. Somebody always thought power could solve it.

"Nah," Cap said finally, voice even. "She's wedged bow-down. Props are too close to the sand. We push her free, get her floating. Then we talk about throttles."

Danny hesitated, "You think it's that bad?"

Cap tapped the rail, once, "Not saying it's bad. Saying it's not the right way. Try backing her off now, we suck up half the bottom, twist her sideways, maybe open the hull wider. We do it clean, by hand, we control the angle. I'm not gambling on diesel and wishful thinking."

He looked back at the others, their faces expectant, waiting.

"We do it the right way," Cap said. "The slow way. The smart way. Once she's free, me and Kid'll get that painter untangled. If we have a leak, not saying we do, we'll plug her with a little duct tape and divine intervention, and we're back in business. We'd have lines in the water thirty minutes from now."

He looked around the deck, reading them. No panic. Some tension. But they still trusted him. That was good.

"Unless somebody's feelin' fragile, in which case you're welcome to stay topside and point at things."

That drew the laugh he was looking for. Not much, but enough.

He turned toward the rail, squinting out over the Sound. The sun was high. The shadows short. The boat was holding, for now.

He needed her to hold a little longer.

* * *

Kid reached for the transom door and swung it open with one smooth motion, the hinges creaking slightly as it parted. Sunlight hit the water in a flat, hard glare, and a thin line of foam lapped at the threshold. He took a step back to let the others through.

Shel was already moving, ducking past him without hesitation, drawn to the open edge like a runner to the line.

But Cap was quicker. He stepped in without raising his voice, one hand shooting out to catch Shel by the arm, firm, but calm.

Like he'd seen something Shel hadn't.

"Whoa there, server of the month."

Shel blinked, caught off guard.

"Quarter," he muttered.

Cap gave a small nod, as if that made all the difference, and then fished his ancient flip phone from his shorts pocket, the casing sun-faded and worn smooth from years of rubbing against boat keys and loose change. He gave it a small shake, like it might rattle with memory.

"Apologies. Tell me, server of the quarter…"

He paused, lifting an eyebrow.

"Is that eight-hundred-dollar phone of yours waterproof?"

A smile tugged at the edge of Cap's mouth, but the message was clear: Don't jump yet.

* * *

One by one, they dropped their phones into a cardboard box, a beat-up produce crate Cap had dragged from under the bait table. The bottom was stained dark from fish blood and brine, the cardboard edges warped and grainy from years of damp. It reeked faintly of old squid, salt, and diesel.

Hesitation lingered, hands closing too long around small, familiar weights before letting go. Someone muttered. Someone stared out past the rail like they were cutting loose from shore. A phone hit the pile with a dull thud, then another. Breath went out in short, uneven bursts as the last few followed.

Jack waited until the end, watching the pile grow. His mouth tightened.

He could already feel what was missing, the quiet pull of a tether they'd all agreed to drop.

* * *

Shel and Larry stripped off their shirts, kicked aside their shoes, and dropped into the Sound. Kid, already bare-chested, followed.

Cap kept his bleached Columbia shirt on, then handed his hat to Jack with a quiet nod. He stepped onto the swim ledge and dropped into the water, the shirt billowing before it clung to his frame.

Jack held the hat awkwardly until Cap surfaced and clapped once, sharp, expectant. Jack tossed it down. Cap caught it clean, pressed it to his dripping head, and swam for the bow.

Jack watched them go, broad shoulders and sunburned necks cutting through the Sound, toward the place where Devildam's hull nestled into the buried sandbar.

Danny was next. He pulled his shirt off in a single motion, quick and practiced. Sunlight caught the tattoo across his chest, Ava's name, scrawled high on the right side in bold, looping script. Faded now, but visible. Still there.

Jack noticed his father hesitate, a beat, glancing in Ava's direction.

She didn't look up.

Danny kicked off his sneakers, stepped onto the ledge. His foot slid on the damp fiberglass, but he steadied himself, then stepped off and dropped into the water. It closed over him in an instant, cool, dark, nearly eight feet deep. He surfaced with a sharp inhale, shook water from his eyes, and started to tread. He raised both hands and looked up at Jack.

"Let's go, champ. Shirt off."

Ava's head snapped toward Danny. Her expression shifted, irritation flaring in her eyes.

"Keep your shirt on," she said. "Not without a life vest."

Colleen, standing nearby, bent down and picked up one of the vests Cap had tossed aside earlier. She handed it to Ava without a word.

Ava reached for Jack, trying to fit the vest around his shoulders like he was five.

Jack stiffened.

Danny clapped his hands, "C'mon, buddy. It's not deep."

"Always cutting corners," Ava muttered.

Jack saw something shift in his dad's face, a flicker, there and gone. Danny's jaw flexed, but he didn't say anything.

"What was that?" Danny asked, voice low.

Ava shrugged, but Jack could see it in her eyes, whatever it was, it wasn't small.

"Nothing," she said. "Just... it's always duct tape instead of a proper fix, right? A borrowed truck instead of a rental. Someone else covering for you instead of planning ahead."

They were doing it again. The same tired rhythm. The same loop they always got stuck in.

Danny didn't answer right away. He stared at her, silent, like he was holding something back.

"You think I planned for this?" he said finally. "You think I wanted this to happen?"

"I think," Ava said, arms crossed, "You're always hoping things will hold together. That somehow, good enough will be good enough."

Her voice wasn't loud, but every word landed sharp and direct. She knew exactly where to aim.

Jack clenched his jaw. Heat bloomed behind his ears. It always went like this, some stupid, sideways fight that started over nothing. Always simmering under the surface, ready to boil over when he was nearby.

Even this, getting in the water. It had to become a battle. And somehow, he was in the middle again.

He yanked the vest from Ava's hands.

"What is it with you two? I know how to swim."

Something in Jack tipped, frustration rising, gathering in his chest like pressure behind a dam.

"You're the one who signed me up for lessons, remember? At the YMCA. I was eight. Every Tuesday and Thursday after school. You used to sit in that plastic chair with your coffee and say I swam like a bullet."

Ava looked like she wanted to say something, but no words came out.

"So, stop acting like I'm going to drown."

He glanced between them, jaw tight, "Can't you be normal parents for once?"

He peeled off his shirt and tossed it aside, the fabric hitting the deck with a wet slap. Then he slung the vest around his neck, cinched the strap, and dropped into the water without waiting.

Danny reached for him, too slow. Jack was already past him, arms pulling in clean strokes, headed for the others near the bow.

Behind him, Jack heard Colleen mutter, "Kids."

He didn't look back. Didn't want to see them, his parents, on that swim ledge, throwing shade behind clenched teeth, pretending they weren't unraveling in front of him.

Again.

Each stroke felt like a statement. Like forward was the only direction that made sense.

He reached the others - Kid, Shel, Cap and Mr. Kealy - who were wading in knee-deep water, inspecting the hull from different angles, trying to make sense of what had gone wrong. None of them said anything when he joined them. That was fine. Jack didn't want to talk.

He stood a few feet apart, chest heaving, water dripping from his hair. The wake from his arrival rippled out and vanished into the murk.

Behind him, he could feel them, two voices, two histories, always tugging in opposite directions. It didn't matter if they were arguing about swim lessons or sinking boats or who forgot the damn sunscreen.

It always came down to the same thing: a rope pulled tight and him in the middle, fraying under the strain.

Always in the middle.

And here, finally alone in the water, he realized how tired he was of trying to hold the ends together.

* * *

Near the stern of Devildam, Ava and Danny were locked in the weight of it, words unsaid pressing between them.

"Cutting corners?" has asked. "Why would you say that in front of our son? Sometimes you don't think."

Ava didn't answer. She stepped out of her sandals, shrugged off the cover-up, and tossed it aside. Easing onto the ledge, she slipped cleanly into the water beside him with barely a sound. She surfaced, slicked her hair back, and gave him a look that said more than words could.

"Nice suit," he muttered, all sarcasm, all sting.

She shook her head, smiling without warmth.

"That's all you've got? Nice suit? That's the kind of clever you get when you work in a damn crab shack."

She turned and started swimming, long, even strokes that pulled her away without a second glance.

Danny stayed where he was, water lapping at his collarbone, jaw tight.

Colleen wriggled out of her shorts, kicked off her sandals, and stepped onto the swim ledge in her yellow one-piece, one hand steadying her floppy hat. Star-shaped sunglasses sat tilted on her nose like a wink at the sun.

She glanced from Ava's retreating back to Danny, pulled the transom door closed, and then hopped into the water. The splash nearly took her hat with it.

"There's nothing wrong with working in a restaurant, Danny," she said, adjusting her sunglasses. "Good, honest work."

Danny gave her a quick, polite nod, his jaw clenched.

Colleen paddled away with slow, deliberate strokes, drifting after Ava with the kind of grace age and practice earned.

She didn't look back.

She didn't need to.

CHAPTER 23

They gathered at the bow, eight of them in the water, knee-deep and squinting against the glare.

The plan was simple, push, but already Danny had doubts.

"How much does this thing weigh?" he muttered, mostly to himself.

Cap had split them up by sides. Port side got the muscle - Cap, Kid, Shel, and Jack. Starboard took the rest - Danny, Larry, Ava, and Colleen. On paper, it looked uneven. Danny suggested swapping Colleen for Kid, but Cap shook his head.

"Not about brute strength," he said. "It's about balance. Symmetry. Even pressure across the hull. We push wrong, we twist her and then we're really screwed."

Danny didn't argue, but it felt off. His side had enthusiasm. The other side had power.

He planted his hands against the warm fiberglass, the hull baked to bathwater heat by the sun. He dug his feet into the shifting bottom, searching for something solid. The water was deeper than it looked, up to his knees, and the sand slid under every adjustment.

Cap's voice cut through it, "On three. Use yer legs."

He counted them in, one, two, then shouted the third, and they drove forward together.

Danny pushed with everything he had - arms, back, legs - but it felt like pressing into a wall. His feet slid backward. Sand swirled beneath him. Water churned white around their legs.

Devildam didn't budge.

Not a tremor.

They fell back, gasping. Jack wiped water from his face. Kid cursed under his breath. Danny threw a glance at Cap, eyebrows raised, palms out.

You really thought we were gonna shove this thing free?

Cap muttered, "Too many captains, not enough crew."

Danny snorted. *Typical.*

"I'm out," Colleen said, already backing off. "These scrawny arms aren't helping."

She pivoted, kicked away from the hull, and floated onto her back. With slow, practiced strokes, she began to backstroke toward the open Sound, away from the men, away from the noise. Her movements were lazy, almost graceful, letting the water carry her where it wanted.

"I'll keep you company," Ava said.

She cut her eyes at Danny and he saw a familiar flicker. That quiet exit. That urge to disappear the moment things got uncomfortable.

Always running.

In their marriage, it had been the same. He'd stayed. Fought. Held things together with tape and willpower. She'd checked out the second things required effort.

Always ready to walk.

Always ready to let someone else clean up the mess.

Ava pushed off and glided toward Colleen without a word.

Danny watched her go, heat rising in his chest.

"Thanks for the help," he muttered.

Mostly to himself.

Mostly to the water.

* * *

Colleen and Ava treaded water thirty feet out as the men regrouped near Devildam's bow. The sun was high now, sharp and warm, glinting off each ripple. Ava's hair clung in wet strands to her neck and collarbone, skin slick with salt and heat.

Colleen let her limbs go loose, the sea lifting her with each swell. She drifted on her back, arms out, fingertips skimming the surface. The water cradled her, cool and steady. She could've stayed like that forever, weightless, untethered, the world held out of reach.

On the shoal, Cap gathered the men close, knee-deep near the bow. He didn't raise his voice. Instead, he used his hands, mapping where to push, how to angle their force, spreading his arms wide before driving both palms toward the stern.

"Boy power!" Ava called, cupping her hands toward the boat. "You guys got this!"

Colleen tipped her head back and looked at the sky, endless and clean, not a single cloud overhead.

"Between us girls," she said, "I didn't pay thirty-two hundred bucks to push a boat stuck in the mud."

Ava laughed, loud and real. The edge went out of her voice.

They floated side by side, their bodies swaying gently, legs moving in slow, unhurried bicycle kicks. Sunlight danced across the water, flecking their skin with gold. It felt peaceful, something that had been rare on this trip.

At the bow, Cap positioned his troops. From where she floated, it looked ridiculous. Like they were trying to dislodge a mountain.

"This is like Keystone Cops," Ava said, shaking her head.

Colleen looked at her from the corner of her eye. That energy, sharp, hot, slightly cracked around the edges, was familiar. Women like Ava ran fast and loud. Burned bright. Left trails behind them. Colleen had known plenty, enough to recognize the pattern. Enough to know how it usually ended.

"You seem super high-strung."

Ava blinked, caught off guard.

"Really?" Ava said. "I mean… Danny and I… things are bad. You can probably tell. Maybe that's the vibe you're picking up on?"

"Girl, that's the vibe everyone's picking up on."

Ava let out a weak scoff, more reflex than humor, "It's a weird time for us."

Back near the bow, Larry slipped. One moment he was braced against the hull, the next he was flailing, arms pinwheeling as he plunged backward into the water. He rose, sputtering and red-faced, with as much dignity as he could muster.

Colleen laughed softly, not at him, but at the moment.

And suddenly she was back, twenty years old, maybe twenty-one, watching Larry try to dive off the edge of a pier at Lake Travis. He'd slipped, back flopped, and popped up grinning like he meant to do it. They were young then, strong and dumb, and so wildly, hopelessly in love it ached.

She loved him more now. Not because he'd stayed the same, but because he hadn't. The softness in his belly, the creak in his knees, the way he tried even when he didn't have to. That was the good stuff. That was the glue.

"That's my man," she said, voice warm. "Used to be quite the athlete."

She glanced toward Ava, then back to Larry, "Time has a way of changing us. Shaping us."

Larry got back into place, shaking water from his eyes, pretending nothing had happened. He didn't look at her, but she knew he felt her watching.

She smiled and adjusted her hat.

God help me, I'd pick him again. Every time.

* * *

Ava treaded water in silence, her thoughts drifting. Time had shaped her, too. She had met Danny young, their love easy and electric in the beginning. Then came Jack, the tiny force that rearranged her universe. And success, more than she ever expected, had followed.

She had worked for it, chased it, and somewhere along the way, it had pushed Danny further behind. She hadn't meant for that to happen, but it had. Success had created space, a chasm neither of them had known how to cross.

And maybe Colleen was right. Maybe the looming divorce had changed her, made her harder, more closed off. She hadn't noticed the walls going up, but they were there.

She could feel them now, separating her from Danny, from Jack. She didn't want to be the reason Jack pulled away. Didn't want to be the thing that made him retreat into himself.

She glanced toward Danny, that tattoo bold above his heart. The ink had softened with time, no longer crisp, but legible, like an old headline you couldn't quite forget.

She remembered the night he got it clear as glass: a sticky summer evening, the two of them buzzing on warm beer and adrenaline, stumbling down a strip of beach bars and neon signs. The tattoo shop had been wedged between a t-shirt kiosk and a shuttered ice cream parlor, the kind of place that smelled like disinfectant and bad teenage decisions.

She'd leaned against the doorframe, giggling, trying to talk him out of it.

"You're gonna regret that by morning," she'd warned, but he'd waved her off, already describing what he wanted to the guy behind the counter.

"I want something permanent," he'd said. "Something no fight can erase."

She hadn't understood what he meant, not really. But the words stuck with her. And now, years later, the tattoo was still there, faded, but unbroken. Like a scar that didn't ache but lingered. A reminder of who they were before things turned. Before real life crept in, quiet and relentless, and rewrote the story in smaller, harder words.

"You guys turned out all right," she said to Colleen.

"Wasn't always easy."

"Yeah, but it all worked out. For you two, I mean."

"Know our secret sauce? I let him be him. He lets me be me. Warts and all. And now look at him... he's grown into one big wart."

Ava laughed, a real laugh, short and sharp, "He's not that bad."

Her gaze flicked to Danny. Shirtless. Fit.

"I don't know you that well," Colleen said, tone casual but direct, "so take this with a grain of salt..."

Ava turned, one brow arching slightly. Her stomach tightened. *Uh oh. Here we go.*

"Sure," she said, voice neutral. "What's up?"

Colleen didn't flinch, "You've got this vibe. Angry. Your sweet boy, Jack? He's no dummy. He feels it. And if you're not careful… he'll start to pull away. You don't want to be the reason he shuts down."

The words hit harder than Ava expected. Not because they were cruel, they weren't, but because they were too close to something she already feared. Something she'd felt gnawing at her in the quiet spaces between work and sleep, in the long silences on the drive to school, in Jack's too-polite replies and the way he always looked out the window when things got tense.

She felt the heat rise to her cheeks, a flash of defensiveness bubbling up.

You don't know me, you don't know what I've carried.

She wanted to say it. Wanted to snap. But instead, her shoulders dropped.

Colleen wasn't judging. She was noticing.

Ava looked away, out toward the open water. Her throat felt tight. She kicked gently beneath the surface, letting the salt hold her up. Her hands floated at her sides, fingers slicing through the water in slow, absent movements. The reflex to cross her arms, to shield herself, flickered and passed.

"Yeah," she said after a long beat, voice quieter now. "You're right."

She glanced back at Colleen, who gave a simple nod, nothing smug, nothing performative.

"Thanks," Ava added, this time with more weight behind it.

And for the first time that morning, the pressure drained from her chest, replaced by the slow tide of a real breath.

* * *

The men had gathered again, chests heaving, feet slipping in the churned-up sand. Cap stood knee-deep at the bow, hands on his hips, watching their faces. Determined, yeah but tired too. They'd

tried everything short of divine intervention, and Devildam hadn't
budged more than an inch. He was about to call it. Call it and come
back with something smarter, tools, time, tide.

But then Danny spoke, "What if we rock her? Side to side.
Like… loosen her up a bit."

Cap glanced at him, brow raised, "Rock her, huh?"

"She's stuck forward. So, shift the weight. Get the hull to shift,
not much, a smidge, break the suction."

Jack nodded immediately, water dripping from his chin.

Cap rubbed his jaw, thinking. It wasn't a bad idea. Breaking the
suction could help, might even be the right next step. He hoped the
hull could take it. She'd already taken one hell of a hit.

"Alright," he said. "What the hell. Worth a shot."

He gave the order, voice cutting through the water, "Port side!
Push! Starboard! Pull! On three!"

They moved in rhythm. Left, then right. Shoving. Rocking. The
hull groaned in protest, like it was waking from sleep.

"Keep going! That's it!" Cap barked.

The boat gave a twitch, small, almost imagined, but Cap felt it.
Deep in the soles of his feet, in the tension of the hull against the
water. It wasn't much. But it was enough.

"Again!" Cap barked, urgency rising in his voice. "Push, damn it!
She's coming loose!"

Kid drove his shoulder into the hull, skin slipping against the
slick fiberglass. Shel worked beside him, grunting with effort, feet
sinking deeper with each shove. Larry lost his footing, cursed, then
threw his weight back in. Jack pressed in too, smaller but stubborn,
matching the rhythm as water climbed his knees.

Cap stayed forward, off the bow, knees bent, both hands
gripping the pulpit rail like he could will her free by sheer force of
command. The sand underfoot shifted with every pulse of
pressure, soft, reluctant, grinding down.

"Rock her! Starboard! Now back!"

The hull moaned, a low, warping creak drawn from deep in her
ribs.

Then…

A sharp report, like bone giving way.

The grinding pull of fiberglass over sand.

Water rushing in to fill the void she left behind.

She broke loose.

The bow rose, sudden and stubborn, like a trapped breath finally released. Water surged around their legs, curling with froth and churn.

Devildam slid backward off the bar, her hull groaning with relief, rocking back into the deeper water on her own steam.

She drifted, slow at first, then with gathering motion, untethered, unsettled. Cap watched her move, jaw tight, the silence around them suddenly louder than any engine.

Free.

Cap's chest tightened. The work wasn't done. Not even close.

"Nice," Shel muttered, almost surprised.

"Appreciate the help, boys," Cap said, exhaling.

Danny grinned and high-fived Jack, water spraying between their palms. For a moment, the tension eased between them, Danny grinning, Jack mirroring it, both of them caught up in the same brief victory.

Cap gave Danny a nod. Subtle. Measured.

"Not bad, Captain Crab Shack. Not bad."

It wasn't much, but it counted.

He caught Jack glancing over, eyes lit up in a way Cap hadn't seen earlier. The boy stood a little taller in the water, shoulders squared, pride flickering across his face like sun on waves.

Cap noted it, filed it away.

Small wins mattered.

Especially out here.

* * *

When Devildam struck the hidden shoal, the Sound went still. She didn't scrape. She didn't jolt.

She stopped.

Cold.

Her hull met something harder than sand, an old section of jetty,
half-buried and barnacle-laced, its rebar skeleton jutting like
exposed bone. Not sharp, but cruel, angled to cause the maximum
harm. Like it had waited for her, knowing exactly how to break her.

She hit it bow-first, and the blow traveled up her frame like a
whispered accusation. The laminate skin of her hull splintered. Not
a clean wound, a twisting, grinding breach that opened aft of the
keel.

Small at first. Manageable. Contained. The packed sand of the
shoal cupped her tightly, disguising the worst of it with pressure
and friction, holding her together like a couple that had long since
stopped being kind, but hadn't yet signed the papers.

For a while, it worked. She looked fine. Her stern floated.

But the crew rocked her. They shoved and strained and loosened
the grip of the shoal, believing they were setting her free.

And they were.

But freedom had a price.

The moment she broke loose, the tension vanished. The sand let
go. The force that had been holding her together now abandoned
her.

The crack widened. Saltwater pressed in, first as a trickle, then as
a stream, dark and insistent. It bled into the bilge like resentment
slipping through a marriage in its final weeks, slow at first, then
impossible to ignore.

The hull, strong in all the ways people could see, had been
compromised in the one place that mattered most.

Below deck, the water slowly rose.

CHAPTER 24

The men stood knee-deep at the lip of the sandbar, breathless and dripping.

The sun glinted off the swirling water around their legs, cloudy from the churned-up silt. They faced Devildam together, watching as she bobbed free in the deeper water, her bow light, her stern steady, like a dog shaking off a bad dream.

Danny bent over, hands on his knees, laughing under his breath. Kid stood beside him, swiping a forearm across his face, saltwater streaming down his chest and ribs.

"Gotta give it to you," he said, catching Danny's eye. "That rocking idea? Solid."

Danny looked up, a little surprised, "Yeah?"

"Yeah. You cracked her open."

Shel let out a grunt of a laugh and ran both hands down his torso, flinging water, "I was about two seconds from saying screw it."

"You did say screw it," Larry chimed in, his thick arms spread like he was about to testify. "Right before we shook her loose."

That brought a ripple of laughter, low and raw, tinged with disbelief. The kind that came not from humor, but from the exhale of shared effort and the miracle of it having actually worked.

They stood there a moment longer, catching their breath, the Sound lapping around them.

Devildam floated free.

* * *

Ava drifted near Colleen, water nudging gently at her chin, arms loose, legs moving in a slow, steady rhythm.

On the sandbar, the men were laughing, slapping backs, raising their arms in half-triumphant cheers as Devildam bobbed free at last. Danny grinned at Cap. Jack let out a whoop that echoed across the Sound.

"Looks like they did it," Colleen called to Ava, her voice bright, drifting a few yards away.

Ava didn't answer. She watched the boat, the men, the ripple of the tide. On the surface, everything looked right.

But something underneath felt... off.

The water had changed.

It wasn't colder, or rougher.

Heavier.

Like it had taken on mass.

She shifted in place, adjusting her stroke, and her legs dipped a little deeper. She kicked harder, instinctively, unsettled by not knowing what lay below.

How deep was it here? She wasn't sure. *Ten feet? More?*

The water was still clouded from the sand they'd kicked up when they grounded. Too dark to see the bottom. That unknowing pulsed in her chest like a second heartbeat.

Colleen rolled upright a few yards away, scanning the horizon, "Do you feel that?" she asked softly.

Ava did. Though she couldn't explain it.

It wasn't a sound or a sight. It was a stillness. Like the Sound had stopped breathing. The gulls had gone quiet. The boat floated without motion. The men's voices sounded smaller.

The sea had gone watchful.

Ava's body stiffened, her movements narrowing to the bare minimum needed to stay afloat. Her skin tingled in places she couldn't name. Instinct whispered.

Colleen stilled next, subtly, like a chord gone slack.

She flinched and her gaze snapped to Ava, and Ava knew.

Something had touched her.

Not drift.

Not debris.

Something alive.

Something with intent.

"Did you…" Ava started.

Colleen didn't respond. She turned slowly, carefully, like a swimmer trying not to disturb the water too much. Her breath came shallow.

Something was down there.

Below.

Close.

* * *

The current trembled.

Judy barely moved, suspended in the cooler, denser layer of the Sound. Above, the water rippled warm and slow, sunlight refracting in broken shafts. The division between layers bent light and muted sound, wrapping her in a pocket of concealment.

She waited there, cloaked in shadow.

Above, disturbance.

Threads of pressure danced along her lateral line. Several sources. Large. Slow. Buoyant.

Not fish.

Not seal.

Not familiar.

She turned slightly, adjusting depth with a tilt of her pectorals, slipping forward through the heavier water. A new current met her, thin, strange. Salt and something richer. Skin oil. Trace metals. Sweat.

Alive.

She flared her nares wide and inhaled. The scent sharpened. Not wounded, but close to it. The chemical whisper of stress.

She angled upward. The pulses grew stronger.

One of them moved closer. Limbs dangled beneath the surface, long, pale, slow. Each flick of its foot sent tiny vortices downward. Her electroreceptors lit with faint electricity, heart rhythms, muscular flickers.

She banked beneath it, passing within a body length. Her dorsal fin remained below the surface, tail coiled tight. She moved in silence, every muscle tuned to the pulse of the water.

She felt it, the kick above.

A disturbance directly overhead. The displacement curved around her flanks, a slow swirl of heat and pressure.

A moment of quiet passed between them.

She turned sharply. Circled. Closed the gap again.

Below the surface, her muscles began to contract.

Jaw loosened.

Teeth parted slightly.

Blood vessels constricted, redirecting oxygen.

Gills flexed, pulling water in tighter rhythms.

* * *

Ava floated forty feet off the edge of the shoal, where pale sand fell away into darker water. Colleen drifted farther out, another ten feet beyond her, body loose, arms sculling in slow, careless arcs.

The distance back to the sand looked manageable. It didn't feel that way. The water between them stretched, slack and depthless, offering no landmarks, no promise of footing.

Colleen's kick shortened. Her arms slowed, then changed, no longer drifting, but holding. Her body drew inward, legs firming beneath her as if the water had thickened around her. The surface stilled at her shoulders. She stayed there, suspended, every muscle quietly awake.

Ava blinked.

"Colleen? What?" she asked, too softly to carry.

Colleen's eyes had gone wide. Not panicked, resigned. She was staring down.

Into the green–black murk.

The water split.

No warning.

No breach.

A sudden, violent distortion.

A thick, pale blur surged upward at a diagonal, and in the space where Colleen had been - her center, her ribs, her middle - there was a mouth.

Not in Ava's view long enough to focus, only the impression of white and grey, the massive hinge of a jaw, the twisting torque of something ancient and inevitable.

Colleen folded around it.

Her star sunglasses and hat shot into the air, flung with such force they seemed weightless. It reminded Ava of a car crash she'd once witnessed on Route 12, a cyclist struck broadside, the bike folding, backpack and shoes flying free, as if the body had simply come apart on contact.

Then the water closed.

And Colleen was gone.

No scream.

Seawater burst upward as Judy's tail slapped the surface, flat and muscular, throwing a fan of droplets into the air. Ava flinched as it hit her face, coughing, her legs kicking back on instinct.

Colleen surfaced for a second, one arm flailing, her shoulder shredded, blood clouding the water around her. She turned toward Ava, mouth open, a sound stuck halfway to words.

One eye met hers.

Raw.

Uncomprehending.

Then she was gone again, sucked under with terrifying grace.

The bloom spread fast - rosy, cloudy, unreal - like food coloring dropped into a basin. Ava didn't know when she started swimming, only that she was, legs driving, arms tearing at the water.

She didn't look back. Didn't dare. The ocean behind her felt like a mouth, open and waiting.

Shouts erupted, sharp, panicked, cutting across the water like flares.

"AVA, SWIM!"

"GO! NOW!"

She kicked harder, legs churning, hands slapping the surface. Her breath came in gasps. The water felt thicker now, grabbing at her, dragging her back.

She clawed forward, not toward safety, but toward the sound of human voices. Anything human.

* * *

Knee-deep on the shoal, Larry saw the end of it.

A flash of water. A twisting shape. The unmistakable violence of something being taken. Colleen's body wrenched under like a rag pulled down a drain.

His mind stalled. One blink, no more than that, and the space where she'd been was empty. Just churned water, already settling, as if she'd never been there at all.

The silence that followed was worse than any scream.

He didn't think about sharks or risk or the years settling into his joints. His mind went to Colleen, her laugh, her voice, the way her sunglasses had sat crooked after the grounding. The way she'd drifted off, trusting the current to hold her.

"COLLEEN!"

The name tore out of him as he dove, arms flung wide, body breaking the surface in a reckless arc. Water closed over his head. The sound of the splash vanished at once. All that remained was the place she'd gone under, the widening swirl of red, the space already empty.

He swam hard, chest heaving after a few strokes. The cold hit first, then the ache. His legs kicked out of rhythm, arms already tiring.

Adrenaline pushed him forward, but his body couldn't cash the check. Everything he'd outrun, late nights, lost sleep, the years themselves, closed in at once.

He grunted, cursed, forced his limbs to keep moving.

Ahead, Ava thrashed through the water, headed back toward the shoal, face wide with panic, arms windmilling in a frantic attack.

Their paths crossed for an instant.

She saw him but didn't stop. Couldn't stop. She kept going, lost in the frantic current of her own terror.

* * *

Ava clawed at the water like it might pull her under at any second.

The sandbar was ahead somewhere, close, maybe, but it felt impossibly far. Her strokes were wild, uneven, more survival than swimming. She didn't think about Colleen. Not directly. Not yet. The image was still forming, too large to settle into anything whole. All she knew was that Colleen had gone under without a sound, and the water had gone quiet in a way that meant something was still there.

Something was still there.

That thought looped, jagged and useless, chasing itself around her skull as she thrashed forward. The water behind her felt wrong, too wide, too full. It pressed at her spine like breath on the back of her neck.

Something was still there.

She didn't dare turn.

A flicker passed through her, gut-deep, irrational, ancient.

Something was still there.

Not a wave. Not a current.

Her heart screamed the word before her brain did.

Shark.

Her breath came in choked gasps. Her limbs felt wrong, heavy and far away but she kept going. Panic had replaced instinct, and now it ruled her completely. The water boiled behind her, even if she didn't look. Even if she didn't know.

"SWIM, MOM! SWIM!"

Jack's voice tore across the Sound.

She drove her legs harder, the water resisting every kick. Her breath hitched, muscles burning, but she didn't slow. The shoal was there, somewhere ahead, and she fixed on it, a strip of sand she

could touch, stand on, claim. Whatever it took to reach it, she
would.

The water turned shallow in a heartbeat.

Her knee scraped bottom, sand, soft but sudden. Her feet
thrashed for purchase.

Then hands, strong, steady, wrapped around her wrist and
yanked.

Danny.

He pulled her forward in one hard jerk, dragging her out of the
deep like he'd done it before. She stumbled once, caught her
balance, and collapsed to her knees in the sand. The sun lit the
spray around her like glass shards, but she didn't see it. Her vision
tunneled. Her heart raced.

Jack threw himself into her, arms tight around her shoulders.

She clung to him, gasping. Shaking. Her fingers dug into his back
like she was trying to stay afloat.

* * *

Larry reached the spot where Colleen had been, where the sea
was red with blood, and spun in place, gasping.

No shadow.

No scream.

No hand to grab.

He dove once, then again, lungs burning, the world reduced to
murk and salt and the desperate hope of one more second.

On the third dive, he opened his eyes against the sting, blinking
through brackish swirl. The water was thick with sediment, silt and
sand kicked up by panic and struggle. Sunlight filtered through in
broken shafts, bending and wavering, offering no clarity.

Shapes floated past. Bubbles. Threads of something darker.

Then he saw it, flecks of red.

Not a cloud, not thick, but scattered. Hanging. Threads of it spun
into ribbons, trailing away like smoke underwater. He reached
toward one, fingers open, heart pounding.

A strip of pale flesh drifted past, no larger than a leaf. He recoiled, then lunged again, groping through the water. A shadow crossed his vision, broad, slow-moving, gone before he could register it.

Too big for Colleen.

Too quiet.

His chest seized. He needed air.

He surfaced, gasped, and dove again, this time lower, harder, twisting through the water like he could find her by sheer will. A tangle of long hair shimmered near the bottom. He kicked toward it. A weed.

He spun in place, arms slashing, turning, searching.

There was nothing.

No movement. No cry.

Only the drifting silt, the ribbons of red, and a silence that felt too deliberate. Too complete.

He surfaced again, gasping, his throat burned raw.

"COLLEEN!"

The name came out wrong, too high, already breaking. He turned in place, eyes skimming the water, searching for anything that might resolve into her.

A hand.

A sleeve.

A ripple that didn't belong.

There was nothing. The surface had settled, smooth and blank, the disturbance already dissolving into ordinary chop.

He said her name again, quieter this time, as if volume had been the mistake. As if the water might give her back if he asked the right way.

Then he filled his lungs and went back under.

* * *

Cap stood waist-deep at the edge of the shoal, eyes scanning the water. The sun beat down hard now, glinting off the surface like polished steel, too bright, too calm. His hands were braced on his knees from the push they'd made to free the boat, but his eyes hadn't left the open Sound since the scream.

Then he saw Larry surface.

Not clean.

Not calm.

Gasping, flailing slightly, his face raw with something Cap recognized too well: loss, disbelief, and something darker, an unwillingness to accept what the sea had taken.

Cap's mind did the math in an instant.

Larry wasn't near the others. He wasn't headed for the shoal. He was closer to Devildam.

Cap cupped his hands around his mouth, voice cutting across the water like a flare, "KEALY! GET TO THE BOAT!"

The man didn't react right away, spinning in place, searching the water like he might find her in the churn. Cap saw it in his shoulders, the hesitation. The refusal.

Cap shouted again, sharper this time, "GET TO THE BOAT!"

Danny looked up, followed Cap's gaze, and added his voice, "Larry. GO!"

Kid was already moving to the edge of the shoal, suddenly chest-deep, pointing toward Devildam, now drifting forty feet off, its hull a ghost against the horizon.

"Current's pulling! Swim now or miss your shot!"

Larry finally turned, face drained of color, water spilling from his hair. His eyes found Cap's and held for a single breath, bare, asking, already knowing. Then he moved. Slow at first, like his body needed permission, then faster, arms tearing through the Sound in long, uneven strokes toward Devildam.

Cap exhaled. His gaze tracked the swells behind Larry.

The shark was out there.

He knew that. Somewhere beneath the chop, probably already wheeling back.

Larry had, maybe, thirty feet to cover.

He's not going to make it.

CHAPTER 25

Judy moved beneath the surface layer, balanced in the narrow gradient where warm and cool water met - not a deep thermocline like in the open sea, but a shallow, shifting threshold formed by the storm's passing and the morning sun.

In the brackish shallows of Pamlico Sound, the barrier was thin, sometimes a few feet deep, more suggestion than boundary.

She had fed - her strike precise, her jaw mechanics honed over millennia. Now, metabolic changes slowed her. Oxygen demand dropped. Muscle groups relaxed in a coordinated cascade.

She was no longer in pursuit. She was metabolizing.

Blood clouded the water, drawn through her gills in thin ribbons as she flushed it from her mouth and spiracles.

The residue lingered, cells, iron, disrupted charge, diluted by the current but still thick enough to foul the field around her.

Too much interference.

Too much noise.

Movement disrupted the surface above. Pressure shifted.

A single foot, pale, kicking, dragged across the ridge of her back, behind the gill slit. The contact was brief, the texture soft, unresisting.

She felt it as a line of displaced water pressure first, then through the contact-sensitive skin along her dorsal curve. Her denticles registered the abrasion: not aggressive, not charged, not prey.

No instinct compelled her to turn and strike.

Her systems were already elsewhere, focused inward, conserving. She felt the foot recede and the turbulence collapse behind it.

She slipped forward into deeper shadow, leaving the chaos of blood and motion behind her.

The Sound folded around her like muscle memory. What remained above would decay or drift. It was not her concern.

The ocean made no judgment. It simply moved on.

* * *

Larry's foot struck something under the surface, dense, slick, unyielding.

Not seaweed.

Not driftwood.

Alive.

He recoiled, lungs seizing, every nerve lighting up at once. His legs kicked out on instinct, arms windmilling to lift himself away.

It wasn't a shark.

It was *the* shark.

The one that took Colleen.

He screamed, raw and hoarse, "It's under me! The shark, it's under me!"

From the shoal, voices exploded.

"Swim, Larry!"

"Go! Now!"

"Move!"

Cap. Danny. Maybe Ava. The words blurred into noise behind the thunder of his heartbeat.

He didn't look back.

Devildam floated ahead, twenty feet, maybe less. Her white hull gleamed in the morning sun, a silent sentinel drifting in the tide. She rocked gently, as if unaware of the blood in the water.

Empty.

Waiting.

It looked so close, but the distance stretched like punishment.

Larry thrashed forward, arms and legs burning, heart hammering inside his chest like it wanted out. The water felt thicker with every stroke, as though it knew. As though it meant to keep him.

The shark was behind him. He could feel it, not in sound or sight, but in pressure, in dread. It clung to him like heat, a presence in the water that didn't have to rush to be terrifying.

The boat loomed ahead. Closer now. A salvation he didn't trust.

He kicked, arms flailing more than swimming, every stroke a scream of muscle and will. The swim ledge drew closer, rising in his frame of vision like a promise. His hand hit fiberglass. Slipped. Hit again. Found the rail.

He hauled himself up, chest scraping the slick fiberglass, knees cracking the edge as the boat shifted under his weight. His arms shook, useless for a second, his breath coming in harsh pulls that wouldn't quite fill him.

He reached for the transom latch and found it by feel. Pulled. Nothing.

It wasn't stuck. It was exacting. A small lift, then a slide. He knew that. He tried anyway, too hard, too fast. The mechanism didn't answer.

Water streamed from his hands. Salt stung the cuts in his palms. He reset, slower this time, but his fingers wouldn't listen. The latch stayed where it was, indifferent.

A sound tore out of him - half grunt, half plea - as he gave up on it and lunged forward. He folded over the transom, stomach burning as it dragged, one knee slamming into something solid. Pain flared and vanished.

He didn't stop.

He spilled onto the deck in a wet sprawl, gasping, the world narrowing to the thunder of his pulse and the hot, empty space where his breath should have been.

* * *

Judy slid beneath the wounded Devildam, her twenty-one-foot body moving with the untroubled certainty of something that had never met resistance. A vast shadow in motion, she swallowed light as she passed, pushing the water aside in slow, heaving pulses.

Her dorsal fin, tall, unyielding, rasped along the underside of the hull, a sound like sandpaper drawn across old bone.

For a breathless moment, her mass pressed there. The fiberglass shuddered. A low, hollow thunk traveled through the boat, more felt than heard, and the pressure shifted, steady, inevitable. Devildam slid ten feet into deeper water, dragged like driftwood caught in a riptide.

The hull scraped, then stopped. The water settled. The shadow beneath thinned and vanished into the gloom.

* * *

Larry lay crumpled on the deck, limbs twitching with aftershocks of panic, muscles locking and releasing like shorting wires. His arms refused to answer him. His chest heaved once, then seized. The breath caught, stuck. He wheezed it out with a strangled noise, more animal than man.

Get up.

He drug an elbow beneath him. The world tilted. A black haze crawled in from the edges of his vision.

His heart hammered, not fast, but hard, like it was being squeezed from the inside. A dense pressure pressed into his sternum, low and deep, unfamiliar and wrong.

Not panic.

Not fatigue.

Something else.

He rolled onto his side and retched. Bloody Marys and seawater sprayed across the fiberglass, burning his throat, the taste coppery and sour.

His body convulsed once, then again.

A cold sweat slicked his face. He pawed at the deck, trying to sit up, to breathe.

CHAPTER 26

The engine compartment of Devildam groaned under the weight of its own decay.

Tight, sweltering, and slick with desperation, it stank of diesel and rust layered over something quieter, wet plywood, sour metal, the slow rot of things left unattended too long.

Overhead, the single bulb swung from its corroded chain, casting jittery light that made shadows dance across the ribs of the hull like ghosts.

Where there had once been a manageable puddle beneath the battery rack, water now sloshed halfway up the lower tier. It lapped gently at the swollen plywood support, inches from the terminals. The sheen of oil floated in broad, rainbow smears, twisting with every slow shift of the boat. The bilge pumps hummed like they still believed they might win. But they were losing.

Steadily.

Quietly.

Surely.

Each pulse of the pumps was like a failing heartbeat, valiant, insistent, but no match for the volume. They weren't broken. Not yet. But overwhelmed. Working harder than they were ever meant to, drowning in a tide they could no longer manage.

It didn't fall apart all at once. No rupture. The slow accumulation of what had gone unattended. The kind of wear you notice when it's too late, small leaks multiplying into something unmanageable. And now the machinery groaned beneath the strain, working past its limits, barely holding off the inevitable.

A hiss of escaping steam whispered from the manifold. A cable trembled in its bracket. Devildam swayed slightly with the swell, her own bones creaking as the Sound claimed her from below, inch by inch.

There was time. But not much.

CHAPTER 27

Larry's consciousness drifted in and out, his body leaden, his breath shallow.

His head throbbed, a slow, merciless pounding at the base of his skull. His muscles ached, knots of pain twisting through his arms, his legs. His chest, *Christ, his chest*, burned, a tight vise gripping his ribs, refusing to let go.

His skin was hot under the sun, raw in places, stretched too tight. No shirt. Nowhere to hide.

A wetness clung to his lips. He swallowed hard, tasted salt, copper. Blood? He spat, a thick, red splatter against the deck. His sluggish mind fumbled for the answer before the memory hit: Bloody Mary.

The world rocked beneath him. The deck slanted, the horizon swayed. He blinked up at the cloudless sky, eyes raw, unfocused. He sucked in a breath, the air thick with the scent of salt, oil… and something else.

Blood.

Death.

This was it.

A lifetime of neglect, of poor fitness, of easy choices catching up all at once. Every missed jog, every extra plate, every adult libation instead of a God damn water, it all clung to him now, dead weight pulling at his limbs. His body wasn't built for survival. He'd let it rot, slow and steady, one small indulgence at a time. And now it was failing him.

A groan crawled up his throat as he moved. Arms shaking, he pressed his palms to the slick deck and dragged the sealed crab bucket closer, more for leverage than intent.

He didn't even register the faint tapping of the creatures on the inside. He leaned into it, hunched over, then shifted enough to sit.

The plastic creaked beneath him, cool against the backs of his legs.

For a long moment he sat there, breathing through clenched teeth, sweat gathering at his brow despite the wind.

Then, slowly, he braced one hand on the gunwale, the other on his thigh, and pushed. His legs screamed, thighs trembling under the weight. He rose in inches. Lungs burned. Head pounding, every heartbeat a hammer blow behind his eyes.

But he stood.

Barely.

He steadied himself. As he did, his gaze landed on the box resting on the deck filled with their phones. It sat there, untouched, precarious, as if waiting for fate to decide its usefulness. He picked it up and set it on the gunwale.

His hand moved on instinct, reaching in, fingers brushing against the cool, smooth edges of technology. His phone. The case was scuffed, edges peeling, a faded sticker of a crab barely clinging to the back. He gripped it, pulling it free, his thumb automatically pressing the power button. The screen flickered to life, smeared with a sheen of moisture from his damp hands.

"Kealy! Mr. Kealy! Over here!"

The voices came from far away. Like memories. Like a TV left on in another room.

The others.

Habit had him drop the phone into his pocket and turn towards the voices.

They stood on the sandbar, sixty feet away now, maybe more, small against the wash of pale sand and moving water. A knot of bodies, tense and unmoving. Waiting.

Cap was easy to pick out at the front, planted wide, hands locked on his hips. He didn't wave or shout. He just watched Larry with that hard, measuring look, the kind that came from having seen men break before they ever said a word.

Danny hovered just behind him, arms folded tight, shifting his weight like he couldn't find a place to stand.

Ava had Jack pulled in close, her arm firm across his shoulders, her eyes jumping between Larry and the water as if expecting it to give something back.

Shel stood apart, hands tangled in his hair, lips moving around words Larry couldn't hear.

And Jack, too still, fists balled at his sides, staring straight at Larry like willpower alone might hold him upright.

They didn't look like a group anymore. They looked like witnesses.

Then it hit.

Colleen.

The shark.

The attack.

His stomach clenched hard enough to make him bend, breath coming shallow and wrong. The world narrowed to the water at his feet, the shine of it, the false calm, his mind circling one impossible thought again and again.

She had to be there. Just below the surface. Caught on something. Waiting.

He scanned the water anyway, eyes burning, heart beating so hard it felt loud, like it might carry. Every ripple became a possibility. Every dark shape a lie he wanted to believe.

He kept looking, not because he expected to find her but because stopping felt worse.

* * *

Cap stood knee-deep at the edge of the sandbar, arms crossed, fingers absently pressing against his ribs. His eyes were fixed on Devildam, far enough away to see the whole of her, close enough to notice the ways she wasn't quite right.

Something was off.

She drifted bow-high, the stern dragging in the water like an old dog favoring a bad paw. Her running lights burned against the pale late morning, faint but visible, green to starboard, red to port, steady as ever, even as the rest of her sagged. The movement wasn't dramatic - not yet - but it was wrong. A half-second slower on the recovery. A little too heavy on the tail end.

Cap squinted and took a step forward, instinct rising like a tide.

The bilge outlet spat a burst of water, then another. Too fast. Too frequent. He waited for the pause that should've come between pump cycles.

It didn't come.

The pumps were running near-continuous now, spitting froth and streaks of oil into the Sound. He knew the sound by heart, what they should sound like, and what they didn't. That wasn't drainage. That was desperation.

She was taking on water.

Cap's throat tightened. Not panic. Not yet. But urgency. The sense that the clock was ticking.

Could be minor. A pipe. A gasket. Something knocked loose when she grounded. He told himself that. Let the thought hold for a moment before it slid away under the weight of what he really knew.

Devildam was listing.

Slight, yes - but unmistakable.

Too much weight aft. Too much water in the wrong places.

Cap muttered to himself, half under his breath, "Come on, girl. Don't do this."

But she already was.

And his gut knew it before his mind caught up.

"She's sinking," he muttered.

The thought landed heavy. Not loud, not dramatic but certain.

He squared his shoulders, turned to the others, "She's sinking."

* * *

"SHE'S SINKING!" Cap yelled.

Larry's head snapped up.

"KEALY! YOU HAVE TO PUMP THE WATER OUT -

NOW! MOVE!"

Cap's voice cracked with urgency, cutting through the distance. He took a step forward, as if sheer will might push Larry into action.

"GET TO THE PUMP! THE HATCH! IN THE SALON! WE DON'T HAVE TIME!"

Larry froze.

His mind spiraled, everything crashing in at once. He had to help the survivors - get the water out, save the boat.

But then, Colleen.

The shark.

The attack.

His breath caught, his chest tightening as the weight of the mental stress threatened to pull him under. His hands hovered uselessly, unsure what to grab, what to fix first.

Cap's voice lashed through the wind, sharp and urgent, "HEY! WE NEED YOU!"

Larry's gaze darted toward the sandbar. The survivors, huddled, wide-eyed, waiting. Hope clung to their faces like salt spray.

"HAVE YOU SEEN COLLEEN!?" Larry shouted.

The sound fell flat. No one answered.

Cap's mouth tightened, the muscles in his jaw jumping once before he looked away. Danny took a half-step forward, then stopped, stranded between movement and fear. Ava's arm cinched around Jack, pulling him in, her gaze flicking back to the water before she could stop it.

The silence told him everything.

They knew. They all knew. But no one wanted to say it.

Deep down, Larry knew, too. He had known from the moment the water churned red. From the way no one would meet his eyes. But knowing and accepting were two different things. If he said it out loud, if they said it, then it was real.

And he wasn't ready for that. Not yet.

* * *

Larry stepped into the salon and crossed to the open hatch, the red cone Cap had set earlier standing guard beside it. He leaned over and looked down.

The dome light cast a weak, yellow wash into the engine compartment, just enough to reveal the water pooled around the engine mounts. It lay black and still, deeper than it had any right to be. The battery rack loomed above it, and the bottom row sat uncomfortably close to the surface

He moved fast.

The portable bilge pump lay where Cap had dropped it, hose still zip-tied to its frame. Larry dragged it closer and set it down hard on the deck.

The pump itself was squat and compact, a metal housing bolted to a rubber diaphragm. A long steel handle was hinged at one end, folded flat against the body when stowed. Larry flipped it upright and felt it lock into place, like the arm of a jack.

He snapped the zip tie, freeing the coiled hose, and carried it across the salon to the side window. The latch fought him before giving way. Heat rushed in. He shoved the discharge hose through the opening until it hung outside the hull, then jammed a rolled dish towel around it, packing the gap tight so the hose wouldn't slide back or spray water into the salon.

Then he turned to the intake.

He uncoiled the second hose and fed it down through the open engine hatch, pushing until he felt it bump bottom.

He dropped to one knee beside the pump and flipped the steel handle upright. It wasn't long, barely a forearm's length, and offered no leverage unless you leaned into it.

He braced the pump with his foot, wrapped both hands around the grip, and pulled. The handle fought him, rubber resisting inside the housing. His shoulders bunched. His back tightened.

He shoved the handle forward again, short and hard.

Nothing.

He pulled once more, slower this time, feeling for the resistance. The pump answered with a wet, hollow gulp. A moment later came the rush, water racing through the hose, a gurgling surge that ended in a heavy splash as it exited the hose and cleared the hull.

Larry stayed where he was, one knee down, one foot planted, working the handle in short, punishing strokes. The motion left no room for thought. Just pressure. Just repetition. Each pull dragged water up from below; each shove forced it out again.

His arms burned.

His grip slipped and reset. He leaned into the work anyway, measuring time not in minutes but in strokes, trying to stay a fraction ahead of something that would not stop on its own.

* * *

Cap watched oily water spurt from the exit hose Larry rigged to the window. It splattered into the sound in thick, sputtering bursts. He exhaled, a tight breath he hadn't realized he'd been holding. It was working. The manual pump was working.

For the first time in the last chaotic stretch of minutes, a thought flickered, maybe they had a chance. Maybe they'd make it out of this yet.

* * *

Larry stayed low, shoulders rounded, weight pitched over the pump. Each stroke burned shorter than the last. Sweat poured down his back, soaking his shirt, blurring the line between heat and seawater until everything felt the same, slick, hot, unbearable. His breath came ragged, wheezing in time with the pump, both of them sounding used up.

She might be gone.

The thought didn't arrive gently. It landed whole.

Colleen was gone.

The Sound had taken her and there was no arguing with that. No strength left to prove. No version of himself that moved faster.

But the others were still out there - Jack, Ava, Kid. Even Danny. And Larry was the only one inside the boat, the only one keeping water from winning outright.

That had to be enough.

He kept one hand on the handle and reached for his pocket with the other. His fingers were numb, clumsy. The phone stuck against the lining, slick with water. He cursed under his breath and yanked harder until it came free.

He braced the phone against his knee and wiped the screen with the hem of his shorts. It blinked awake. His thumb hovered, trembling.

Nine. One…

The pump handle slipped.

It kicked forward under his grip and slammed into the deck, the jolt snapping up his arm. The phone wobbled, weightless for half a second too long.

"No…"

It dropped into the engine compartment with a soft splash.

Larry lunged, heart spiking.

For an instant, the screen glowed beneath the surface, pale and warped by oil and ripples, then flickered once and went dark.

Gone.

He stayed bent over the hatch, breath tearing out of him, the pump forgotten by his knee.

"Oh my God," he whispered.

He leaned close to the water and plunged his arm into the engine compartment.

The smell hit first - diesel and rot, sharp with battery acid and mildew, undercut by something sweet and metallic that turned his stomach. His fingers scraped blindly across cold metal, hose clamps, slick machinery. Cables slid against his wrist. Slime coated his skin.

Nothing.

He leaned farther in, chest tightening, groping at the dark as if the phone might still be there, hovering just out of reach.

It wasn't.

* * *

The survivors stood in eerie silence, eyes fixed on Devildam.

She floated beyond reach, bow high, listing slightly, something off in her posture. They could all see it now. Like she knew she'd let them down.

No one spoke.

Their breaths came shallow, nerves strung tight. All attention was fixed on the boat, waiting, watching, for any sign of Larry.

The only proof of his effort was the bilge hose draped through the cabin window, spurting oily water in fitful bursts. Each discharge felt like a small defiance, man forcing back the sea, inch by inch.

The next burst didn't come.

No sputter. No warning. The hose sagged, heavy and motionless.

What followed was worse than sound: stillness.

A long, suffocating pause settled over the group. No movement on the boat.

No sign of Larry.

Only quiet.

Ava tightened her grip on Jack. Shel's hands dropped from his head, fingers flexing at his sides. Cap's stance shifted forward, his muscles taut. The air itself seemed to hold its breath.

Larry emerged from the salon, his body heaving, one hand pressed to his side, trying to hold himself together.

Danny squinted, brow furrowing, "Something's wrong."

Even from a distance, Kealy looked horrible.

His skin was a blotchy, sweat-slicked red, his chest heaving as he stumbled to the gunwale and collapsed against it. His arms shook, his fingers digging into the fiberglass for support as he tried to steady himself. His breathing came in quick, shallow bursts, each one lifting his shoulders in sharp, uneven jerks.

After a moment, he forced himself upright, eyes darting wildly. His gaze landed on the box of phones perched on the gunwale. He reached in, rifling through the contents, his movements frantic. He pulled one free, held it up high.

His mouth moved, but the wind ripped his voice away.

His expression twisted in frustration. He squared his shoulders, sucked in a breath, and bellowed over the rising wind, "WHAT'S THE CODE!?"

"What's he saying!?" Ava asked. "MR. KEALY! WE CAN'T HEAR YOU!"

"Aw, Christ," Cap muttered. "He's in bad shape."

* * *

A hot sheen of sweat glazed Larry's face, his skin pale and waxy beneath the flush creeping up his neck. His breathing had turned shallow, short, sharp pulls like a man trying to pull air through a cracked straw.

He stared down at Jack's smartphone in his hand, the boy's grinning face frozen on the lock screen. Below it, glowing in clean, merciless white:

ENTER PASSCODE

Larry's thumb hovered uselessly. He didn't know it. He hadn't thought that far.

His other hand gripped the edge of the gunwale, knuckles bloodless. He opened his mouth to shout, but the words came jagged, tangled in pain.

"I said…" His chest spasmed mid-sentence. A guttural cry tore loose, raw and involuntary.

His hand snapped to his sternum, fingers digging in. The pain radiated outward, jaw, arm, ribs.

Not pressure.

Not discomfort.

Fire.

He stumbled, knees knocking against the console, nearly pitching forward. He caught himself on the gunwale, trembling. His breath wheezed in and out like a torn bellows.

"I said…" he rasped, voice cracked and watery, "It needs… a… a passcode…"

Across the water, Cap's voice cut through the haze, "USE THE RADIO! IN THE COCKPIT!"

Larry turned, everything spinning, his vision greying at the edges. He moved because stopping wasn't an option.

He turned toward the wheelhouse, his sluggish mind latching onto Cap's order, *The radio. I need to find the radio.*

His legs felt like lead as he took his first step. Every muscle ached, his chest too tight, but he forced himself forward. One foot in front of the other. He could do this. He had to do this.

Then something in the water caught his eye, a flicker of white twisting in the current.

He stopped, breath snagging.

Colleen's sun hat.

Ten feet off the stern, bobbing gently, turning in slow, careless circles. Untouched. Intact. As if it had simply drifted loose and waited.

The sight of it hit him harder than the water had. Harder than the silence. Something inside his chest lurched, once, twice, then broke rhythm. A sharp, blinding jolt tore through him, stealing his breath mid-inhale.

Larry staggered. One hand clutched his sternum. The other reached for the rail and missed.

Heat tore across his chest, up into his jaw, down his arm. His fingers curled uselessly against his chest. He tried to breathe and couldn't get enough air to matter. The boat tilted. Or maybe it was him.

He reached again, toward the rail, toward the water, toward the hat.

His knees gave out.

They hit the deck with a hollow thud. One leg kicked wide, striking the crab bucket. It tipped and clattered, the lid popping free and sending the fiddler crabs across the fiberglass.

Larry pitched forward, dropping hard to his knees. One hand slapped the deck, skin burning as it slid. The other reached blindly over the rail, toward the hat, toward the small white circle turning just out of reach.

Colleen's name rose in him and stopped there. What came instead was her face: laughing that morning, leaning over the rail, eyes narrowed against the sun, salt spray caught in her hair.

The memory flared too bright to bear.

His shoulder bumped the cardboard box of phones.

It tipped, rocked once, then slid over the edge in a slow, unreal arc.

The splash was soft.

The water closed over it without hurry.

Larry stayed where he was, kneeling, half-folded over the rail. One arm stretched out over the Sound. The other lay slack against the deck.

A thin breath slipped out of him and didn't come back.

The fiddler crabs didn't scatter this time. They stilled in the corners and seams of the deck, half-hidden beneath coolers and coils of rope, their jointed legs angled toward him.

A few crept closer, cautious, testing the space he no longer claimed.

The boat rocked once, gently, as if settling.

Then nothing moved at all.

CHAPTER 28

The phones drifted downward, turning slowly in the murk.

Some tumbled end over end, others fluttered like leaves, catching brief currents before sinking lower.

Tiny bubbles rose from their seams, silver threads unraveling toward the surface, bursting soundlessly.

Screens flickered, blue-white glows dimming with each foot of depth.

A text half-sent.

A lock screen lit and beckoning.

Then dark.

CHAPTER 29

Larry's final breath rasped out in a long, shuddering hiss.

His body sagged, weight sinking into the gunwale, one arm draped lifeless over the water.

His fingers, once curled with desperate reach, unspooled toward the Sound.

Jack's phone slipped from Larry's open hand, slick with seawater and sweat. It tumbled once, twice, then struck the water with a faint splash.

A flash of reflection, then nothing. It joined the others at the bottom of the Sound.

A few feet away, Colleen's sun hat spun on the surface, its brim catching light as it drifted in slow, indifferent circles.

CHAPTER 30

The survivors stood knee-deep in the shallows, the sandbar barely holding them above the vast reach of the Sound.

Water curled around their legs, cool, deceptively gentle. But beyond the narrow strip of sand, Pamlico pulsed with something darker.

Steady.

Waiting.

Beneath their feet, the ground shifted, softened by the tide's relentless pull. A step too far in any direction would send them plunging into deeper water, where the currents lurked, twisting and waiting.

Sixty feet out, Devildam rocked gently on the swells, her hull slick with seawater and streaked with rust. Larry's body slumped against the gunwale, head and shoulders visible above the rail, the rest of him swallowed by the fiberglass wall of the port side.

His arm hung limply over the side, fingers a few inches above the water as the boat swayed. The gentle motion made it seem as though he might be alive, reaching for something unseen. But the unnatural angle of his neck and the quiet in the half-lidded eyes told the truth. The sea rocked him like a thing already claimed, already forgotten.

The world had grown still except for the whisper of the wind and the rhythmic breath of the tide.

No one spoke.

The water held them, stranded between the living and the dead.

* * *

They stood scattered in the shallows, legs stung by salt, water nudging gently at their calves. The silence wasn't shock, it was the mind tripping over itself, trying to arrange the impossible into a shape that made sense.

A shark took Colleen.

Larry made it to the boat.

Got a manual pump running.

Then it stopped.

He yelled something - passcode?

Then collapsed.

He knocked the box of phones overboard.

Now the phones were gone.

Lost.

All of them.

Ava couldn't make it fit. The sequence. The speed. Less than ten minutes had passed since the massive fish rose and took Colleen. It felt like watching a storm surge swallow a bridge just crossed.

Next to her, Shel let out a strangled sound, half gasp, half growl, and turned, eyes wide and unfocused.

"What...? What the hell happened?" he whispered.

His hands shook at his sides. He ran them through his dripping hair like he could scrub the moment off his skin.

Then louder, his voice breaking apart, "What in the hell happened!?"

No one answered. Pamlico Sound stretched around them, wide and glittering, serene as a painting. Unmoved by Shel's questions.

Shel turned a slow circle, pleading with the others' for something, confirmation, denial, anything.

"Somebody say something! Did he... keel over and die? Just like that?"

No answers.

Ava stepped forward without thinking. She wrapped an arm around his shoulders, pulling him close, her other arm curled tight around Jack. She didn't say a word. Held them both, feeling Shel sag into her, trembling. Jack leaned in, too, his arm wrapped around her waist.

It was more comfort than contact. The only tether they had left.

And she felt it, quiet and crushing, that whatever came next, she was the one holding the line.

* * *

The water cradled them, bodies half-submerged, minds drifting somewhere between exhaustion and disbelief. Danny sat with his arms resting on his knees, gaze fixed on the lifeless figure aboard Devildam.

The water, cooled by the hurricane's passing, seeped into his bones. A shiver curled through his chest, sharp and mean. Instinct kicked in. His balls crawled higher to escape the chill, a reflexive, ancient reaction that might've made him laugh if there were anything left to laugh at.

But there wasn't.

The water had taken Colleen. Then Larry. And it wasn't done.

"Someone will come," Danny said, his voice barely carrying, brittle even to his own ears.

He didn't know if he believed it. He said it because it sounded like something a man should say.

From a few feet away, Kid gave a dry swallow and shook his head, "Not so sure."

Danny didn't need to ask what he meant. There were no planes overhead. No boats slicing the horizon. Only the bright, empty sprawl of the Sound and the feeling that the world had forgotten they were out here.

The idea of rescue suddenly felt like a fairy tale, something he used to believe in, like Santa or the idea that things always worked out for the good guys.

Cap stood nearby, legs wide for balance, his face unreadable.

"No one is coming," he said simply.

Shel let out a tight laugh, "They were good people. Nice people. Didn't deserve…"

He trailed off, voice cracking, the sentence unfinished.

Cap didn't flinch, "Sea don't care, son. Good, bad. She takes 'em all.”

"Hey, Mr. Barton? Cap?" Danny said sharply. "Enough with the Pirate Pete bullshit, okay? People are dying, and you're standing there dishing out platitudes."

He didn't know why he snapped. Only that it had been coming. And for once, he didn't back down.

He felt Ava glance his way, a flick of acknowledgment, but that was enough. Enough to register that she'd noticed. That maybe she even approved.

Danny had spent years second-guessing himself, shrinking around her disappointment, but this time he didn't fold. And that flicker of recognition from her, brief, quiet, struck deeper than he expected. It stirred something he hadn't felt in a long time. Not love. Not longing. Something closer to being seen.

Cap met his eyes, jaw working once. Then he gave a small nod, "You're right. Apologies."

Cap glanced to Devildam, the wreck of it, then back at the broken circle of survivors clinging to the sandbar like driftwood.

"Didn't know 'em well. But they seemed like fine folks."

He pulled off his cap and ran a hand through the wisps of hair clinging to his scalp. Then he dipped a hand in the Sound and rubbed seawater across his head like it might clean something deeper.

Danny froze.

He hadn't noticed it before, the missing hair, the thin papery skin along Cap's temple. But now it clicked. The memory slammed back: Ava's father in that hospice recliner, sunken, quiet, the chemo having stripped him bare.

Danny remembered the way Ava had curled up beside the man, whispering like her voice could anchor him in place. Danny had stood there, fists tight, useless. That was the first time he'd really understood what it meant to be powerless.

Now, looking at Cap, he saw it again. That same surrender. That same timeline narrowing.

Their eyes met.

Cap didn't speak. He didn't need to.

Danny swallowed hard, the taste of guilt rising like bile.

I'm sorry, old man. I'm so goddamn sorry.

Cap nodded, barely more than a twitch, then turned to scan the horizon.

"You're gonna get thirsty," he said. "Don't drink the water."

There was no judgment in his tone. No drama.

"Get you sicker than a dog," Cap added, and then gave Danny a dry glance. "Not a platitude."

Danny said nothing.

Above them, the sun climbed higher.

The water glittered, empty and wide.

And time, merciless as ever, kept moving.

CHAPTER 31

The sun crawled across the sky, indifferent to the suffering underneath.

It burned, steady and relentless, dragging its heat across the water, baking the sandbar where the survivors huddled. There was no mercy in its gaze, no pause in its slow march westward. Like the sea, it didn't care.

"Oh my God. There it is."

Kid's voice cut through the thick, stagnant air. He pointed toward the open water, fingers stiff with tension.

All eyes followed.

The dorsal fin cut the surface twenty feet out, moving with eerie precision. Even from here, that familiar shape was unmistakable, blunt where it should've tapered, scarred from some old violence. Behind it, the SPOT tracker clung to the bottom of her dorsal, blinking once, then again, beaming its quiet signal into the sky.

Instinct took over.

Feet slid backward, a collective retreat, though the water remained too shallow for the predator to reach them.

For now.

* * *

Cap's breath hitched.

He'd seen adult great whites before, off Hatteras, near the Gulf Stream, even once out near the canyon wall, but never one this size, and never this far inside the Sound.

His pulse thudded in his throat as he watched her move - fluid, deliberate, impossibly calm. She didn't thrash or dart. She didn't need to. Every shift of her body read like intent.

He'd bumped into big fish in his life, tuna the size of bathtubs, bull sharks that looked like they'd been carved from stone, but this one was different. Not for her size. It was the way she carried it. Measured. Watchful. Like she'd already figured out who they were and what they were worth.

"Sometimes we get whites in the Sound," he said, more to himself than the others. "But nothing like that."

* * *

"Maybe that tracker will alert someone. Send them a signal," Jack said.

Ava watched the red light blink, steady, patient, almost hopeful.

"Maybe…" she said, though she'd seen lights like that before. Blinking.

Alerting. Sometimes, no one came.

Jack's voice rose, thin and brittle, "That tracker, on her fin. We've seen that, dad. Remember? The one with the missing tip. We saw it on Shark Week."

His eyes narrowed as he tried to recall…

"Judy. That shark is Judy."

He didn't shout it.

He barely breathed it.

His recollection was hazy, lost in thousands of television shows, TikToks, and YouTube videos. He recalled the sleek white shark arcing out of the water, salt spray catching the light.

The camera panned across her dorsal, the tip truncated, ragged. A man in wraparound sunglasses and a weather-beaten shirt stood on the deck of a research boat, gesturing like a magician.

"This girl," he'd said, voice loud with pride, "She's the queen of the deep. Let's see where she goes."

Jack remembered the way the man had looked, not afraid, exactly, but reverent. Like he understood something no one else did.

Now Jack understood, too.

His eyes stayed fixed on the fin cutting through the Sound. His mouth felt dry.

The water suddenly felt colder.
It wasn't just a shark.
It was the queen.
And she was here.

* * *

The words tugged at something in Danny.
Shark Week.
Those had been good times. Pizza. Video games. Jack curled up next to him on the couch, both bleary-eyed from too much sugar and too little sleep. No showers, no rules, the two of them lost in an endless loop of sharks breaching, scientists tagging, narrators droning on about apex predators.

Jack used to rattle off facts as if he were training for some future marine biologist exam. Danny would fake-argue and claim he could take on a shark with his bare hands. Jack would call bullshit, and they'd laugh until their stomachs hurt. Back when things were simple. When Jack still looked at him like he was the center of his world.

As if answering to her name, Judy's fin sank beneath the water, vanishing without a ripple.

* * *

Ava watched the fin vanish, a final ripple curling outward like a closing eye. Around her, the others exhaled, shoulders loosening, breath returning. Relief, or the shape of it. But she stayed still. Eyes fixed. Muscles braced. Something deep inside her refused to ease.

She's not gone.

It wasn't a thought so much as a knowing. A low pulse behind her ribs, ancient and automatic.

Judy hadn't left. She was circling.

Watching. Ava could feel it, not with logic or evidence, but with a quiet sense that had followed her since girlhood.

184

Women's intuition, her mother used to call it, half-mocked and half-prized. Ava had come to trust it. It had warned her when something was off with Jack's health, when a doctor was bluffing through questions he should've known, when the foundation of her marriage began to crack beneath the polished surface.

It stirred again now, low and insistent. Not panic. Not yet. Just the sense that the water hadn't finished moving.

She glanced sideways at Danny and Jack, father and son folded close in a way she had never quite reached.

Shark Week had been their ritual. She remembered the sound of their laughter more than what played on the screen, the way Jack pressed in against Danny, rattling off facts, both of them talking over the narration like collaborators instead of viewers.

Danny would nod along, correct the scientists, spin theories half-serious and half-joking. It was easy. Effortless. Their rhythm.

Ava had hovered at the edges. Bringing popcorn. Asking questions that slowed things down. Sharks, she'd realized even then, were their mythology, something thrilling but contained, reduced to graphics and commentary and commercial breaks.

Safe.

Explained.

She hadn't felt afraid watching with them. Just slightly out of step. As if something real had been flattened into entertainment, its teeth dulled by repetition. Standing there now, the water rolling in its slow, unreadable calm, she wondered what it meant that the queen of their shared mythology had risen long enough to look at them and hadn't finished speaking.

Ava shifted her stance. The current brushed her thighs, cool and heavy. She didn't know what to do. *How could she?*

This wasn't the kind of danger that came with instructions or exits. This was ancient.

Wordless.

A thing that waited.

She kept her eyes on the water, body alert, instinct tightening its grip.

She couldn't be part of Danny and Jack's world before, not really.
But maybe now, in this impossible moment, it would be enough
that she could see what they couldn't.

* * *

Cap sloshed through the knee-deep water toward the bright
orange marker Kid had earlier planted near the bow of Devildam.
It rocked weakly in the warm breeze, half-submerged in the
sandbar's shifting floor.

He yanked the marker free and turned toward the group,
"C'mon."

They waded toward the sandbar's center, where Cap drove the
marker into what he judged to be the highest ground. Danny
squinted, trying to make out the edges of their fragile submerged
island, but the glare off the water and the constant shifting of the
tide made it impossible.

The sandbar blurred into the Sound, dissolving into the vastness
around them. He hated not knowing exactly where the drop-off
started, where solid ground ended and deep water began. The
uncertainty gnawed at him, made his skin crawl. They were
standing on borrowed time, and he could feel it slipping away
beneath their feet.

The water licked past the two-foot mark.

Danny took a slow breath, "We need to know what we're
working with."

Cap nodded, "Agreed."

* * *

Ava stood knee-deep near the orange marker, one hand braced
against its sun-warmed surface, the other shielding her eyes as she
watched the men spread out in opposite directions. Their voices
drifted back to her across the glassy surface of the Sound, calling
out distances like explorers in some post-apocalyptic game of tag.

They looked purposeful. Brave. Like they were doing something that mattered.

And here she stood.

Beside her, Jack squatted in the sand, running a fingertip through a tiny rivulet of water that traced lazy lines between the shallow ridges of his footprints. He wasn't asking questions. He wasn't panicking.

But Ava could see the tension in his shoulders, the way he kept glancing at the deeper water as if it might shift again, as if something might rise from it.

She wanted to stay by him. Needed to. The instinct was primal. Maternal. Her job now was to make sure he didn't see more than he could process. That he didn't lose one more thing today.

But even as she stood guard, something inside her curled into a knot. Not at Jack. Never at Jack. But at the unspoken assumption that this was her place. That she was the one who watched while the men measured. That her role was to stand near the child, soothing, steady, sidelined. That she was the soft place. The afterthought.

She glanced again toward Danny. Toward Cap. Toward Kid and Shel.

They hadn't asked if she wanted to help. Hadn't looked to her for insight or instinct. They left her here. By the marker. As if the only thing she could offer was comfort.

She hated that it stung. Hated more that it felt familiar. Like all the other moments when her voice was measured but ignored, when her ideas were nodded at but never acted on. When her value was wrapped in the shape of her care, not the sharpness of her mind.

But she didn't move.

Jack needed her.

And maybe, for now, that was enough.

* * *

The men mapped out their prison.

It started with careful steps, slow and deliberate, each spreading out toward the edges, probing the limits of their fragile ground. Cap, Danny, Kid, and Shel each took a direction, moving outward, counting paces from the center pole before the sandy bottom gave way, marking the edge of their safety.

"Twenty-five paces north!" Cap shouted, his voice sharp against the quiet.

"Ten east!" Kid added, eyes squinting toward the late morning sun.

"Twenty-two south," Shel called, already retreating a step from the ledge.

"Twelve west," Danny said grimly. "That's it."

Forty-seven paces long, twenty-two wide at the center, tapering to five at the ends. The shape was unmistakable now, a long, narrow oval, almost like a football, floating beneath the water's surface.

The sand beneath them shifted with every step, soft and treacherous, its form ever-changing beneath the restless tide. The shallowest parts barely reached their knees, but at the edges, it plunged off in sheer drops, a silent, unseen cliff leading down into the cold, dark depths of the Sound.

* * *

Shel stood at the far edge of the shoal, separated from the others by a strip of shallow water and nerves. The tension was thick, grief and fear coiled around them like wet rope, and he hated it. Hated the silence. The look on everyone's face, like they were already halfway gone. So, he cupped his hands and called out, voice loud and deliberately chipper.

"She's a real fixer-upper! We can put the bedroom over there. The kitchen on that side—"

No one laughed. A few heads turned. Not amused.

He smiled. Couldn't help himself. That's who he was. The guy who broke the silence. Who made people grin when they didn't want to. Who said the thing that made the awful a little more bearable. He knew it might not be the right time or right place, but a smile and a laugh could go a long way.

And if not me, who?

He turned to add something else, maybe a joke about a pool in the middle of the shoal, when he spotted it. Bright orange. Bobbing lazily beyond the edge of the shallows.

The life jacket drifted just beyond the edge of the shoal, waterlogged, half-submerged, rolling gently with the tide like it had nowhere left to go. Its straps trailed beneath it, pale and wavering, more like jellyfish than rescue gear. It didn't look like safety. It looked like something that had already given up.

Shel squinted at it, the grin fading as he judged the distance. Close enough, he thought. Close enough to be useful.

He stepped forward.

Some small, sensible voice tried to rise, quiet, easily ignored, but the jacket was right there, and maybe grabbing it would help. Maybe someone would need it. Or maybe he just needed to do something, anything, in a day that had stripped choice down to instinct.

The sand softened under his foot. Then thinned.

"Shel—" someone said, sharp and sudden, but Shel's weight had already shifted.

Cold water surged up his legs, stealing the ground from under him. His stomach lurched as he pitched forward, arms flinging out for balance, for the edge of the bar, for something solid - but there was nothing to catch.

The current took hold and pulled.

For half a second, the whole Sound went quiet.

From the dark, Judy rose - huge, fast, unstoppable.

The water peeled away like silk, and her snout broke the surface, broad and brutal, followed by jaws vast and pink, lined with teeth like shattered glass.

He didn't even have time to scream.

CHAPTER 32

Her snout slammed into his chest, hard, massive, like getting hit with a sledgehammer wrapped in steel. The air ripped from his lungs as he flew backward, spine smacking the packed sand with a thud that knocked the thought clean out of him.

Water exploded around him.

Cold.

Frothing.

Violent.

He tried to suck in air, to scream, to do something, but there she was again. That shape. That impossible mouth.

It came for him, pink and gaping and full of teeth.

Too many.

Too big.

His hands clawed at the slick sand, fingers tearing through it, desperate to backpedal, to get away, but his foot slipped...

SNAP.

Her jaws clamped shut inches from him. He felt the wind of it. The force.

Then she came again. Lower this time. No warning. No breath between attacks.

He felt her teeth enter him, grinding into his thigh, cracking through bone like it was nothing. A crunch so deep it echoed in his skull.

And then the pain. *God, the pain,* white-hot and endless, not sharp but total, like his body couldn't process what was happening and was trying to shut down around it.

He shrieked as she shook him, side to side, fast and brutal, like a dog with a rabbit, his flesh peeling away in strips, nerves lighting up in strobe flashes of agony. His world narrowed to that one point of contact, that awful grip.

Then, suddenly, release.

His body flew, hurled across the shallows, skidding hard until it came to rest half-submerged, the sky above spinning in dizzy, sun-streaked arcs.

He couldn't feel his leg. Couldn't look.

But he knew.

The water pulsed warm around him, thicker by the second, turning red, dark and deep and wrong. He tried to lift his head, to see past the haze, but everything was noise.

Distant shouting. The throb of his own blood. The breath he couldn't quite catch.

The world tilted, weightless and slipping away.

Then he saw her silhouette again, brief, massive, sliding away into the deep like a curse disappearing into the dark.

* * *

Danny was already moving, but Judy's attack was so fast, so violent, that by the time he surged forward, it was already over.

He plowed through the water, heart hammering, legs burning as they slipped and dragged against the sand. The shallows surged around him, frothy and warm, slapping high against his chest as he closed the distance.

Beside him, Cap and Kid followed, but Danny barely registered them. All he could see was Shel, crumpled, bleeding, face twisted in pain.

Please God don't let him die…

It looped in his head with every lunging step.

Please God don't let him die…

Shel groaned, one hand grasping at his thigh, no, the place where his thigh had been. Blood surged out in heavy bursts, darkening the water with each pulse. Danny dropped to his knees in the churn and clamped his hands over what was left.

The musculature of the thigh was gone.

Just…gone.

A brutal cavity where there should have been flesh. Tendons

hung in limp strands. Muscle was shredded, and the bone...

Jesus.

Danny's stomach flipped. He tasted bile. But he didn't back off. No time for shock. No space for fear.

Please God don't let him die...

He pressed his palms into what was left, trying to stanch the blood, trying to make his hands do something other than tremble.

"Is it bad?" Shel's voice was barely a rasp.

Danny didn't answer. Couldn't. Shel's eyes rolled back. His body slackened, eyelids fluttered, and he passed out.

"Shel!" Danny lunged, grabbing him under the arms, wrenching his head back above water.

Dead weight. His arms were useless, flopping like rope.

Cap reached them first, then Kid, both dropping beside Danny in the blood-warmed shallows. Cap slid his hands under one arm, Kid under the other.

Together, they lifted Shel and dragged him back from the edge of the shoal. The water fought them, warm, thick, slick with blood. With every step, Danny felt the current tugging, trying to pull Shel from their grip, as if the Sound itself meant to take him back.

They made it five paces before they dropped to their knees again. Shel's head lolled. Each breath was broken, wet. Danny pressed him upright, trying to keep his airway clear.

"Tourniquet! Tourniquet! Tourniquet!" Kid's voice cracked the air like a starter's pistol.

Cap unbuckled his belt. Whipped it through the loops. He tossed it to Kid, who caught it mid-air and looped it high on Shel's thigh. Danny could see the skin pinch tight under the pressure. Shel's body twitched. A low groan escaped his lips.

Cap tore off his shirt and shoved it into Danny's hands. He balled the fabric and pressed it into the wound, the cloth darkening almost instantly.

He pressed harder.

Blood leaked through his fingers, unstoppable, as if the body had already given up. His hands slipped on the slick heat of it, like trying to hold on to something that didn't want saving. But he didn't stop.

He kept pressing.

Ava appeared beside them, breath shallow, eyes locked on the wound. Jack hovered behind her, fists clenched, frozen. Danny saw the shift happen, his son's face collapsing from adolescent back to child.

The terror, the disbelief. It undid Danny for a moment.

But Ava, she didn't look away.

He remembered that look. A fever night, years ago. Jack burning up, struggling to breathe. Ava had stayed up with him for hours, refusing sleep, her own body wrecked with the flu. She'd sat upright in bed, cradling him against her chest, whispering nonsense and lullabies through cracked lips and a raw throat. She had anchored them both with a look. And now, she did it again.

"His thigh... where's his thigh?" Her voice caught on the words, thin and rising.

Danny didn't answer. He met her eyes and saw her steel herself.

Shel sputtered out a breath. And didn't inhale again.

"Jesus," Kid whispered. "He's not breathing!"

Cap dropped to his knees beside Shel and leaned over him, one hand sliding to the center of his chest, the other bracing as he positioned himself. He interlocked his fingers, set his palms where he'd been taught, between the nipples, over the sternum, and locked his arms straight.

He pressed down.

Hard.

Fast.

Each compression drove Shel's body into the sand, ribs shifting under the force, the impact traveling back up Cap's shoulders. Sweat spilled from his face, darkening Shel's skin where blood and water already streaked it.

The chest rose when Cap let up, fell again when he pushed but nothing answered him. No gasp. No twitch. No sign that anything inside was willing to come back.

Cap kept going anyway, jaw clenched, counting without numbers, forcing motion into a body that had already begun to refuse it.

Cap gritted his teeth, "C'mon now, boy! C'mon!"

His voice was raw, strained. He kept going, relentless, pushing oxygen through failing lungs, forcing blood through shattered veins.

The seconds stretched, unbearable.

"Breathe, now! Breathe!"

Danny realized Jack was watching Shel die in front of them.

He turned to Ava, voice tearing from his chest, "Get him out of here!"

* * *

Ava scrambled, pulling Jack away, shielding his face with her hand as she rushed him towards the depth marker in the center of the sandbar. Her arms wrapped tight around him, one hand cradling the back of his head, pressing him into her side like she used to when he was small enough to tuck under her chin.

She moved on instinct, protect, shelter, hide, but it was already too late. He'd seen everything. She could feel it in the way his small frame trembled against hers, in the panicked rhythm of his breath, sharp and shallow against her ribs.

He wasn't speaking. Wasn't crying. He clutched at her, his fingers curled tightly into the skin of her side, breath hitching as if each one came with a cost.

She kept moving, kept whispering nothing-words, "It's okay. I've got you. I've got you."

She wasn't sure if they were for him or for her. The water lapped above her knees. Somewhere behind them, voices shouted orders, but Ava didn't turn around. She couldn't.

She sank down near the depth marker, settling into the cool, wet sand, easing Jack down with her. He wouldn't meet her eyes. He stared blankly at the shifting surface of the water, his mouth parted, his breath heavy.

She reached up and cupped his cheek, gently guiding his gaze back to her. His skin was cool. Too cool.

"Jack," she said softly. "It's okay. I've got you."

His lip trembled. He nodded, barely, but his fingers tightened again, twisting into her skin like he couldn't bear the thought of letting go.

And in that moment, she was back in the old nursery, dim light, soft breath against her collarbone. Jack, days old, his whole body curled into the crook of her elbow, eyes wide and unfocused, trusting her with a kind of blind, total faith she hadn't been ready for. He used to fall asleep that way, face tucked beneath her chin, his whole world small enough to fit between her heartbeat and his.

Now the world had opened and shown him what it could take.

She pulled him closer, pressing her lips to the crown of his head, holding him like she had when he didn't yet know that monsters existed.

* * *

Pumping.

Blowing.

Breathing.

Sweat traced down the weathered lines of Cap's face.

Then, a twitch. A shudder in Shel's limp frame. A wheeze, sudden and desperate, rasped from his lips. His chest hitched, then another breath dragged in.

A violent cough wracked his body, his head jerking as his lungs fought for air. His eyelids fluttered. He was back, barely.

"We got him! We got him!" Kid gasped, relief cutting through the panic.

Cap slumped forward, breathing hard. He rocked back onto his heels, hands hovering over Shel's chest before dropping to his sides. His arms shook. Sweat ran through the grit on his face, carving pale streaks in the dirt.

He drew a long breath, slow and shuddering, eyes blinking hard against whatever threatened to spill over. For all the years and bodies, this one had taken more.

Danny pressed his fingers to the makeshift bandage, feeling the weak throb beneath. The wound still bled, the skin wet and dark, but the arterial bursts had weakened to a shallow, intermittent flow.

He peeled the edge of the shirt away enough to glimpse the ruin of Shel's thigh. The muscle was barely holding together, skin torn and raw, but at least the worst of the bleeding had stopped.

"Bleeding's slowing."

Cap stood. Swept seawater and sweat from his face.

He turned to look over at Ava and Jack by the depth marker, "Maybe we're out of the woods."

Kid met his eyes. Shook his head, *No way he survives.*

Cap held his gaze, the unspoken truth settling between them like an anchor dropped into deep water. Cap had pulled men from the jaws of the sea before, had seen their eyes go glassy as life bled out of them, and he knew.

They had stopped the bleeding, but there was too much gone. Shel wasn't going to make it.

Not out here.

* * *

Danny turned. Across the sandbar, Ava and Jack sat near the depth marker, backs slightly hunched, the tide lapping gently around them.

The sight caught him off guard, hit low, beneath the armor he'd built over the years. Jack was curled into her side, his shoulders rising and falling in jagged rhythm, not quite crying, but close. The life preserver hung around his neck, bobbing awkwardly with each breath.

Ava held him close, one arm wrapped tight across his back, the other hand gently stroking his damp hair. She rocked him, slow and steady, the same rhythm she'd used when he was an infant in the middle of the night, colicky and inconsolable.

She was whispering something soft, rhythmic, for Jack alone.

Danny couldn't hear the words, but he saw the shape of her mouth, the calm in her eyes. And then, impossibly, a flicker of a smile broke across Jack's face. Not joy but a moment of comfort, of connection.

Danny's breath caught. The ache that followed felt old, familiar, like scar tissue pulling tight.

A memory surfaced: Ava in her birthing room, soaked in sweat and shaking, hair stuck to her temples, one hand clenched around Danny's wrist and the other reaching out, reaching for Jack the second his newborn cry broke the air. Her face had crumpled then, not in fear or doubt, but in something almost holy. She'd looked at that baby like she'd always known him. Like some part of her had been waiting for him her entire life.

He hadn't understood it then. Not really. He'd tried. He held Jack, changed diapers, warmed bottles but there had always been something deeper between Ava and their son.

Something elemental.

A language he couldn't quite speak. He told himself it was because she stayed home at first, while he picked up extra shifts, tried to make things work.

But the truth was harder. Jack came to her first. Always had. And now, watching them through the veil of everything that had happened, through the wreckage of their marriage, through the shouting, the silences, the things they never said, Danny felt that divide all over again.

Danny and Ava were two shapes that used to fit together, now with too many edges. But this, this part of her had never changed. She hadn't softened. She hadn't quit. She was still his son's island.

Even here.

Even now.

And for all the ways their love had eroded, for every bitter word and late-night argument and lawyered-up signature on a line that ended things—he couldn't deny the one thing that mattered most.

Ava North was a damn good mother.

And she always had been.

CHAPTER 33

Jack had stopped trembling, though he clung to her with both arms, face pressed against her side.

Ava held him loosely now, one hand on his damp hair, the other resting on the crown of his back, eyes scanning the darkening water.

She glanced toward Shel and saw Cap looking back at her. For the first time, she saw him bare chested.

It startled her, not the nakedness, but the state of him. His frame looked carved down. Lean in places that shouldn't be. Shoulders broad, but the meat had thinned off them, and the muscles beneath his skin seemed borrowed, like they didn't belong to him anymore.

A thin scar curved low across his belly, pinkish-white against the sun-darkened skin. Higher up, near the collarbone, a second mark, smaller, puckered, where a port must have been.

His chest rose and fell with sharp, shallow breaths. Sweat glinted on his ribs. Veins stood out in his forearms. He didn't look fragile. But he didn't look well, either.

She felt Jack's gaze shift toward the men.

He wouldn't stop looking back, toward the others, toward the blood in the water, toward what had happened. She kept one hand on the back of his head, gently steering his eyes away.

"You're okay. It's okay. Don't look," she murmured, but Jack shook his head hard.

"It's not okay! It's not!" His voice cracked, raw and high. He curled into himself, fists grinding into the wet sand.

Ava pulled him closer, "Shhhh. Don't make this…"

"Judy's gonna get us. That's a… a damn fact." His breath hitched. "She's out there, and she's going to eat us. We c-c-can't get away. We're trapped."

A shadow passed over them. Danny.

"Hey, you two." His voice was scraped raw. He knelt beside them. "Shel's... he's... I mean, he's okay for now."

Ava didn't look up.

She rubbed Jack's back in slow circles, "He thinks the shark is going to get us."

Jack's voice came again, hollow, "We're trapped."

Danny looked around, then leaned in, "Are we, though?"

Jack blinked up at him, confused.

Danny's mouth ticked up, "I don't think we're trapped. We've got the high ground. Remember what Obi-Wan said to Anakin in Revenge of the Sith? 'I have the high ground!' Right?"

Ava felt Jack soften against her.

"Yeah. Right. We have the high ground."

Danny ruffled his hair, "Damn straight. You remember that. I'm going to go help with Shel. You guys hang here. You don't want to see that sort of stuff."

Danny stood and walked back toward the others. Ava felt Jack watching him, silent, holding his breath. He didn't speak.

But she could feel the words straining at the edges of his silence. *Don't leave. Stay with us. We need you.*

"I wanna go," he said instead, his voice small. "Go home..."

She rested her forehead against his, "Me too, buddy."

"Where it's normal..."

"Yeah." She kissed his temple. "But listen to me, okay? You need to get your breathing under control or you're gonna make yourself sick."

The words came automatically, an old reflex. First grade. Drop-off.

Jack clutching her hand, eyes brimming, "Don't go! Momma, please!"

She'd knelt then too, like now, "Breathe. Just breathe. Control what you can control."

And he had done it.

Now she watched his chest rise and fall, slower, steadier.

"We're here. We're alive. We're gonna make it."

Jack nodded, "Anakin... he..."

She tilted her head, "What?"

"It wasn't over. Anakin killed Obi-Wan. In A New Hope. On the Death Star."

Ava sighed, pulling him close again, "I know he did, honey. But I need you to stop now. Your dad means well. That shark..."

"Judy," Jack whispered, the word small but certain.

She exhaled slowly, her eyes tracing the broken horizon, "I wish you didn't have to see that. Didn't have to know that world."

She paused, fingers moving gently over his shoulder, "But Judy is just doing what Judys do. And we're going to outsmart her. We're going to win."

The words came automatically, meant for comfort. But inside, another voice, the one she couldn't say out loud, whispered back, *Judy doesn't care if we outsmart her.*

That was the truth, wasn't it? Nature didn't hate. It didn't punish. It didn't care. It simply was. Unfeeling. Indifferent. It surged forward, took what it wanted, and left the rest to pick up the pieces.

Like the storm that was ending their marriage.

It hadn't been one big fight. It had been a slow, relentless wearing down. An emotional erosion. Danny hadn't meant to hurt her any more than the ocean meant to drown people. He was... himself.

Danny being Danny.

He had drifted, and she had clung, and when the riptide came, neither of them had the strength to claw their way back to shore.

She stared at the water now, at the place where Shel had taken one step too many, and felt it again, that same numb helplessness.

The sea didn't care who you were. Whether you loved or tried or prayed.

It didn't care.

It took.

But Ava still had Jack and her fragile circle of survivors, adrift on a patch of sand no wider than their grief. And she would fight, not because they deserved to live more than anyone else, but because her son deserved better than to learn, so early, how cold and brutal the world could be.

She kissed the top of his head.

"We're going to win," she said again, softer this time. "Because that's what moms do."

Jack's fingers clutched her side again. It hurt, but not in a bad way, "That's what…"

"No. Stop." She kissed the side of his head. "No more Star Wars quotes. Positive vibes, okay? Mom needs positive vibes. Maybe a Harry Potter quote or something."

"I'm too old for Harry Potter."

She smiled, a flicker of sadness behind it, "Yeah. I know. Too old."

A voice cut through the silence.

"Little help?"

Ava turned. Danny was waving her over, urgency in every line of his face.

CHAPTER 34

It began closer than anyone realized.

Off the submerged slope of the shoal, where the sandbar gave way to deeper water, a cluster of blue crabs hid among the eelgrass and oyster rubble, dozens at first, waiting out the heat and chaos like they always did.

Benthic scavengers, opportunists by design, they knew to hide when larger predators stirred the water. But when the world settled again, when the Sound grew quiet, they began to move.

One twitched first, then another. They turned upstream, drawn by something fresh, trace molecules in the current, microscopic filaments of blood and damaged tissue. Shel's wound had begun leaking the moment Judy flung him aside, and now, the scent radiated outward like a slow, uncoiling signal.

To the crabs, it was information.

Urgency.

A call.

Their chemoreceptors flared, tuned to pick up amino acids from decaying flesh in trace-level concentrations. They didn't know what they were approaching, not in any conscious way but something had broken. Something had begun to die. To unspool. And that was enough.

They moved in jerks and waves, not as a horde but as a behavior, one crab triggering another, then another, each body following the trail like fingers on a pulse. More joined from the nearby slope, their numbers grew, a swarm in motion now, skittering, crawling, pulled forward by scent and instinct and the ancient knowledge that flesh never stayed uneaten for long.

They headed for the top of the sandbar. For Shel. For what the water promised them.

CHAPTER 35

Cap stood next to Shel's prone form, knees aching, hands on his hips, squinting toward Devildam.

The boat floated, but low, too low, and listing harder now to port. He'd spent his life reading water, reading boats, and what he saw wasn't good.

Not terrible.

Not yet.

But getting there.

Fast.

He turned toward the others and found himself watching Ava and Jack wade toward them from the center of the shoal. They moved like people used to moving as a family, close but unsure of the rhythm. Ava held Jack's hand, steady, guiding. Cap clocked it in one glance: that boy was rattled to the bone.

Jack hesitated, his eyes locked on Shel's crumpled form, and Cap watched Danny move instinctively, angling his body to block the view of the worst of the wound. Good on him. The kid didn't need more cruel images burned into his head.

Cap straightened and addressed Ava first, "We been talking and we agree, we gotta find a way to get to the boat."

He saw her flinch.

Damn.

Misstep.

"You agree, huh? Thanks for including me."

Her voice was tight, controlled. But the heat behind it was unmistakable.

Cap raised his hands, palms out, "Wasn't that we weren't including you, Miss. You were watching after the boy."

He tipped his chin toward Jack, "Surely that's job one?"

He meant it to reassure, but he could see the old bruise behind her eyes. The way she squared her shoulders, jaw clenching for a beat too long. Cap had known a hundred men who dismissed women at sea, hell, he'd been one of them when he was a buck, dumber. But not anymore. Not after what he'd seen. It was a mistake to underestimate a strong woman.

To her credit, Ava took a breath and let it go, "Yeah. You're right. I'm sorry."

Cap nodded toward Jack, "Swap in for Kid and Danny boy? Keep the head and foot elevated."

He softened his voice, "Can you do that?"

Jack looked uncertain, but Ava gave him the smallest of nods, and that was all it took. He moved closer, careful steps through the swirling water.

Cap knelt beside Shel, "Kid, let's do it slow. No sudden drops."

Kid cradled Shel's head, holding him steady, arms trembling with the effort. Cap watched as Jack moved in behind, kneeling carefully in the shallows.

Cap steadied the transition, one hand at Shel's neck, the other guiding Jack into position. Kid eased out, slow and precise, and Jack took the weight. Shel's head settled into Jack's lap, limp and heavy. Jack's hands hovered for a moment, unsure, then rested gently on Shel's shoulders.

His jaw was tight. His eyes stayed locked on the water.

Cap turned to Ava, "Take the leg?"

Without hesitation, she dropped to her knees beside Danny and took over, gently lifting Shel's leg above his heart. She kept her eyes on the movement, not the damage. Cap respected that.

"Thanks," Danny muttered.

She nodded, focused, already adjusting her grip.

Cap saw the way Jack refused to look at the wound. His shoulders were stiff, fingers trembling slightly where they steadied Shel. Cap squatted again, knees popping.

He met the boy's eyes, "And don't you worry, Captain Jack. That shark, just a matter of time before she gets bored and swims off. She ain't gonna hurt us no more, okay?"

Jack's voice was low, "Judy."

Cap blinked, "Say again?"

"Her name is Judy."

"Just a fish, Jack," Ava said.

Cap nodded, "Ayuh, Judy. Lisa. Nancy. Just a fish."

He studied Jack's face, "That mind of yours is a-churnin' a million miles an hour. I can see it. You know the Ten Commandments?"

Jack shrugged.

"The Bible stuff? Well, I got me an eleventh commandment: Don't worry 'bout things you can't control. Know the twelfth?"

Another shrug.

"Sleep when ya' can. Those are wise words, my friend. True words."

Jack's lips twitched, just slightly.

Cap ruffled the boy's damp hair, "Now you take care of this fella best you can. Right now, it's about all you can do, okay?"

Jack nodded. His hands stayed firm on Shel's shoulders.

Cap met Ava's eyes. She was watching him closely. There was gratitude in her look, but something else too, raw, tired trust. A silent message passed between them. She needed him to steady this ship, and he would.

He tipped his hat, turned, and sloshed away toward the others.

* * *

Jack watched him go, then turned to Ava, "He seems nice. Is he sick?"

Ava didn't answer right away. Her eyes stayed on Cap, tracing the way he moved, stiff through the knees, slow through the spine. Not old-man slow. Not lazy. The kind of slow that came from pain. Quiet pain. The kind people learned to carry without comment.

She had caught a glimpse of the pendant dangling on his chest, a small silver compass, dull with age, swinging on the thin silver chain as he shifted. It glinted once, then settled against his skin. Not decorative. Worn. A reminder, she thought, of where he'd been. Or maybe where he planned to go.

She thought of the way he'd rubbed his scalp earlier, the thin patch of hair, the drawn look around the eyes. That paper-thin skin across the temple. The stillness in him. Not the peace kind of still, but the kind you saw in people who'd stopped expecting things to get better.

She'd seen that look in her father once, near the end. And in herself, sometimes, during the recent months of arguments, when the fight left and the quiet set in, and there was nothing left but to keep going.

Cap had that same worn look. Like something had been stripped away from him, slowly, until only the essential parts remained.

"Yeah," she said softly, more to herself than to Jack. "I think he is."

She didn't mean sick. She meant hollowed. Weathered down by something too big to beat.

But still here.

Still trying.

Like the rest of them.

* * *

Danny, Kid, and Cap stood beside the depth marker in the center of the sandbar. The water lapped hungrily at their knees. In the distance, near the far end of the bar, Ava and Jack tended to Shel, their backs to them.

Cap exhaled, eyes drifting again to the listing silhouette of Devildam. Her bow still floated, barely, but the stern rode too low now. The running lights stayed on, red and green steady against the haze, doing their quiet job as if nothing had changed.

Below them, the engine compartment was likely half full, if not worse.

She wouldn't hold much longer.

"We've gotta find a way to get to the boat," he muttered, mostly to himself but loud enough for the others to hear. "Before she loses power."

Danny exhaled, dragging a hand through his damp hair, "Did you, uh... did you tell the harbor master? Or, you know, whoever handles that kind of thing? About our change of plans? The Sound instead of the sea?"

Cap didn't answer right away. His eyes stayed locked on Devildam. The boat rocked gently, her fiberglass sides scuffed and worn.

Larry's body sagged over the gunwale, limp and empty. A lifeless warning. The whole vessel looked hollow now, gutted, spent. A ghost ship.

"A float plan," Cap said finally, as if the words had taken the long way around.

His voice was flat, "No. No float plan."

Danny stiffened, "So nobody knows we're here?"

Kid scoffed, dry, "Nobody files a float plan..."

Danny's voice turned sharp, "I wasn't asking you."

Cap raised a hand, cutting them both off, "Enough. We're in a bad way. We don't work together, we go down together."

He let the words settle, then added, "No. Nobody knows we're here."

The weight of it landed hard. Danny's mouth closed. Kid looked away, jaw set. The Sound stretched around them like a bowl with no edge, no echo.

Cap stepped forward and reached out toward the depth marker. His finger, tacky with Shel's blood, dragged a slow line across it, about eighteen inches above the current waterline.

"Water's here in two, maybe three hours. High tide, we got nowhere to run. Boat's out of reach."

He wiped his hand in the shallows, voice tightening, "When that happens, Judy's gonna swim right up and give us a great big ol' how-do-you-do."

Danny inhaled, slow and steady, "We sit tight. Someone will find us."

Kid snorted, "And if they don't? Who put you in charge? I signed on with Cap…"

Danny's jaw tightened, "How's that workin' out for you?"

Cap laid a hand on Kid's arm before it could go further, "Easy now."

Danny faced him, "I can't put Jack and Ava in danger. I can't risk leaving a son without a dad. We're not equipped to do battle with… something like that. That size. When the tide starts to shift, if nobody shows, when we have to, then we take action."

Cap watched him. The man wasn't posturing. He wasn't flailing. This was conviction. Cap looked toward Ava, saw her crouched at Shel's feet, trying to keep Jack occupied, to keep his mind off of anything other than what was right in front of him.

He gave Danny a nod, "Alrighty, then. Agreed."

Across the bar, Ava's voice rang out, urgent.

"Hey! Something's moving!"

CHAPTER 36

Cap, Kid, and Danny turned, expecting to see Ava pointing at Judy's dorsal slicing through the water - but she wasn't.

She pointed past them, toward the far end of the sandbar.

They turned in unison.

At the edge of the bar, the water quivered, ripples spreading in quick, chaotic bursts. The surface popped and splashed, as if something heavy stirred below. The disturbance stretched wide, a circular patch nearly fifty feet across, rolling and swirling as it crept toward them.

"What is that? Is it fish?" Danny asked, squinting against the glare.

Cap sloshed forward without answering. The water clung to his calves, thick with silt. He'd seen stranger things, nets full of torn flesh, stingrays folded like linens, turtles missing half their shells.

What had tested him most hadn't happened offshore. It had come later, on land. Sitting still while something ate at him from the inside.

Needles.

Hours.

The slow humiliation of waiting to see if your own body would cooperate. Compared to that, this, whatever it was, felt familiar. Tangible. Something he could put his hands on.

He stopped at the edge and looked down.

"Crabs," he said. "A lot of 'em."

Danny's breath caught, "What are they doing?"

The water darkened. At first it looked like a few dozen, but the shoal kept shifting until the sand crawled with crabs—, close to a hundred, maybe more. Most were no bigger than a man's palm, shells glinting cobalt and rust in the sun. A writhing, armored mass. Driven. Hungry.

"Whatever they damn well want," Cap muttered, stepping back.

Kid and Danny retreated with him, eyes fixed on the oncoming swarm.

"Where can we go?" Danny asked.

Cap gave a helpless shrug, "Go? Nowhere to go, sir. Nowhere to run, 'less you wanna swim with gentle Judy."

He looked toward Ava and Jack, at the edge of the bar, "Tell them not to panic."

Danny cupped his hands, "Ava! Jack! Be still! It's crabs! They won't hurt you!"

Cap heard it before he saw it, the change in the air. A faint whistle of wings, then a single gull, circling high above. It banked once, slow and watchful. A second joined. Then a third. Cap squinted upward.

Within seconds, there were five.

Then ten.

Then more.

He'd seen it before, this sudden gathering. Not a sound had called them. No signal had gone out. But the birds always knew. Movement, glint, the faint signature of opportunity. It was never one. You saw one, you'd get twenty.

Their cries sharpened, thin and pointy, and the sky itself seemed to churn. One dove. Then another. Then the rest.

A storm of wings collapsed onto the crabs. The silence shattered.

Gulls stabbed into the swarm, beaks tearing with jerking precision. Water sprayed. Shells cracked. Claws snapped open and shut, useless against the onslaught. The gulls were fast and tireless, wingbeats loud and overlapping.

Cap turned his shoulder as one skimmed past his head. Another landed near his boot, yanked a crab in half, and was gone before he could react.

He swatted one from his shoulder. Danny ducked and covered his head as a pair of gulls wheeled past, wings slicing the air inches from his scalp.

The sand writhed with movement. The sky beat with wings.

The crabs had swarmed the men first - Cap, Danny, and Kid stomping and shoving through the tide - but now the mass was shifting, spreading, closing in on Ava, Jack, and Shel.

The boy flinched as the first one brushed his foot.

"They're here," he said, voice rising.

"We got this," Ava said quietly, trying to hide the rising panic, scanning the swarm as it fanned out across the shoal.

Another crab crept past Shel's leg. Then three more. Jack whimpered, his grip tightening

The crabs reached her feet, spilling past the high point of the shoal like water breaching a rim. A ripple turned their way, then more. Dozens broke from the main swarm, drawn by heat, motion, breath.

Jack gasped as cold, spindly legs brushed his ankles, then his knees. The water churned around him, alive. Crabs scaled his thighs, piling into his lap, three, four deep, scrabbling over one another in blind, urgent hunger. Legs scraped skin. Pincers tugged at the straps of his life vest.

Shel's chest vanished beneath them. Crabs clambered over his face, dragging legs across his eyelids, flexing mandibles near his mouth.

And with them came the stench, the thick, throat-coating reek of brine and rot, of something long dead and left to warm in the sun. Ava gagged as it hit her, sharp and sour and clinging.

Above, gulls shrieked and dove. The air split open with wingbeats and snapping beaks, the wet crack of shells crushed midair. Birds wheeled and plunged, talons locking onto the larger crabs and wrenching them skyward.

Some flailed, legs windmilling. Others were dropped, crunched, or dragged screeching across the sand in a blur of wings and foam.

"Mom!" Jack screamed.

"Don't move! Close your eyes!" Her voice cracked, thick with fear and disgust.

Crabs writhed up her back, tangled in her hair.

She reached for Jack, tearing them from his arms, his chest, his face. Claws raked her palms, but she didn't stop.

A shadow swept past, a gull, shrieking as it dove. It latched onto a strap of Jack's life vest, mistaking it for a crab. It yanked once, hard enough to pull him off balance.

Jack gasped, pulled sideways, his hands slipping away from where they supported Shel's head.

"No!" he cried, twisting around, searching the water.

For a second, Shel was gone, submerged, face tilted beneath the surface, hair drifting like kelp.

Jack plunged both arms down, fingers scrabbling. He found him - skin, hair, scalp - and hauled upward with all he had. Shel's face broke the surface, his head limp and heavy. Jack cradled it in his lap, blinking water and panic from his eyes.

He retched.

Almost puked.

A crab clung to his collarbone. Another clattered across his cheek. A few veered toward Shel's leg, drawn to the blood-dark cloth. They clacked at the tourniquet, snapping blindly.

Jack knocked them away, each slap sending a crab flying in a spray of water and legs.

Then, silence.

The swarm passed as suddenly as it had come, scattered by beaks and wings, broken apart across the shallows. Gulls hovered and screamed, ripping at the stragglers still twitching in the surf. Bits of shell littered the waterline.

A single crab, half-crushed, spun in a tightening circle near Ava's knee.

"Get them off..." Jack whispered, eyes shut tight.

"They're gone, baby. They're gone." Her voice shook.

She cupped his cheeks, brushing away salt and tears and slime.

His eyes opened, red-rimmed, wide, "Why'd they do that?"

Ava hesitated.

"I don't know," she whispered.

She did know. They weren't looking for anything but food. No malice. No choice. Just the pull of need. The way they'd closed in, patient, relentless, stirred something she didn't want to name.

It reminded her of the divorce, of motions filed and deadlines set, of fighting for ground inch by inch without ever calling it a fight.

She ran a hand through Jack's soaked hair and pulled him closer.

"Sometimes things move toward what they need," she said. "That's all."

Jack nodded slowly, blinking through tears, "Yeah. Well. It was gross."

Ava managed a smile, "Super gross."

CHAPTER 37

Cap, Kid, and Danny slogged through the shallows, hurrying toward Ava, Jack, and Shel.

The tide had left the sandbar slick and uneven, the churned-up silt clinging to their feet and ankles, every step a fight. Water dragged at their legs, slowing them when all they wanted was to move faster.

Shel lay cradled between Ava and Jack. His breaths came in thin, rattling gasps, the rise and fall of his bare chest so slight it was hard to see. His mouth hung open, lips pale. Eyes barely open. Unfocused. Rimmed in red. The skin had taken on a dull sheen, as if it no longer belonged to him. He looked less like a person than something left behind.

Ava knelt beside him, one hand wrapped around his ruined leg, elevating the wound above his heart. The blood had slowed, but it seeped in dull pulses through Cap's shirt tied tight around the wound.

Jack didn't speak. He sat stiffly, one arm cradling the back of Shel's head, the other hand resting on his shoulder. His eyes stared straight ahead, wide and unblinking, as if he hadn't noticed their arrival at all.

Danny stopped a few feet short, unsure whether to speak.

"You guys okay?" Kid asked, voice low.

Ava let out a breath, tight and shaky, "I guess. No more crab. Ever."

Danny tried to smile, but it barely stuck.

"Yeah," he said. "I'm definitely out of the crab business."

He stepped closer to Ava, noting the way her hair clumped and twisted, streaked with salt and stuck to her face.

A small blue crab clung to one of the knotted strands, its legs twitching weakly.

He reached in, plucked it free, and flung it away with a grimace.

Ava didn't even blink. She looked spent, dark circles around her eyes, arms trembling with fatigue.

Overhead, the gulls wheeled, screeching, riding the thermals stirred by the moving tide. Two broke off and glided down, landing on Devildam ten feet from where Larry lay slumped across the gunwale. They cocked their heads, eyeing him with sharp, suspicious movements, uncertain if he was meat or threat.

One stepped closer, then stopped. The other let out a thin, reedy cry. The boat shivered beneath them.

Danny turned his attention back to Jack.

His face had gone slack, lips parted enough to hold the ghost of a breath. He didn't blink. Didn't move. Danny studied him for a long moment.

He's in shock.

The realization hit like a gut punch. He should've seen it earlier. The silence. The too-wide eyes. Jack wasn't okay. Not even close.

Danny's stomach tightened as he crouched beside him, searching for something to say and finding nothing that wouldn't sound thin.

Jack's mouth was moving, soundless at first, like he was trying to push a word through water.

Danny leaned closer, "Hey. Jack. What is it?"

Jack didn't look at him. His eyes stayed locked on the water beyond the shoal, pupils blown wide.

"She's…" He swallowed.

Tried again, "She's back."

Danny followed his gaze.

CHAPTER 38

Jack's words were flat.

Dull.

He was looking past Ava and out toward the water.

Danny followed his gaze.

Judy's dorsal sliced the water silently, barely rippling the surface. Coming back around. Closer this time.

She meandered lazily near Devildam, her crescent tail carving slow, deliberate sways through the water. The boat's stern rode low. Not yet awash, but heavy, weighted by the water pooling below deck.

The bow had lifted slightly in response, giving her a strange, wounded posture, like a horse trying to favor a broken leg. Her name was still visible across the transom, half-submerged, peeling paint catching the sun in dull flashes. A faint slick of oil trailed outward into the Sound.

Larry's body hung over the port gunwale, limp and twisted. His arm dangled toward the water, wedding band flashing once before the swell rolled him back into shadow.

Danny swallowed hard.

It was obscene, how casual death looked. A man one minute, then this: weight, meat, emptiness. A boat that had once been full of laughter, shouting, motion, now silent except for the occasional knock of wood and metal as it shifted in the water. Devildam wasn't sunk.

But she was no longer theirs.

Not really.

Not anymore.

Ava's voice cut the air, "What if… what if he's alive?"

Cap didn't answer right away. He kept his eyes on the boat, his expression fixed, jaw set.

When he finally spoke, his voice was low and certain, "Crabs know, Miss. They know."

Danny frowned, not understanding. He followed Cap's gaze back to Devildam, to Larry's shape slumped over the rail, still, wrong somehow.

For a second, that was all he saw.

Then the movement registered.

Small.

Fragmented.

At first it looked like the deck itself was shifting, shadows where shadows shouldn't move. A twitch. A ripple of motion along Larry's legs, his side, the slack hand hanging near the fiberglass.

The fiddler crabs.

The ones Kid had scooped from the shoal. They were out of the corners now, no longer skittering or hiding. They clung to him, climbed him, testing skin and fabric with blind persistence.

Danny's stomach dropped.

They hadn't come to scatter.

They had come to feed.

* * *

They came one by one, at first.

Larry had freed them as he fell. His foot struck the bucket, sending it skidding sideways. It tipped, rolled, the lid popping loose on impact and spinning to a stop near the scupper. The bucket rocked, clattered, then spilled.

Fiddler crabs poured out in a dry, clicking rush, scattering across the fiberglass in nervous, sideways bursts. They spread without pattern, probing corners, seams, shadows, following instinct more than direction.

For a moment, they wandered. The deck was foreign, the air wrong.

Then one reached the still shape at the rail.

Another followed.

The boat was small. The signal was unmistakable. What began as accident became convergence.

They gathered.

Larry had collapsed against the gunwale near the stern, right shoulder and arm propped over the rail, fingers drooping inches above the water. The left arm was inside the boat, hanging down, fingers brushing the deck.

His flesh was pale, waxy and slack. But not yet cold. The arm hanging over the water had warmed under the sun and its reflections, and the blood pooled in the muscles had kept a residual warmth, enough to interest the crabs.

The first crab climbed from the deck up his left arm, trundled across his shoulders, and continued along his outstretched right arm. At the knuckles, it paused, claws testing the air.

One jointed leg brushed a spongy fingertip, then another, before it backed away. Moments later, it returned with two companions. They crept down the length of his extended arm and along the curve of his hand like they were navigating a sand dune, claws flexing, antennae twitching.

Their claws, small but sharp, found the soft webbing between his thumb and index finger. They pinched and picked, breaking the skin, opening shallow vessels beneath the surface. Blood rose in beads, gathered, then slipped from his fingers in slow, deliberate drops, falling into the Sound below, vanishing without a ripple.

More fiddler crabs came, twelve, then fifteen, drawn across the deck by an instinct older than memory. They scaled his hip, scattered across his back, scuttled down the length of his arm in fitful bursts. They picked at the torn skin along his elbow, where he'd scraped himself while falling.

One climbed to his shoulder and perched there, antennae twitching. Another balanced on his head and batted clumsily at his ear with its smaller claw. A third wedged itself into the crook of his elbow and peeked out from the shadow.

Two reached his face, where a dab of blood had dried at the corner of his mouth. Their claws moved gently at first, probing, then pinching.

None of it was coordinated. There was no plan. No hunger in the way a predator knows hunger. They were opportunists, ancient and tireless.

They tested everything.

Softness.

Moisture.

Warmth.

The nerve endings were dead, but the tissues still gave way.

Below, blood slid from Larry's slack fingers in slow, patient drops, one, then another, each ring widening as it touched the Sound. The current took it gently, thinning the color, carrying it outward. Not gone. Just traveling. A signal released into water that knew how to listen.

* * *

Danny blinked, trying to make sense of it.

At first, it didn't register, not what he was seeing. The pitiful, slumped figure hanging over the edge of Devildam's stern.

Then his gaze dropped to the fingers. The spindly crabs. The same crabs they'd meant to use for bait. The same creatures they'd planned to toss overboard and forget, now they were tearing at the man who'd brought them here. Picking him apart. Starting small. The way scavengers always do.

His eyes followed the slow drip of blood slipping from Larry's fingertips, fat, dark drops that struck the water with soft plips. A steady rhythm. Almost like a metronome. Almost like a countdown.

He took a step back, heart knocking hard behind his ribs.

Blood in the water.

Judy rose, her dorsal slicing through the Sound with quiet purpose.

For a breathless second, the fin eclipsed Larry's body entirely, a wall of dark gray, smooth and unwavering, passing between them and what was left of their friend.

Then it dipped again, vanishing into the Sound as if she had never been there.

Danny didn't move.

He couldn't.

All he could think, as the water calmed and the blood kept falling, was that Judy had seen it too.

* * *

The water had changed.

Not the scent, though that, too, had shifted, but the pressure. The sound. The rhythm. There was no thrashing, no panicked wake.

But above, something lingered. Something leaked. Blood. Weak and pulsing. It came in slow threads that spiraled down like plankton, warm and fragmented.

She drifted low beneath the hull, pectoral fins spread wide, tail swaying in slow, deliberate beats to counter the surge. The boat creaked and listed, its shadow heavy above her, fiberglass straining in the tide.

From below, she detected a shape at the edge, something suspended. Something hanging.

She rolled, slowly banking upward, following the trail.

The limb extended above the water, slack, pale, and dripping.

It hung motionless except for the occasional shiver from the breeze. Above the waterline, blood beaded and dropped, rhythmic, predictable. The scent tugged at her.

Not fresh kill.

Not struggling prey.

But tissue breaking down. Something dead. Maybe long dead. No panic in the chemical trail. No cortisol. No muscle flicker.

But... protein.

Warm.

Exposed.

She adjusted her approach.

At depth, scent ruled. But near the surface, sometimes light told

220

more than blood.

She angled upward, arching through the water until the drag thinned across her snout. A measured sweep of her tail steadied her rise. Her pectorals tipped, fine adjustments against buoyancy and glare.

The surface touched her eyes.

She did not break through in a breach or surge. She lifted just enough, rostrum cutting air, eyes clearing the meniscus, holding herself there in a brief, costly balance. It burned energy. It exposed her.

But it gave her what scent could not.

Shape.

Contrast.

Movement.

The world above wavered in heat and glare. Hull lines. Sky. Shadow.

And there, pale against the boat's flank, the slack limb, suspended inches above the water.

And on that limb, movement.

Small.

Pale.

Crawling.

Creatures. Not fish. Not threat. They scurried over the flesh, picking at it. Pulling at the edges. Their movements registered on her electroreceptors, a flutter of twitching contact, minute discharges. Feeding.

She held her position, buoyed beneath the surface, head exposed from the tip of her snout to behind the eyes. Her spiracles pulled water across her gills as she hovered, tasting the air. Her body remained fixed below, her musculature taut to maintain balance.

She watched.

And what she saw didn't flee. It didn't resist.

It offered.

She held her position one heartbeat longer, then let gravity take her back beneath.

She turned once.

And then rose with intent.

* * *

Cap had seen calm water before, dead calm. Water with weight. Like the sea was holding its breath.

The gulls rose together, wings slapping the air, lifting from Devildam's rails and canopy in uneasy silence.

Cap knelt beside Jack, "You look away now, Captain Jack. Look away."

Jack didn't ask why. He turned into Ava, pressing his face to her ribs. She wrapped her arms around him and held tight.

Judy's jaws breached first, no warning, no swirl, a blur of sudden violence. Her snout slammed into the hull, teeth locking onto Larry's dangling arm with a sickening crunch. Bone gave. Flesh tore and parted in a single brutal wrench.

She jerked once and disappeared below, the limb ripped clean from the shoulder.

Devildam rocked violently, groaning under the impact.

Cap stepped forward instinctively, even though he knew better. Nothing he could do.

The water pulsed again.

Her shadow swelled beneath the hull, rising with the lift of a slow, deliberate kick. Then she broke the surface, head and open jaws clearing the water, teeth flashing wet in the sun.

She closed on Larry where his body hung over the gunwale. No thrashing. No warning. Just the full, crushing certainty of the bite.

The pull came after.

Judy sank with her prize, dragging Larry with her. His weight peeled over the rail, ribs scraping fiberglass as his center of mass tipped past balance.

Devildam answered at once, her stern yanked down hard, the transom flooding as seawater rushed across the back deck in a single, choking surge.

For a heartbeat, it looked like she might follow him.

The sound reached them a second later: a hard run of snaps that couldn't be anything but bone being pulverized. Ribs, maybe, small failures in quick succession, followed by one heavier crack that stopped everything inside Danny for half a breath.

Nobody moved. Nobody spoke. The water kept its rhythm as if it hadn't heard a thing.

Freed of the load, Devildam rebounded. Her stern rose, coughing water back through the scuppers in foaming sheets that slapped and drained away. The deck cleared.

Along the starboard rail, the gunwale sagged where it had taken the bite, fiberglass crushed inward, splintered and raw, a fresh white wound scored with blood and tooth marks.

The hull groaned once, low and resentful, then settled back into its lines.

Below, the shadow thinned and vanished into deeper water, buoyancy restored, damage done.

She didn't vanish immediately. She rolled, dragging the body beneath her, belly pale as she twisted in the red churn. Her wide pectoral fins rose and fell like wings slapping at the foam.

Her tail followed, a massive, crescent arc, sick and shining, lashed the air and slammed flat against the surface with a thunderclap.

A wall of bloody spray lifted high, arced outward, and pattered down on the stunned survivors.

Cap wiped the warm mist from his face with the heel of his hand, smearing red across his cheek. He stared at the droplets clinging to his arm, salt and iron, bright against sun-dark skin. Proof of what she'd taken.

He didn't look at the others. Didn't need to.

The sea settled.

No one spoke. There was nothing to say.

The thought came quiet and uninvited: we're all going to die.

* * *

Ava stood motionless, arms wrapped around Jack, her breath shallow, eyes locked on the blood-slicked water. Her limbs felt heavy, waterlogged with dread.

Danny and Cap flanked her in stunned silence, but she barely registered them. Her gaze traced the rippling trail where Judy had vanished, the froth tinged with red. Somewhere beyond that, the sea went back to being itself, as if nothing had happened.

A white gull circled above, then descended in a slow spiral and landed in the gore. It floated easily. Its feathers absurdly clean against the sullied surface. The bird turned its head toward them with a blank, unblinking eye, as if bearing witness to their insignificance.

Ava couldn't look away. It reminded her of something, a photo she'd once seen in a magazine waiting room, the kind that made tragedy look elegant. That quiet moment before the world moved on.

The gull flapped twice and rose, leaving a ripple behind.

Ava looked down.

Her hands, trembling, wet, were dotted with red. The water around her knees was tainted with blood. She wiped her palms on her bikini bottoms, once, then again, harder. It didn't help. She wasn't even sure if it was Larry's blood or Shel's anymore.

Maybe both.

Then she turned, and her breath caught.

Shel's face was still, empty. His chest didn't rise. His eyes, half-lidded, stared blankly at nothing. She didn't need to check his pulse. She could feel it, the absence.

"Shel's gone..." she said, voice barely audible, but the weight of the words rang in her ears.

Jack sat cradling Shel's head in his lap. He didn't blink. Didn't move. His face was pale, empty, like something vital had leaked out of him.

Ava stepped forward. She knelt beside Jack, the water sucking around her calves. Carefully, she reached out and touched his cheek. His skin was clammy. A line of blood had dried along his temple, matted into his hair. She wiped it away with the side of her thumb, brushing at the salt and tears that streaked his face.

He didn't flinch, but he didn't lean in, either.

Then, with the quiet grace of someone handling something holy, Jack let go. He eased Shel's head from his lap and lowered it gently into the water.

The man who had made them laugh that morning slipped beneath the surface without a sound. A few bubbles escaped his lips, rising lazily, bursting with faint pops. Ava watched as the water closed over his face.

Gone.

"It's okay, Jack," she whispered. "We did the best we could for him."

The words felt thin. She didn't know if they were meant for him or for herself.

Cap let out a long, tired breath beside her.

She glanced up, following his gaze as it drifted past Devildam, sagging, waterlogged, barely upright, and toward the widening gray horizon.

Her eyes returned to her son, and she brushed his hair back, smoothing it from his brow with a gentleness she didn't feel.

The water around them had gone calm, but inside, everything was trembling.

CHAPTER 39

"This shoal's shaped like an oval," Cap muttered, more to himself than anyone else.

He looked down at the wet sand underfoot, tapered at both ends, widest in the middle where they stood.

"Two long sides."

His gaze drifted to Devildam. One of the internal bilge pumps had kicked on, sending a thin, steady stream through its built-in discharge line and into the Sound, rhythmic as a metronome. Not much force behind it, but enough to catch his attention.

That meant the pump was running.

Which meant the batteries were alive.

And if the batteries were alive... the radio should be, too.

He felt the weight of that thought settle somewhere deep in his gut.

Her list was bad, sure, she'd most likely taken on more than she could shed but she hadn't lost power. Not yet. That told him the water hadn't crested the upper battery rack. Might be lapping at the lowest terminals by now, maybe two or three inches from knocking the whole system out.

The portable bilge would buy them time, but not much. Thirty minutes, maybe. Forty if they were lucky and the wiring held.

But luck hadn't been with them all morning.

"If we can get the shark on the far side, away from the boat, I can make a swim for it," he said. "Might be able to reach the radio."

Ava turned, studying him with an expression that knew too much. She didn't answer right away. She took in the tremor in his hands, the too-careful way he shifted his weight.

"You'll never make it," she said quietly.

Cap didn't argue. He'd been told that before.

Gloria, '85 - when the storm curved in hard and sudden, and

Miss Maribel, a twenty-six-foot Sisu with a soft hull and a stubborn engine - had been too far offshore to run. Cap had been chasing kings that day, late season, long drift, too much pride to turn back.

Forty-eight hours of hell, a torn shoulder, cracked ribs, saltwater in his lungs but he'd brought her home. Half-dead maybe, but upright.

"I might be sick, Miss," he said with a hoarse chuckle, "But I got me an extra gear when I'm racin' the devil."

Even so, doubt stirred like smoke in his chest. She was right. He wasn't sure if he really did have that gear anymore. Not where it counted.

"I'll go," Kid said, stepping forward.

Cap turned. The boy didn't flinch.

He judged Kid's face, steady, not cocky. Ready. Maybe even more ready than Cap had been at that age. That stirred something in him. Not pride exactly. Something older. Something closer to faith.

He'd always known there was a moment like this waiting out there. A moment where some kid would step up and take a job that was never meant to be his.

And Cap, he was supposed to say no, protect him, shoulder the burden himself.

But he couldn't. Not this time.

He studied Kid's face, how his jaw was set, how he didn't fidget or crack a joke or fill the silence like he normally did. The boy had found something inside himself.

And Cap wasn't going to take that from him.

"I always knew there was somethin' special about you, André," Cap said, quiet and certain.

If they moved fast. If the boy swam true. There might be a chance.

"You get to the boat, straight to the wheelhouse," Cap said. "Starboard side, behind the helm, there's a metal panel. Flip it. Radio's mounted inside, Uniden. Probably sticky from the salt, so give the toggle a solid flick. Watch for the needle to flutter. When it does, you hit channel sixteen."

Kid's eyes didn't waver.

"You say Mayday. You say your name. You say we're five souls stranded on a shoal south of marker thirty-four. Say we've had casualties, three dead. Say the vessel's taken damage, and we're exposed. Say it again. Even if no one answers. Keep sayin' it."

Cap gave him a long look, gauging the steel in him.

It was there.

If they could distract the shark. If they could draw her off.

Cap glanced toward Shel's ruined body, his jaw clenching.

There'd be a price. But Good Lord up above, don't let it be André.

"Don't screw it up," Cap said, and clapped Kid on his muscular shoulder.

"Now if you can get the shark to cooperate," Danny muttered. "What are you going to do? Whistle? Ask if she'd mind swimming to the other side of the sandbar?"

"Sort of," Cap said.

The words landed flat.

He tried to hold the grin that usually followed a crack like that, but it didn't come. Instead, his gaze drifted to the water, and something in his face darkened, a shadow passing behind his eyes, subtle but deep. The kind of shift no one else might have noticed, but Cap felt it. Felt it settle in his chest like a stone.

Because he knew.

This wasn't about outsmarting a shark or buying a swimmer a few extra seconds. It was about an offering. A trade: flesh for time. A goddamn deal with the Gods of the deep.

He hadn't told them, not yet, but he'd already made up his mind. Shel's body, limp and pale, was going to draw Judy off. That was the plan.

He'd shove it toward the far side, send it drifting just enough to catch her attention. Enough to make her turn. She'd take the offering.

And in that small, brutal window, André might make it.

And if she didn't take the bait?

Cap didn't finish the thought. He didn't have to.

He could already feel the guilt rooting in him.

Shel wasn't cold yet. And here he was, looking at the body like it was chum, something to be measured, handled, tossed overboard.

Cap had buried men at sea. Friends. Shipmates. But this wasn't burial.

It was barter.

He exhaled, sharp and quiet, and wiped a hand across the back of his neck, more out of habit than need.

"Sort of," he repeated, softer this time.

No one asked what he meant.

CHAPTER 40

Cap squatted in front of Jack, his knees crackling softly as he lowered himself.

Jack sat half-submerged, water at his shoulders, the life vest rising and falling with the swell. Ava stood behind him, one hand steady on his head.

The boy didn't speak. He only looked up, wide-eyed, quiet, already carrying more than he should.

"Hey there, Captain Jack," Cap said, his voice rough as weathered rope but soft at the edges, a quiet gravel that carried warmth beneath the grit. "I need to borrow this for a bit."

He nodded to the life preserver looped around Jack's neck. For a beat, none of them moved. Wind threaded through the silence, tugging at the straps of the faded orange vest. Somewhere behind them, the Sound sighed, relentless and alive.

Cap reached out, slow and deliberate, fingers brushing Jack's collarbone as he curled them around the strap. The boy didn't resist, but Ava saw it, the way his chest hitched, the way his chin tucked down, as if bracing against a truth he couldn't yet name.

"You might not get this back," Cap said. "But she's headed for a good cause."

He lifted the preserver free with the care of someone handling something sacred. It wasn't the flotation device that mattered, it was what it had become.

A shield.

A comfort.

A symbol.

Cap straightened and stepped to Ava. He lowered his voice so Jack wouldn't hear.

"Things like this," he murmured, "Can leave a mark. You'd be doing a favor if you kept his eyes averted."

There was no bravado in his tone. No false comfort. Just a man who'd seen his share of goodbyes and knew how to handle them with grace.

Ava met his eyes and gave a small nod, quiet, steady. She understood.

She extended a hand. Jack took it without a word, and she hauled him gently to his feet, the water falling away in sheets. Without the life vest, he looked smaller, shirtless, pale, ribs faint beneath skin creased and worn from the water. His soaked shorts sagged on narrow hips, knees knocked slightly as he stood.

A boy trying to be brave.

She remembered him at six, the day his bike bucked on a gravel trail behind their old duplex. He'd come limping up the sidewalk, palms bloodied, helmet askew, tears caught in his lashes but never falling. He hadn't cried then, either. He stood there, breathing hard, waiting for her to tell him he was okay. Waiting to believe it.

She gave his hand a squeeze, "Come on, baby. Just a little farther."

Danny and Cap turned toward Shel's body.

Jack hesitated. His gaze flicked to Danny, "I can help."

Ava opened her mouth, but Danny stopped and turned back.

"Yeah. I know you want to," he said, his voice low, steady. "And that means a lot. It really does. Wanting to help, wanting to be brave, that's what men do. But being brave also means knowing when to hold back. When to trust the people who love you to take on the hard part."

Jack blinked, his lip trembling. Danny reached out, one hand on the boy's shoulder, grounding him.

"You've already done more than most grown-ups would," Danny continued. "You stayed calm. You listened. You looked after the others. That's not small stuff, kiddo. That's leadership. That's heart."

Ava felt it then, a kind of settling inside her.

She watched Danny not just speak to their son, but truly see him. Every word was measured. Intentional. He wasn't putting on a show. He wasn't parenting to prove something.

He was being… real. Present.

"If there was more you could do," Danny said, "I'd be the first one to hand you a rope. But right now, the best thing you can do, the strongest thing, is stay safe. Got it?"

Jack's eyes filled, but he nodded. A small, determined nod.

Danny smiled and squeezed his shoulder, "That's my guy."

Ava swallowed hard, eyes stinging. She hadn't seen this version of Danny in a long time.

Or maybe she hadn't been willing to.

The quiet strength. The emotional fluency. The way he knew exactly how to speak to Jack's heart without talking down to him.

And for the first time in what felt like forever, she let herself wonder, not with nostalgia, but with clear eyes, if maybe she hadn't been entirely fair.

Maybe Danny wasn't just the right father for Jack. Maybe he was the kind of partner she'd been looking for all along.

* * *

The fan above the fryer clattered like it always did, too weak to move the oil-choked air hanging through the crab shack. Danny wiped sweat from his brow and glanced out front, where Shel leaned on the counter and smiled at a woman who looked ready to come unglued.

Her order was wrong. Too much spice, not enough butter, something about her kid having allergies. Her voice carried, sharp and shrill. Danny tensed, waiting for Shel to cut her off, maybe throw her a refund and move on.

But he didn't.

Instead, Shel nodded, slow and patient, like he actually cared about what she was saying.

"That's on me," he said. "I was rushing. Let me fix it for you."

No eye-roll. No huff of breath. He turned back to the kitchen and pulled a fresh basket without a word, hands moving quick and sure.

As he worked, he started talking, soft stuff, easy stuff. Asked how old her kid was. Said he had a niece who was picky, too. Made a joke about crab legs having a personal grudge against him.

It wasn't long before the woman laughed, really laughed, and when she left with her new order, she thanked him like he'd saved her day.

Danny stood by the sink, half-stunned. Not by what Shel had said, but by how easily it came. The generosity. The patience. That lightness. It wasn't performative. It wasn't strategy. It was who he was.

Shel caught him watching and raised his eyebrows.

"What?" he said, grinning. "You want me to be mean to the next one so you don't feel bad?"

Danny shook his head.

"Nah," he said, voice low. "You're just... good at this."

Shel shrugged, like it didn't mean anything, "Sometimes folks just need a little room to put their guard down."

* * *

Cap and Danny lifted Shel's corpse without a word and carried him to the far side of the sandbar, as far away from Devildam as they could manage. The water lapped above their knees as they worked, the tide inching higher.

They moved in silence, each step a careful negotiation with the uneven sand beneath their feet. Danny gripped under Shel's arms while Cap took the legs, the two of them working in rhythm, breathless, their feet slipping in the wet grit.

The memory clung to Danny like mist, Shel behind the counter, laughing, softening someone's worst moment with nothing but kindness. Sometimes folks just need a little room to put their guard down. That line kept repeating, low and steady, louder now in the quiet.

Danny kept his eyes away from Shel's face. The gray pallor, the emptiness, it was easier to focus on the task than the reality.

Together, they wrestled the body to the sandbar's far edge and gently laid Shel down. His head lolled to one side, eyes half-lidded and lifeless. The dull, unnatural color of his skin seemed to drain what little warmth remained in the air.

Danny swallowed hard, forcing down the rising bile in his throat.

Cap moved with deliberate care, as if handling something fragile. He fitted the life preserver around Shel's neck, the bright orange fabric against Shel's cold skin, a final indignity that somehow seemed too bright, too alive, for a man so still.

In the distance, Jack and Ava waited near the depth marker, their backs turned to the grim business unfolding nearby. Kid loitered beside them, standing close enough that Danny knew what he was doing, trying to use his body to block Jack from catching a glimpse of what they were up to.

Danny watched Kid for a moment and felt a pang of something close to hope. If Jack grew up to be like Kid, steady, calm when things got hard, Danny knew he'd be proud.

"Almost time, André!" Cap's voice rang out.

Kid turned toward Cap, giving a quick thumbs-up.

Kid told Danny and Ava, "See you in a bit."

The words barely reached his ears, but Danny caught them.

Kid sloshed to the edge of the sandbar closest to Devildam, the water swirling gently above his knees. He shot a final look toward Cap and lifted his thumb again, ready.

Cap turned to Danny, "Once we see ole Judy near Devildam, we'll send Shel off. It won't take long for these currents to have their way with the body. With a little luck, she'll catch the scent and come about."

Danny stared down at Shel, his gaze heavy.

Sometimes folks just need a little room to put their guard down.

"He was your friend?" Cap asked.

Danny swallowed, "No. Yes. He was. I mean, we were co-workers. But he was nice to me. Nice to my family. A fun guy. Funny. So, yeah, he was my friend."

Cap reached out and placed a firm hand on Danny's shoulder.

His fingers dug in, not rough, but strong - an anchor. The weight of that grip felt solid, certain, as if Cap were pouring every ounce of his own resolve into Danny. His eyes locked on Danny's, steady and sure.

"Sorry for your loss," he said quietly. "You'll meet again, of that I'm sure."

He gave Danny's shoulder one last squeeze, not a quick pat, but a lingering hold, something meant to remind Danny that he wasn't alone in this.

"Just not today, okay?"

Danny forced a tight smile and nodded.

* * *

Ava and Jack sat together in the shallow water by the depth marker, shoulders pressed close.

The cool tide washed over their legs, sending shivers up Ava's spine, but neither moved. Both stared silently at Devildam, barely sixty feet away, tilting low in the water like a beast wallowing in pain.

Kid stood between them and Devildam, quietly focused. His eyes locked on the wreck, scanning the water where Judy might lurk. He rolled his shoulders, stretched his arms, shook out his legs, trying to stay loose, ready to swim.

He looked calm, almost relaxed, but Ava knew better. He had to be scared, terrified even, yet here he was, volunteering for the most dangerous job of all. She swallowed hard.

Brave, she thought. *The very definition of brave.*

Cap and Danny weren't far behind them, fussing with Shel's body. Ava sensed them working, the subtle splashes of water, the occasional muttered instruction. She tried to tell herself it was only a body now.

An empty vessel.

Nothing more.

But she couldn't make herself believe it. Her mind slipped to her father's funeral. She remembered standing by his coffin, staring down at him, willing herself to believe he was gone. But she couldn't. She'd waited, half-expecting him to sit up, smile that crooked smile of his, and tell her everything was going to be alright.

When it hit her that he never would, that she'd never hear his voice again, it hollowed her out. That same feeling twisted in her chest now, the aching certainty that Shel was gone, death was close, and there was nothing left to do but survive.

"This seems wrong, Mama," Jack said quietly.

His voice was small, uncertain.

Ava squeezed him closer.

"Doesn't it, though?" she murmured. "But you know what? Shel's already gone. Already in heaven. He'd want us to be safe, don't you think?"

Jack pressed deeper into her side, "Yeah... I guess."

She stroked his hair, whispering, "He would."

Kid's body suddenly tensed and his arm rose stiffly as he pointed toward the water.

"There she is," he said lowly. Then louder, "There she is!"

Judy's mangled dorsal fin cut through the surface near Devildam. The crooked, jagged tip swayed like a torn flag in a slow, ominous rhythm. The fin drifted past the battered boat, the water barely rippling as her bulk shifted beneath the surface.

Each lazy sweep of her tail seemed deliberate - confident - like she knew time was on her side.

CHAPTER 41

Cap and Danny stood in the shallows, water lapping mid-thigh as they stared across the sandbar.

Shel's body floated between them, empty eyes reflecting the pale sky above.

Beyond the curve of sand, Judy's mangled dorsal fin moved in slow arcs through the water, steady and unbroken.

Cap locked on the fin, his fingers flexing at his sides. He didn't need to say it. Danny already knew, one wrong move, and the shark would be on them. Shel might be the bait, but if they failed, the rest of them were meat, too.

"All right then," Cap muttered.

Together, they moved Shel's body deeper into the Sound. The sandbar dropped away faster than expected, solid footing turning to soft pull in a few steps. Cold water surged up their thighs, then their waists. Another stride and it hit their chests, stealing their breath. The current tugged stronger here, swirling and insistent.

Shel's body bobbed between them, his limbs loosening in the water, weightless and slick. Cap's grip tightened on the dead man's arm, his knuckles pale beneath the chill.

Danny shifted like he meant to let go, to launch the body, but Cap caught his arm.

"Word to God?" Cap asked, his voice low.

Danny hesitated, "I'm not..."

Cap closed his eyes.

He hadn't been a churchgoer. Still wasn't. Never trusted the performance of it, the suits and sermons, the collection plates passed like judgment. But in the quiet moments, especially lately, he'd found himself talking upward. More questions than answers, sure. But at least he was talking.

Maybe it was age creeping in. Or maybe it was the growing sense that something waited beyond the dark. He bowed his head. His lips moved in silence, barely a breath escaping.

Take him quick. Don't let him feel more than he already has. Give the boy peace.

"Amen," Cap whispered.

"Amen," Danny echoed, awkward but sincere.

Cap reached for his belt cinched around Shel's thigh and pulled it free with a sharp tug. Then, gently, he peeled away the wadded shirt pressed into the wound, his own, once faded white, now dark crimson and heavy with blood.

He stared at it for a beat, then slid the sodden bundle beneath the edge of Shel's life vest, tucking it into place as if leaving a tribute.

Not for Shel.

Not for himself.

For her.

Below, dark blood unfurled into the water like ink, slow and deliberate. It didn't pump, Shel's heart had stopped long ago, but it seeped, curling into ribbons that drifted toward the deep.

They pushed the body forward.

The current took him. Shel spun once, slow and unresisting, before the water carried him farther out. For a moment, it almost looked peaceful, a drifting procession with no mourners, no words.

His limbs moved gently with the tide, his body circling as if guided, slipping toward whatever waited in the depths.

The Sound lifted and lowered him, steady as breath.

Cap and Danny watched. No one spoke.

Without a word, they turned and waded back.

The current fought them harder on the return. Cold bit into Cap's joints, and his soaked shorts pulled heavy at every step. When they finally reached the shallows, he stopped, breathing hard, letting the silence fall over them.

"Used to be," Cap said, voice rough, "A lot of things didn't matter. Specter of death changes you. Makes a man evaluate what's important."

He looked toward the sandbar. Jack was laughing, actually laughing, at something Ava said. She smiled, tired but real, brushing a hand over his messy hair. The sight hit Cap square in the chest.

His mind flinched toward a different time. His daughter's face. Her wild braids. The way she used to shriek with joy when he came through the door.

Too long, he thought. *Too many years lost to pride and work and silence. If I get out of this, I'll find her. I'll see her again.*

He clung to that promise like a lifeline.

Cap's eyes stayed on Jack and Ava, the boy's laughter echoing faintly across the water. The sight of them, alive, together, landed deep in Cap's chest.

"That right there," he said softly, more to himself than Danny, "That's what matters most."

* * *

Danny followed Cap's gaze.

Ava's arm curled around Jack's shoulders, pulling him close as she coaxed another tired laugh from their son. Danny felt a lump rise in his throat, they'd all been dragged through hell, but Ava found a way to keep Jack steady. Her strength wasn't loud. It was subtle, patient.

And it worked.

Whatever tension lingered between them, the old arguments, the distance, it felt irrelevant now. Out here, survival flattened everything.

He nodded. Cap had spoken the truth. Of course, Jack mattered most, no question there, but Danny knew it wasn't that simple. Ava mattered, too. She always had. Jack without Ava was like a boat without a keel.

They were a unit, built to weather storms. Together, they were stronger. Messy, flawed, imperfect but strong. The kind of strong that got people through the worst things.

And this? This was the worst thing.

Whatever came next, they had to survive it as a whole. The three of them. Otherwise, none of it would mean a damn thing.

"She's coming!"

Kid's voice cracked the silence like a whip.

Danny spun, heart jamming in his chest.

Judy's jagged dorsal fin was rounding the tip of the sandbar now, mangled, unmistakable, slicing through the water like a scythe on the swing.

She moved with calm precision, slow strokes pushing her closer to Shel's drifting corpse. The fin swayed with each beat of her tail, a predator's rhythm.

Then the fin began to drop, gradual, deliberate, slipping beneath the surface without a ripple.

Danny squinted, scanning the water, *Maybe she hadn't noticed Shel's body? Maybe she was cruising.*

He clung to the thought like driftwood, *Sharks weren't smart, not in the way people imagined. No grand plan. Meat-seeking missiles wired for hunger and heat. Judy was just a fish - huge and dangerous, sure - but still a fish.*

"Maybe she…" Danny started.

The Sound erupted.

One second, Shel's body drifted gently in the tide. The next, it vanished. Judy hit with no warning, a blur of white and gray surging upward from below.

Her head burst from the water, jaws already locked around Shel's midsection in a devastating, bone-snapping grip.

Danny froze.

For a single, sickening heartbeat, time slowed.

He saw Judy's eyes - black, dead things - and yet… not empty.

Not completely.

Something moved behind them.

Not thought, exactly, but something colder. Something ancient.

He felt it hit him like a chill in the marrow. She was looking at him.

Not through him.

At him.

It made no sense - but it felt real.

I see you, her eyes seemed to say. *And I'll see you again.*

Judy twisted in a brutal spiral, kicking up a cyclone of red.

The water frothed pink and scarlet.

With one final flick, she dragged Shel's body under.

The water sealed shut above them like a mouth swallowing a scream.

Nothing left but smoke trails of blood drifting across the Sound.

"Now, Kid! Now!" Cap roared.

CHAPTER 42

Kid took a final fix on Devildam's battered silhouette, drew a deep breath, and launched forward.

Cold closed over him like a fist, biting sharp at his ribs. He gasped but didn't stop. His arms stretched long and fast, pulling hard, legs pumping beneath him. He felt quick. But not quick enough.

His brain screamed logic: Judy was on the far side of the sandbar. That's where she'd struck. That's where Shel had gone under. But fear didn't care. Fear whispered she could be anywhere.

She could be right there, beneath him.

The thought slammed into his chest. He imagined her below, not drifting, but rising, deliberate, jaws open. He kicked harder, strokes coming sloppy now, water splashing into his mouth. The image came sharp and sudden: the fin slicing the surface, those black, unblinking eyes locked on him.

Memories of violence came rushing back: Larry's limp body slung over the rail, blood dripping from his fingertips; Colleen's scream cracking the air, gone in an instant; Shel, leg torn open, raw bone and wet meat.

Was he next?

Would his blood stain the water?

Would Cap and Danny have to drag Jack away, shielding the boy from whatever was left of him?

He swam harder. Faster. His breath came in hissing gasps. His limbs burned.

Fifty feet…

Debris closed in around him, plastic cups bobbing, beer cans spinning in lazy arcs. Tangles of fishing line snaked like jellyfish tentacles. He twisted to avoid a crushed foam cooler, only to catch sight of the crab bucket drifting past, lid gone.

A fiddler crab clung to its edge, scrambling helplessly. The cooler had come open too, bait bags, wrappers, and between them, something pale. Something wrong.

The plastic bag bumped his face.

He recoiled, a muffled scream bubbling from his throat as his momentum carried him straight through it.

Flesh, cold, unyielding, pressed against his cheek.

He shoved the bag aside, fingers brushing something slick and solid beneath the surface. It shifted, rolled, drawn by the current.

The shape turned toward him.

A face.

The juvenile shark's head.

Small eyes stared from the murk, clouded, glassed over, no longer seeing. Plastic sealed tight around the head, stretched thin across its snout. The mouth gaped open, teeth bared in a crooked frenzy, as if caught mid lunge.

Where the neck had torn free, strands of muscle drifted like sea grass.

Reaching.

Retreating.

Writhing.

Kid kicked hard, breath gone ragged, limbs burning. But the bag followed, slow and indifferent, pulled by the current he was creating, as if it had chosen him. He batted it aside…

Forty feet…

His lungs burned. Cramped. He forced his face down and swam.

Breathe.

Stroke.

Breathe.

Stroke.

His hands felt numb. His legs shook with exhaustion.

Twenty feet…

He knew she was close. He couldn't see her. Couldn't hear her.

He felt her.

Every nerve screamed that she was there—just below, waiting. Rising. His mind howled, *GO GO GO,* a pure survival chant.

Something scraped his arm.

He hadn't realized how close he was. The dinghy bobbed low beside Devildam, barely seaworthy, one side flooded, hull half-sunk. The painter stretched from its bow, slipped beneath the surface, and vanished under the transom.

Somewhere below, it had looped around the prop, then surfaced again, taut and green with algae, where it wrapped tight around the aft cleat. It dipped now and then, tugged by the tide, or something else.

He shoved the thought down and reached. His fingers found the cold metal rail of the swim ledge, slick with seawater, barely there. He slipped once, caught it again, then hauled himself up. The transom scraped his ribs as he crawled onto it.

He crouched on the narrow ledge, breath sawing in and out. On the other side of the transom, the back deck tilted gently toward the stern, low and heavy in the chop. A slick film of seawater shifted with the hull's motion, pooling at the scuppers, dark with oil and grit.

He climbed into the transom and leaped to the deck.

His body hit hard. The deck groaned beneath him, soft, unsteady, wrong. It dipped under his weight, a sluggish give that shouldn't have been there. Water sloshed.

He lay still for a moment, stunned, chest heaving, staring up at the sky.

Then he moved, crawling across the slick fiberglass, hands and knees dragging through sun-warmed seawater. He pushed upright, legs trembling, and grabbed the gunwale as the deck tilted again beneath him.

The whole boat felt off-kilter.

Hollow.

He scanned the Sound.

Endless blue.

Flat.

Empty.

Nothing moved.

No fin.

No splash.

Silence.

The silence was worse than any noise.

His eyes found the sandbar. Cap. Danny. Jack. Ava.

They stood together near the marker, small figures against the sprawl of water. Ava had Jack wrapped in her arms. Cap patted Danny's shoulder.

They were alive. And they were watching him.

Kid blinked fast, swallowing the knot in his throat.

He wasn't safe.

Not yet.

But for the first time since he'd hit the water, he remembered why he was doing this.

Why it mattered.

He raised one arm, waved, and then turned and headed for the wheelhouse.

CHAPTER 43

Beneath Devildam's weather-beaten deck, the water level had been creeping higher for hours.

The pumps, already strained, had fought a losing battle, cycling endlessly, drawing on dying batteries, buying minutes instead of hours. The engine compartment had turned into a brackish soup of seawater, fuel, and drifting debris. The battery rack was on its last legs. The wood shelf bowed. Fittings creaked.

The boat groaned under its own weight, listing slightly to port, but nothing had yet pushed it past the edge.

Then came Kid.

His desperate leap from the transom landed hard amidships, the full weight of him crashing onto the flooded deck. Devildam shuddered. The stern dipped another inch. Water surged aft in a dull, heaving rush.

Deep inside the engine space, that inch was everything.

The battery rack gave way.

It didn't shatter, it slumped, one side collapsing as the wood split along a screw line. Two deep-cycle marine batteries tilted hard and fell with a wet, shuddering thud, smashing sideways into a pool of saltwater already dancing with stray voltage.

The water hissed. A spark jumped. Then another. One battery vented in a sharp puff of acid mist before its cells shorted completely.

The systems failed in a cascade. The bilge pumps stopped mid-cycle, impellers spinning to a halt. In the wheelhouse, the VHF radio spit a burst of static and died. The fish finder flickered once. Then nothing. Even the navigation lights, already dim and unreliable, cut out entirely, leaving the boat one step closer to invisible.

Above, Kid crossed the deck heading for the salon. Each footfall sent ripples through the water gathered below.

CHAPTER 44

Cap had watched it happen - Kid crouched on the transom ledge, soaked and trembling, then he sprang for the deck with everything he had left.

The landing hit like a hammer. Devildam shuddered, the stern dipping hard as water surged aft in a slow, punishing sheet.

That was the blow that did it. The one that tipped her past the point of no return.

The coup de grâce.

His girl had already been dying. But the boy had unintentionally hurried it along.

Cap had felt that shift deep in his gut. Not the motion, the meaning. A final bend in the spine. A sound a boat shouldn't make.

Kid headed into the salon as the running lights blinked out. Not all at once, one by one, like eyes closing.

The bilge lines along the hull stalled.

Stopped.

No spray.

No sound.

The slow hush of surrender.

Cap stood there, watching.

The boat he'd raised like a child, fought storms with, trusted beyond anything else, was done.

He pictured the wheelhouse: dark, lifeless. The boards would be blank.

No nav.

No GPS.

No bilge readout.

No radio.

Maybe there was a backup battery built in, something he'd never noticed before.

Probably not. Kid would find silence and salt, that was all she had left to give.

Fair seas, girl, he thought. *I'll see you again, wherever the good ones go.*

He didn't say it aloud. Didn't need to.

Danny stepped beside him, saw something in Cap's face, and placed a hand on his shoulder, quiet, steady. No words.

Cap didn't look over.

He gave a small nod, jaw tightening, eyes fixed on Devildam as the sea began to take her, slowly, deliberately, like it had been waiting its turn.

CHAPTER 45

Kid stepped into the salon and was struck by how loud the silence had become.

No pumps.

No fans.

No hum behind the walls.

The living murmur of the boat, always there, even in sleep, had vanished. In its place: the soft, irregular lapping of water. The sound of failure, moving with the boat's slow breath.

He paused, letting his eyes adjust. The air was thick, foul in a way that clung to the back of his throat, seawater turned sour, bait gone to rot, the metallic tang of something deeper giving way.

At the open hatch, he looked down into the engine space. Water swirled shy of the lip, dark and littered. A rag floated like a drowned jellyfish, barely intact. A film of oil spread out in trembling rings, broken by the rise of slow, deliberate bubbles - like the boat was exhaling underwater.

The portable bilge pump Kealy had rigged lay curled and useless near the hatch, its hose draped across the floor, slack as a cut limb.

Kid didn't touch it. Didn't need to. He already knew.

He climbed the steep stairs to the wheelhouse, hand dragging along the wall for balance. The steps creaked beneath him, groaning with every shift.

The air changed again, warmer, deader. It smelled like scorched plastic and spilled beer, the bite of electricity long since bled out.

The wheelhouse felt abandoned. Not by people, by purpose. Tools had rolled into corners and stayed there. One panel hung open, limp on its hinge, wires exposed like sinew. But there was no flicker, no smoke. No sign of life left behind.

No Springsteen growling on the speakers. No defiance. No motion. Silence claimed the space, thick as oil.

He stood for a moment, taking it in.

His eyes drifted over the instruments until they found the radio.

It looked intact, no cracks, no burn marks, but the screen was black. Utterly, indifferently black. Buttons gave beneath his touch with no resistance. Nothing clicked. Nothing fought back.

He stared at it longer than he meant to. There had to be something, a backup battery, a delay, a flicker of hope. Boats weren't supposed to go quiet. Not all the way.

But Devildam had.

Still, he lifted the mic.

"Mayday, mayday, mayday," he said, barely recognizing his own voice. "Can anyone hear me?"

The silence that followed was not emptiness, but weight.

He stood there with the mic in his hand, listening to nothing.

No hiss of static.

No chirp.

No echo.

Only the quiet churn of the water rising below.

CHAPTER 46

The tide pressed above Cap's knees, cool and steady, wrapping his legs in a soft, unrelenting pull.

His bare feet gripped the sand without thinking, toes curling for purchase as if that might keep the rest of him from going under.

Devildam slumped offshore, her hull riding low, stern tilted low. She looked smaller now. Beaten. As if her bones had softened.

Kid stepped out of the wheelhouse onto the narrow wraparound ledge, bracing against the tilt. From that height, the list was even more pronounced, a slow sag to port that told Cap everything he needed to know.

The boy cupped his hands and shouted into the wind, "She's dead! No power! No radio!"

The words tore and scattered, carried in pieces across the Sound. But Cap heard enough. He'd known it already, known it the moment the bilge pumps quit and the lights blinked out. But hearing the words carried on someone else's breath made them sharper. Less deniable.

Danny leaned forward, squinting, "What'd he say?"

Kid shouted again, louder this time, his voice thinning at the edges, "Dead! No power! No radio!"

Cap looked down at the water milling about his thighs.

"Game over," he muttered.

Danny turned.

"No," he said. "Game not over."

He stepped close, voice low but urgent, "I'm not giving up. I'll swim for help if I have to."

Cap met his eyes. There was nothing left to say, not really. The sea would take what it wanted.

"I don't think we're gonna MacGyver our way outta this one, Mr. North."

Cap gave a dry grunt, more breath than laugh. He started to turn away, but something held, an itch at the edge of thought.

His mind clicked into motion.

MacGyver.

Improvising.

Tools.

Weapons.

The shotgun.

Cap's stomach dropped. He cupped his hands.

"Kid! Above the wheel! The shotgun!" he called.

* * *

Kid moved through the wheelhouse like it was a mausoleum. No smoke. No sound. Just a deep, unnatural quiet, the kind you find around a body after the breath is gone.

He padded across the slanted floor, every step echoing through the soles of his feet. The Remington 870 was where it had always been, cradled in the bracket above the helm. He reached up and took it down, smooth steel, heavier than he remembered.

He turned without thinking and descended the steep stairs to the salon.

Debris cluttered the floor: broken tackle, busted foam coolers, coffee-stained paper charts gone soft with rot. He dropped to his knees near the galley and yanked open a storage bin. Rags. Empty cans. A crusted box of expired flares.

He crawled over to a collapsed gear pile in the aft corner, rods tangled in line, a spool of bent hooks, a fillet knife with rust chewing through its spine.

Then he saw it. Half-buried beneath a knotted tangle of trawl net, rotted and slick with slime: a coil of nylon rope.

He grabbed it, testing the weight. Damp but sound. It would hold.

* * *

The back deck was half-flooded, its low lip taking water in slow, rhythmic pulses. Kid eased the salon door open and stepped out.

The cold hit his feet first, water sweeping over the deck and slapping against his ankles, swirling around his toes like it wanted to take him, too.

He crouched and looped the rope through the shotgun's trigger guard, tying it tight, hands moving fast despite the numbness setting into his fingers.

Across the stretch of gray water, Cap stood in the tide, bare-chested and waiting, the others gathered behind him in the rising water.

Danny. Ava. Jack. Motionless silhouettes. Their world had shrunk to that patch of sand

Kid stood at the rail and swung the shotgun over his head in a tightening arc. The soaked nylon hissed, flinging droplets of water in wide spirals.

He took one last breath. Squared his stance. Aimed for Cap.

Then he let it fly.

* * *

Cap watched the shotgun arc through the air, the rope trailing behind. For a fleeting moment, hope flickered, one more chance, one more shot at saving themselves. But that hope twisted into something else.

What would go wrong this time?

Every plan seemed to crumble, every idea unraveling at the worst possible moment. His gut told him something was coming, some cruel twist they hadn't seen yet. He sloshed forward, stepping deeper into the water.

He reached one hand back for balance, Danny grabbed it, steadying him.

The shotgun smacked into Cap's outstretched hand, but he fumbled it. His grip faltered, fingers numb and clumsy. One of the cruel side effects of his cancer treatments, tingling and deadened extremities, had stolen the steadiness from his hands. He tried to clutch the gun tighter, but it twisted loose, splashing into the water at his feet.

"C'mon, Mick! Ya bumbleclod!" Cap barked at himself, cursing as he plunged his hands beneath the water and groped blindly for the shotgun.

The cold closed over his wrists, the chill slicing through his bones. He squatted lower, chin nearly touching the surface, unable to see a thing beneath the murky water. His fingers dragged through the sand, brushing against rocks, shells, nothing.

He imagined Judy's broad grey back gliding beyond, circling silently. For a heartbeat, he swore something moved in the darkness, something big, but then his fingers struck cold metal.

He gripped the shotgun and yanked it free, water cascading from the barrel as he stumbled upright. Before he could steady himself, Danny was there, grabbing him under the arm and hauling him back toward the shallows.

Cap staggered, water dragging at his legs, but Danny kept him moving. By the time they reached their marker, Cap's legs buckled and he slumped to his knees, chest heaving. He turned the shotgun in his hands, slick with seawater, and wicked the moisture from the action and barrel with both palms, careful, methodical, like every second counted.

Danny swallowed hard, "Will it work?"

Cap looked down at the gun, soaked, battered, full of questions. He didn't answer right away.

"Maybe," he said at last, voice low. "Maybe once."

Cap glanced at his watch: 3:00 PM.

CHAPTER 47

Kid stood at the gunwale, knuckles white on the rail.

The salt-slick metal bit into his palms. Wind knifed past his ears, sharp and cold, lifting spray into his eyes. He didn't blink it away. His breath came fast and shallow, chest tight with fear.

Just sixty feet away, across the narrow run of wind-rippled water, Cap stood thigh-deep on the sandbar. Danny, Ava, and Jack clustered behind him, too far to see their faces, but close enough to read their expectation.

They were waiting.

Watching.

Cap's voice cut through the wind, "I said… Take the dinghy! Row east! East! Away from the sun! Get help!"

Cap's voice reached him in shreds, torn by the wind, half the words made it across. But the rhythm of them landed hard.

Urgent.

Final.

Kid strained to hear more. Nothing came. The slap of water and the creak of a dying boat.

East.

Away from the sun.

Get help.

The message was there, even if the words hadn't made the full trip.

Kid sloshed across the slanted back deck, water swirling around his bare calves, the surface tilting gently with every shift of Devildam's weight. The transom door was closed, half-submerged, trembling on its hinges with each pulse of the tide.

He gripped the top of it, hauled himself up, and swung a leg over, cold water slapping higher as he straddled the rail. Then he dropped.

His feet hit the swim ledge two feet underwater, slick, narrow, gently canted, and a shock ran straight through him. Outside the boat, everything changed. The hull loomed like a wall. The sea pressed in on all sides.

He felt exposed, like something dangling.

Vulnerable.

The dinghy bobbed against the port corner of the transom, half-swamped and barely afloat, its nose jammed tight against the hull.

He turned back toward the boat and crouched low, twisting his body so his face hovered inches from the hull.

The painter trailed from the dinghy's bow into the water and vanished, pulled taut beneath the surface. He reached underwater, wrapped his fingers around the algae-slick rope, leaned farther in, and pulled.

The painter was seized fast, wrapped hard around the propeller shaft, the kind of bind that only came from steel and torque.

Something shifted. Not a noise, a pressure. A density in the water, sudden and close.

Kid froze. Breath held. Arm underwater. Fingers wrapped around the painter.

To his left, through the murk, a shape swelled into being.

Not rising, approaching.

Horizontal.

Massive.

Judy.

She entered the narrow run between Devildam and the sandbar on a perpendicular line, cutting towards the dinghy and swim ledge.

It was as if she'd never left. No splash, no warning, just the silent pressure of presence. Her head glided below the surface, dark and certain, and then her back rose, broad and smooth, breaking the water like the hull of an overturned skiff, rising from the deep as if summoned.

Instinct took over.

Kid, stood and turned toward the water, shifting until the back of his thighs pressed against the transom. The fiberglass dug into his spine. His toes curled over the slick lip of the swim ledge.

Judy passed directly beneath the dinghy.

The little boat lurched as her back lifted it from below, just a nudge, a slow, rolling rise that tipped the bow sideways and bumped it into Kid's hip.

He didn't move.

Couldn't.

She was too close.

Her head slid past, unseen in the murk, and then the dorsal rose in front of him.

It wasn't sudden. That was the worst part. It lifted with calm authority, a dark blade easing through the surface, nearly three feet tall, thick at the root where it grew straight out of muscle meant to end things. The water parted around it without resistance, as if it knew better.

Up close, it wasn't sleek or cinematic. The skin was scarred and worked-over, rubbery with old damage, proof not of weakness, but of survival. This was a thing that had been tested and kept going. The tip was gone, torn away years ago, healed smooth into a blunt curve that made it look unfinished, improper, like a weapon that had already done its work.

Near the base, the SPOT tag caught the light for a dull instant, half-buried in scar tissue, human interference reduced to a footnote, a pin stuck in something far larger than intention or control.

The fin moved past him with measured patience.

Kid reached out. An impulsive move.

His hand moved like it had been waiting, drawn not by curiosity, but something older.

Reverence.

The deep kind. The kind you feel alone in the woods, in the hush before a storm. His fingers brushed the trailing edge of her fin, warm, alive, striated with muscle beneath the leathery skin.

She didn't flinch. Didn't change course. She kept moving, parting the water like it belonged to her.

And for the first time in his life, he knew what it meant to feel small. Not in fear. In awe.

He remembered standing on the seawall behind his uncle's house in Morehead City. Just nine years old. A hurricane had passed. The sky green, the bay like blown glass. Then it appeared. A waterspout, thin at first, then thickening, twisting out of the Gulf like a fist made of wind.

No sirens.

No warning.

Just that sudden shape on the water, rising slow, impossible, and irrefutable.

He hadn't run.

Couldn't.

He stood there with his hand on the rusted railing, breath locked in his chest, heart hammering.

That had been the first time he saw it clearly. The world didn't ask to be understood. It didn't even notice him.

This moment felt the same.

She didn't charge.

Didn't threaten.

She moved like something with no equal. Like a current. Like time.

You don't fight nature. You endure it.

Trailing behind her, knotted around the base of her caudal fin, was the life vest Cap had fitted on Shel. The orange had bled toward rust, the black stenciling of DEVILDAM ghosted and uneven across the back.

As she slid past the swim ledge, the vest dragged under Kid's feet, close enough for him to catch the heavy roll of her tail, the dense muscle working beneath the skin with each deliberate stroke.

The jacket lagged behind her, half-submerged, tugged and worried by the current like a thing undecided about sinking.

It caught once on the edge of the swim ledge, fabric stretching tight, then ripped free.

The vest bobbed back to the surface and began to turn in slow, empty circles as Judy moved off into deeper water, taking the weight with her and leaving the color behind.

He exhaled all at once.

His legs buckled.

He sagged against the transom, heart hammering like a struck bell.

* * *

Kid stepped onto the swamped back deck, water swirling around his ankles, the surface pitching gently beneath him like the last breath of something settling into its grave.

He crouched into the mess strewn across the deck, tackle, snapped rods, broken plastic bins, coils of wet line, all of it useless now. But near the scupper, tangled beneath a web of nylon netting and rusted pliers, he found the machete.

The grip was cracked. The blade was spotted with corrosion. But it would do.

He stepped to the edge of the swim ledge and took the painter in both hands. The rope was stiff with salt and algae, the fibers swollen and reluctant to give.

He set the machete against it and began to saw, short, forceful strokes, the blade biting through layer after layer. The first passes barely scored the surface. But with each pull, the fibers frayed, weakened, began to part.

On the final stroke, the rope gave with a sudden snap. The dinghy drifted off, released from its strain like an animal finally let off the chain. It bobbed once, then hung there, close, waiting.

Kid stood with the machete in his hand, bare feet planted wide on the slick edge of the swim ledge. The blade hung at his side, dripping saltwater.

What if I'd had this when she swam by?

It wasn't a wild thought. He'd killed before. Lots. Fish pulled flapping onto decks, bled out by the dozens. Sharks, too. He'd seen their eyes go dull, their bodies stiffen. It was part of the job, part of the water, you hunted, you cleaned, you kept going.

But Judy was different.

She wasn't meat. She wasn't sport. There was nothing dumb or panicked about her. He could still feel her under his palm. The rawness of her skin. The slow, tidal force of her passing.

If I'd had the blade... would I have used it?

He wanted to believe that when the time came, he could do what had to be done. But the truth sat quieter than that. It was murkier, half-formed, like something hiding under a pier.

She hadn't attacked.

She'd shown him something instead - not mercy, but awareness. A presence. The sense that she could've taken him, easily, and simply chose not to.

Because the moment didn't require it. Not yet.

She wasn't rage.

She wasn't punishment.

She was death, unhurried, the old kind, vast and indifferent.

A fact older than memory.

Older than fear.

He looked down at the blade again. It felt smaller now. Not useless, just symbolic. A gesture of resistance in a world that didn't need one.

A ripple passed under the hull, slow, deliberate.

His grip tightened.

She could come back. She would come back. He didn't know when, or from where. That was the part that sat deepest, not the size of her body, or her teeth, or the memory of what she'd already taken.

It was the waiting.

She was in no hurry.

She had all the time in the world.

* * *

In the salon, Kid unhooked the portable bilge, looped the hose around the body, and tucked it under one arm. He made his way back to the swim ledge, glanced once at the water, then stepped into the dinghy with a quiet splash.

He knelt and fit the intake beneath the pooled water and set the outflow hose over the dinghy's transom lip. He worked fast, hands moving without instruction.

The pump coughed once, then caught and water began to flow.

He steadied it with one hand, the other resting against the dinghy's damp interior, eyes scanning the water. Watching for the swell. The flash of motion. The silence felt thinner now, stretched over something too large to see.

He stood, feet braced wide against the low, slick floor. The machete felt heavier. He raised it above his head, not as a threat but a question.

"You want me to bring it!?" he shouted, voice battling against the wind.

Cap was sixty feet off, barely more than a silhouette in the gray wash, but Kid saw the answer clearly. Cap lifted the shotgun, slow, deliberate, and held it in both hands like a flag.

Not angry.

Not desperate.

But clear.

We got what we need.

The wind carried no words, but the message landed.

Kid nodded once. Not a big gesture, a quiet acceptance. He gave a short wave, two fingers, quick, then crouched low.

He set the machete down in the stern, positioned himself on the narrow thwart, and reached for the paddle.

* * *

Kid dug in hard, muscles screaming in protest. He pointed the bow east, rowing away from the sun as Cap had instructed. His palms pressed against the rough wooden shaft, burning as they slid with each pull.

Sweat dripped from his brow, stinging his eyes. Panic surged in his chest, fueling his strokes. The dinghy lurched forward, sluggish but moving.

He glanced back, Devildam's stern slumped low, bow almost clear of the water, fighting her final battle against the inevitable.

Pamlico Sound opened around him in all directions, a flat, breathing expanse with no edges he could trust. Distance lost its meaning out there, water and sky folding together until it felt like he could row forever and never reach anything solid. Every dark patch beneath the surface tugged at his attention. Not shapes, exactly, possibilities.

Judy didn't need to be anywhere specific. She could be anywhere at all.

The paddle peeled back calluses to reveal raw, stinging flesh. Blood seeped from the open wounds, slipping between his fingers and dripping steadily onto the dinghy's deck.

Red droplets splashed and spread across the fiberglass.

Kid stopped, chest heaving, and stared at his hands. Skin flayed and peeling, raw and inflamed.

For a moment, it felt impossible to keep going.

His arms trembled, muscles spent. He clenched his teeth, flexed his fingers, and re-gripped the paddle.

Then he drove the blade hard through the water.

CHAPTER 48

The tide was rising.

It always was. Or falling. That was the rhythm, ancient, mechanical, indifferent.

On paper, high tide was scheduled for 5:55 PM, data that came from tables centuries in the making, the result of gravity's slow arithmetic. The moon drew the ocean in a great heave across the planet's face, matched by a counter-pull on the far side. Add in the sun's influence, Earth's rotation, and the shape of the seafloor, and the result was a pulse.

Predictable.

Repeatable.

Implacable.

But the sea was never entirely obedient.

The storm had passed, but not without leaving fingerprints. Barometric pressure had dropped, lowering the weight of the air itself. Winds had pressed hard from the southeast for hours, piling water against the coast. The tide would come higher today than the charts expected, not a surge, but a quiet overachievement. Enough to matter.

Over the last hour, the climb would steepen. What had been a slow, creeping rise through the afternoon would quicken, filling every dip, pushing over every exposed flat. The difference between two feet and four could pass in less than sixty minutes.

Enough to drown a shoal. Enough to erase a margin of safety.

And there was nothing to stop it.

No plea.

No prayer.

No paddle.

CHAPTER 49

Cap stared east across the Sound, eyes narrowed against the shimmer where sky met water.

The shotgun rested in the crook of his arm, one hand loose on the grip. No sign of the dinghy. No glint of movement. Heat lay flat and blinding on the water, the sun burning down the back of his throat as he waited.

Kid was out there somewhere.

Or he wasn't.

Maybe he made it.

Found someone.

A boat.

A signal.

Maybe not.

The dinghy could've taken on water again. Paddle snapped. Wind turned.

He could be drifting in circles or gone under.

Or maybe Judy caught him after all, slow and silent, the way she liked it.

Cap rubbed the side of his jaw, eyes on the horizon.

Kid had the machete. Not much but something. If she came for him, maybe he got in a shot. Maybe that mattered.

Probably not.

Pictures, violent and red, crept into his mind. Cap pushed them away.

Didn't matter. Not now. Not until the Sound gave up a sign one way or the other.

Cap let out a slow breath and lowered his gaze.

Jack knelt in the shallows at his side, hands pressed flat to the water as if he could hold it still.

He didn't speak. Didn't cry. He stared into the surface, shoulders locked, arms trembling with the effort of not coming apart.

Cap lifted his eyes again, past the boy, back toward the center of the shoal.

Danny sat braced beside the depth marker, the same pole Cap had driven down what felt like a lifetime ago. The water lapped at his chest now, nearly to his armpits, rocking the marker gently with the tide. Its orange paint was blistered by sun and salt, and about halfway up a dark ring of dried blood circled the shaft.

Shel's blood. The high-water mark. When the sea reached it again, there would be nowhere left to go.

Ava sat close beside him, her shoulder pressed to his, one hand spread against his back. She leaned in briefly, her chin resting at his shoulder as they watched Jack.

"Hey," Danny called.

Jack straightened and waded over, water dragging at his legs.

Danny reached out, no words, no hurry, and drew the boy in.

Jack didn't resist. He folded into Danny's lap, collapsing like a sail losing its last breath of wind. Danny wrapped his arms around him and held on.

Cap turned back toward the Sound.

Toward Devildam.

The old song drifted up uninvited - *Regrets, I've had a few* - and he almost snorted at the timing. Funny what surfaced when there was nothing left to do but wait. He watched the boat sit low in the water, scarred now, wounded in ways he could name and others he couldn't.

A lifetime of decisions pressed in on him at once. Most of them felt defensible. A few didn't.

Footsteps sloshed behind him.

Cap didn't turn right away. He felt Ava stop a pace back, the water nudging at her waist.

"What are you thinking?" she asked.

Cap didn't look at her. He kept his eyes on the horizon.

"Time," he said. "You think you've got some say in it. Then one day you don't."

He let the words hang there, soft and final.

"Wish I'd spent mine better."

Ava didn't speak. She stood with him. Kept him company. He appreciated it.

He glanced at the bloodline on the marker. The sea hadn't reached it yet, but it would. It always did. The last inches would come fast, like they were trying to make up for lost time.

He felt the water move in the sand shifting under his toes. The way the current curled higher around his knees.

"Been slow so far," he said. "But that last foot's the one that buries you."

Twenty feet out, Judy's dorsal fin rose through the water, slow, precise, quiet. Her body stretched beneath like a continent, a moving distortion across the sandy bottom.

Just beneath the surface, the red light of her SPOT tracker blinked.

She was circling.

Watching.

Waiting.

Cap squared his stance in the shallows, water curling around his thighs. He racked the shotgun - clack-chunk - the sound sharp, mechanical, final. The gun felt heavy with purpose, the metal slick against his callused palms. Water beaded along the barrel and slipped free, vanishing into the Sound.

He brought the gun to his shoulder, bracing the stock tight, and tracked the shark, slow and exact.

Ava, a few paces behind, raised her hands to her ears.

Cap let out a breath. Felt the calm.

And fired.

FA-POW!

The blast cracked across the Sound, sudden, thunderous, brutal. The recoil punched his shoulder, the barrel kicking high. A spray of seawater exploded where the shot struck, sending up a wide fan of mist and foam. Smoke lingered in the air, drifting sideways on the wind.

The echo rolled out flat and low. Then silence.

CHAPTER 50

Something struck her - sharp, scattered, blunt at the edges.

A bloom of pressure rippled along her side, below the dorsal.
Not pain.

A wrongness.

Her receptors flared and logged the disturbance.

The outer layers tore. Flesh split. Blood leaked from the wounds,
slow and heavy, curling outward in dark, deliberate ribbons.
Shredded dermal denticles and skin fragments peeled away and
drifted into her wake, suspended in the water she displaced.

The damage stayed shallow.

Her skin was thick, layered for abrasion. Beneath it, muscle held
tight, dense and coiled. Cartilage beneath that remained intact. She
had taken worse, harder strikes, deeper scrapes, the grinding
violence of hulls and reef.

This was injury, not threat. Something to shed, something to
move past.

This was different.

Not dangerous.

Not yet.

But unfamiliar.

A scatter of force. A shift in pressure. Her blood in the water.
The sound that followed. The shape above.

She turned slightly, dropping deeper. Pectorals shifted. The water
cooled. The signals quieted.

But she saw. Above her.

Upright.

Motionless.

Her ampullae tracked faint current flows along limb-like shapes.
Subtle pulses. A living field. Recently made. Familiar.

Not food.

Not yet.
But known.
Marked.
A signal to file.
An object in motion that might block, or strike, or take.
She didn't wonder.
She didn't wait.
But she remembered.
And if the shape returned, if it moved wrong or rose between her and what she needed, she'd correct the imbalance.
Without thought.
Without mercy.
Because that's how the water worked.

CHAPTER 51

Cap lowered the shotgun, smoke curling from the barrel, and stepped back from the edge.

His ears rang. The echo of the shot hung in the air a moment longer, then was gone.

Out where the Sound deepened, a faint haze of blood drifted, thin and curling, already unraveling in the tide.

He watched it fade, gave a slow nod. Not victory. Confirmation.

The shot had touched her.

Done something.

Not enough.

He knew better. Knew the range was too long. Knew better than to waste a shell.

But he'd fired anyway. Let the tension break through his arms and into the trigger.

A foolish move.

Five shots left.

He heard rustling behind him, movement in the water.

By the depth marker, Danny sat in the shallows, Jack folded into his lap like something rescued from a fire.

Ava dropped next to them and threw an arm over Danny's shoulder for warmth. The tide licked at the top of their chest.

The bloodline now just an inch above the water.

Danny said something quiet to Jack, then gently shifted the boy into Ava's arms. Jack didn't resist. Ava held on tight.

Danny stood. Waded over to Cap.

Cap didn't speak.

He lifted the shotgun, laid it across the back of his neck with both hands hooked over the steel. It was slick in his grip, warm from the shot.

"What's next?" Danny asked.

Cap stared at the water where she'd gone under.

Flat now.

Quiet.

He'd led boats through hurricanes, buried friends, seen engines fail miles offshore with no one coming.

He'd known danger you could chart and track.

But this…

This was something else.

"I don't know," he said.

CHAPTER 52

Danny stood near the depth marker, the water brushing his midsection.

Jack stood beside him, the tide too high to sit, his body sagging with exhaustion even as his eyes tracked the slow, relentless rise of the water.

Danny ran a hand through the boy's matted hair, smoothing it back. The motion caught on something familiar.

A Sunday, years ago. Jack asleep across his legs while the Ravens played a tight one on the road. Danny on the couch with a beer sweating into his palm, his fingers moving through Jack's hair in the same absent rhythm. Ava beside him in her purple jersey, second-guessing calls, shouting at the TV like the coach might hear her. The room smelling of popcorn and carpet cleaner.

Nothing important happening.

And that had been the beauty of it.

The whole world folded down to one small, unremarkable moment, the kind you never think to protect until it's already gone.

The water had reached the bloodline on their marker.

Ava stood near, her shoulder warm against his, both of them staring out over the bright water.

She hadn't spoken since the shot, since Cap had raised the gun and fired at the shadow moving offshore. The sound had echoed, then faded into the wind, lost in the rhythm of waves and distant gulls.

It hadn't stopped her. Nothing had.

Danny looked down at Jack's sun-splotched scalp. The boy's head rested warm against his chest, his breath shallow, his skin hot from the sun.

He glanced at Ava, face red, drawn tight with sun and fatigue, and then out at Cap, standing at the drop-off, the shotgun balanced across his shoulders like a yoke.

He thought about all the time he'd wasted, months knowing his marriage was slipping, doing nothing while the space between them widened. Hoping silence might fix what honesty wouldn't.

But this was different. This was a chance to save something.

To do more than sit and wait.

This was it.

"It's time," Danny said.

* * *

Cap turned toward them as Danny's voice faded. There was no argument in the words. No drama. It was the kind of simple truth that lands hard.

He waded back toward the depth marker, water curling above his waist, warm and rising. The rope Kid used to sling the shotgun to Cap was looped there, dry in places, salt-stiff in others. He tugged it free with a slow, practiced motion, the length sliding loose and settling into the water.

Danny, Ava and Jack stepped forward.

"Okay, then. We draw her in," Cap said. "Bring her close. Close enough to end it."

He coiled the rope in one hand, squinting into the windless sky, judging angle and depth, whatever margin they might have left. "You tie this around me," he said, holding up the line. "Good and tight. I go out five, maybe ten feet. Enough to get her to commit. She follows me in. She'll try to surge."

He looked at the others now, steady and slow.

"Soon as she lunges, you haul the rope. Yank me back. Fast as you can. She beaches herself in the shallows, right there in front of you. And then…"

He patted the shotgun slung across his neck.

"You finish it."

"It should be me," Danny said. "I'll be the bait. You handle the gun."

Cap turned, studied him. The man looked serious.

Not puffed-up or posturing but calm, resolute, and scared in the right way.

Cap glanced at the rope in his hands, then out at the water. The sun had slipped behind the haze. Shadows stretched long across the bar.

He let out a breath.

"No. Not this time," he said. "It's gotta be me."

He saw Danny's protest forming and cut it off, "I've lived my years. Had a good run. And I'm dying anyway, whether she eats me or not. Cancer's already halfway there. You got Jack. You got Ava. You got a reason."

Cap moved toward him, the shotgun wet and heavy as he slid it down from across his shoulders, "Take it."

Danny reached out. The gun was heavier than it looked. Denser. Like it had stored every moment of violence it had ever promised.

He cradled it awkwardly.

Cap gave a half-grin, dry as salt, "You ever handled a gun?"

Danny shook his head.

Cap nodded like he'd expected that, "Alright. First things first, safety's here, see that? Push it off. You'll hear it click. You rack it, shoulder it, then pull the trigger. Don't jerk it. Let it break clean."

He spoke low, steady. Like it wasn't the first time he'd handed someone a weapon who didn't want one.

Danny nodded again, slower this time, eyes locked on the shotgun like it might wake up.

Every part of it looked foreign. The metal too black, too slick. The weight wrong in his hands.

But he was listening.

Soaking it in like instructions to deactivate a bomb.

Cap clapped a hand to his shoulder.

"Point blank," he said. "Don't think. Don't flinch. When she's there, when she's too close, too big, and everything in you's screaming run, you stand your ground. You blast her. Right through her God damn eye."

Danny nodded.

"Do what's right, Danny." Cap said.

"Do what's right," Danny repeated.

* * *

Ava watched from a few feet away, water at her midriff. Jack clung to her side, but he wasn't shaking anymore. He was quiet now, eyes locked on Cap and Danny, taking it all in without blinking, like he knew what it all meant.

She'd known Cap was going to say it. The plan. The sacrifice. The rope. It made a terrible sort of sense, and that was the worst part, that it was logical.

And then Danny had said he'd do it.

That was what almost broke her.

Not because it was so wrong, but because it was so him. So completely, stupidly, achingly him.

The man she'd fought with over bills and schedules and silence at the dinner table. The man she leaned on when her father died. The one she blamed when things cracked, then blamed herself when they didn't mend.

He'd disappointed her, amazed her, held her up when she was too proud to ask, and now he was ready to hand over the last thing he had. Not for recognition. Not even for her. For Jack. For the boy leaning against her, ribs showing, skin burned and raw.

Danny would walk into the jaws of a nightmare to give him one more hour, one more chance.

Cap must've seen something in her face, because he turned toward Jack and knelt slightly, dropping into the water with a grunt and resting on one knee.

He looked the boy dead in the eye.

"Listen here, Captain Jack," he said, his voice low and certain. "I go out there, and I wave her in. Real gentle. She comes running, like a bull after a red flag. And when she thinks she's got me, the three of you are gonna haul my old ass back like you're reelin' in a marlin. Boom. Judy's stuck. And your pop? He uses that scatter gun. Right through the eye. Lights out. Shark season's over, mate. Over."

Jack stared at him, wide-eyed and silent.

Cap smiled, soft and worn, "Yeah. I know it sounds scary. And maybe it is. But I've lived through worse. I promise you, I ain't going nowhere I don't choose to go."

Jack didn't speak. But he nodded, once.

Cap stood again and turned toward the Sound. The rope dragged behind him in lazy coils, each one catching light as the tide tugged it forward.

He started tying a knot around his waist, slow, deliberate, hands steady in the water. It wasn't courage. Not really. It was resignation given shape and purpose.

Ava watched, awed not by the plan but by the quiet certainty of it. This man, a stranger, practically, was walking into the water for her family.

For Jack.

For Danny.

For her.

He had no stake in their future, no obligation to protect them. And yet, here he was, tying himself to a line so they might live.

Her throat tightened.

She turned to Danny. His hands were wrapped around the shotgun now. Clumsy, tense. But sure. He met her gaze and nodded once. Not for comfort. Not for approval.

For readiness.

Ava looked at both of them - Cap wading out, Danny steadying the gun - and the question rose in her, *I see what they're willing to do. What am I willing to do? Not just to survive, but to save our marriage. Our son. Our family.*

She'd spent years clinging to quiet resentments, pulling away in inches, assuming there'd be time to mend things later. But later was gone.

The tide was rising.

CHAPTER 53

Cap took a deep breath, deeper than any he'd taken in a long time, and let it out slow.

The air scraped through his chest, rough as gravel, stinging his throat and lungs. It filled him with something sharp and cold and final.

There'd been a time when breaths like that had meant new beginnings, fresh mornings on the water, clean air, the promise of something earned. Now it felt like the last clear space between one world and the next.

He didn't know if this was redemption, or one more failure dressed up like purpose. Maybe it didn't matter. He was here. He was breathing. And he had one thing left to give.

He turned toward the water, gaze fixed on the deeper edge where the sandbar dropped off into Judy's world.

The rope wrapped around his chest, snug under his arms with a knot cinched tight between his shoulder blades. Danny had done the tying, his fingers slow and deliberate. They both knew this knot mattered more than most. This knot meant life or death.

The slack trailed back fifteen feet to Ava, Jack and Danny, a lifeline in the truest sense. Cap forced himself not to look back at them. If he did, he might lose his nerve.

He fished a small lock-blade knife from his pocket and flicked it open with a snap. The blade gleamed dull in the fading light, its edge uneven from years of sharpening. His fingers curled around the worn handle, knuckles pale and tense.

One step forward and the water reached his stomach, cold and heavy. Another step and the chill climbed higher, swirling against his ribs. The water crept further up his chest, pressing against his heart like a tightening fist.

He paused, gripping the knife tighter. His breath came faster now, faster than he wanted. Gritting his teeth, he ran the blade across the palm of his free hand. The sting flared bright and sharp.

Blood, dark and syrupy in the dimming light, spilled down his arm. Thick droplets dripped from his fingers, splashing into the water, twisting into crimson spirals that coiled and stretched outward, fading into nothing.

Cap slapped the water hard with his bleeding hand, sending a sharp crack rolling across the Sound. The impact stung his palm, but he ignored it.

"Come get it, then! C'MON!" Cap roared, the shout tearing out of him like a growl.

The day's horrors, so vivid, so devastating, boiled up inside him and spilled out in that roar.

Fury.

Grief.

Desperation.

It all fed the words, his voice raw. The shout wasn't a challenge, it was a demand, a curse, a man spitting in the face of death. His voice wavered, but the anger behind it held firm.

The wind died.

The faint slap of water against their bellies faded. The whole world seemed to hold its breath. The surface of the Sound smoothed to glass, dark and slick as oil.

Fifty yards out, beyond the wounded silhouette of Devildam, Judy surfaced.

Her dorsal fin broke first, black, jagged, tall as a post, gliding forward in a slow, relentless line. The water parted around her bulk, the swell of her back rolling beneath the surface. As she passed, the ruined boat tipped gently in her wake, a slow rock that traveled bow to stern, as if acknowledging her presence.

She kept moving, straight, sure, and silent, bearing down on Cap like a promise about to deliver.

Cap's fingers twitched around the knife handle. Fear clawed its way up his throat, a cold fist that squeezed hard. His breathing thinned, parched air scraping over his tongue with every breath.

He forced himself to swallow it down, that gnawing panic, swallowing it like bile. It settled in his gut like a lead weight.

He'd been in tight spots before, but this was different. He'd stared at his own sickness, felt the weight of death pressing closer with each bad test result.

But this?

This was worse.

This was teeth and muscle and raw, relentless power - and it was coming for him.

He swallowed hard and whispered to himself, "Okay, then. Let's do this."

"Here she comes!" Cap shouted. "Ready, steady, now! Ready, steady!"

He didn't turn to look. He couldn't. But he heard movement behind him, the shifting of bodies in water, the sound of breath catching, the rope going taut. Felt it, too, the pull against his ribs, firm and responsive.

He imagined Danny wrapping the rope around his wrist, holding the shotgun with both hands, awkward but committed. He pictured Ava braced at the front, rope clenched in her fists. Jack somewhere between them, small and burning with nerves, pretending not to be afraid.

Cap took a slow step back, dragging the rope with him. The pull of the rope tightened, their rhythm syncing behind him. No one shouted. No one hesitated.

Good.

Judy's dorsal fin cut the water cleanly, twenty feet away now. Her back rolled behind it, black and massive beneath the surface. The wake she threw pushed out in widening arcs, splitting the tide like a plow through wet earth.

Fifteen feet.

Cap shuffled backward, toes digging through silt, water curling up to his chest. The rope cinched hard beneath his arms.

Ten feet.

The water surged forward, lifting in a sudden hump of muscle and mass beneath the surface.

Cap saw the break in her movement, saw the moment she angled up.

The water bulged and rolled around her snout, frothing with air and force.

She lunged, jaws agape, her teeth streaked with blood, gnashing at the water with mechanical violence.

Cap caught flashes of white, bits of flesh dangling between her teeth.

Her gullet pulsed, a tunnel of slick, flexing muscle ready to drag anything alive into permanent dark.

"NOW!" Cap roared.

CHAPTER 54

Cap felt the sudden violence of the rope snapping tight, torso cinched hard, pressure crushing the breath from his lungs as the current tore past his ears.

He shot backward across the surface like a hooked fish, spine cracking in protest, and slammed down onto his tailbone.

His cap tore from his head, whipped away in the rush.

Judy's jaws slammed shut a breath too late.

Spray slapped his face, stinging his eyes, blinding him for a beat.

She hit the shoal hard, her bulk slamming into sand with a deep, bone-heavy thud. Mud and grit erupted around her midsection as the bottom gave way and then held.

Water burst outward. Her tail lashed, driving, searching for purchase, but found none. The shoal had taken her weight and refused to give it back.

Cap's gaze locked on her open mouth, darker than any night sky, wide as a grave. Not a mouth, but an entrance to nothing.

A void where even memory would vanish.

She snapped, and Cap rolled hard to his right.

Her head landed on his planted right foot. Everything below the ankle disappeared beneath her weight, bone, flesh, tendon, all pinned between sand and thousands of pounds of thrashing, prehistoric muscle.

The bones shattered, first the metatarsals, then the finer joints of the ankle, folding in on themselves like dry twigs under boot heel. Ligaments tore free from moorings, a sickening unzipping deep in the meat. The tendons snapped like cable, pulled too tight and too fast.

Cap clawed at the bottom but it wasn't to escape. It was to stay conscious.

He didn't yell.

Couldn't.

A raw, guttural cry burst from his chest, more rupture than voice, all nerve and shock and breath.

He thrashed, but it was like pushing against the hull of a ship, solid, unmovable.

Water surged over his face. He lurched back, fought to keep his head above the chop. Salt scorched his throat. He coughed, spat, gulped another breath before the next surge collapsed over him, thrown by the chaos of her body rolling inches away.

He swung blindly, fists hammering at the broad curve of her snout, dense cartilage, slick and unfeeling. His knuckles skidded and split, but he kept swinging.

Each blow jolted his shoulders, rattled up through his spine.

She didn't flinch.

He tried to buck his hips sideways, twisting hard, trying to shift the weight. Nothing gave. The pain in his ankle was blinding, white-hot, but he rocked anyway, back and forth, using his torso like a lever, anything to keep his mouth out of the water.

He swung his left leg up and slammed his bare heel into her rough hide. Her sandpaper skin scraped his foot raw, the impact jarring through the bones of his ankle.

She didn't flinch.

She was solid as a reef, all mass and instinct and motion, like hitting a boulder wrapped in broken glass.

She didn't look at him.

Her dark eye stared past, unfocused, wide and lifeless. Her jaws snapped again, blindly, inches from his left foot. Her tail slammed the water, beating the Sound into froth.

Cap felt the pull of the rope around his waist. A new angle.

Judy twisted, and the rope moved with her.

Cap blinked against the spray, squinting through water, pain, and salt.

The line was snagged. Caught in her mouth. Somewhere between those sawblade teeth, it had threaded itself into the ruin. Cap was on the wrong side of the line.

Cut off.

Isolated behind muscle and motion.

And now…

They were pulling.

Ava. Danny. Jack.

Each desperate yank on the rope tugged him forward, not to safety, but closer to the jaws.

The tension wrenched his ribs.

Judy thrashed.

The rope jerked again.

"No! No! No!" Cap shouted. "Stop! Let go!"

He slapped the water with his free hand, fingers clawing through the silty bottom, fighting to keep his face out of the surge. His leg spasmed beneath her.

The pain came in waves now, blooming outward from the point of pressure, white-hot and endless.

"Shoot her, Danny!" he screamed. "Shoot her!"

* * *

From the shallows, they watched the mound of water roll toward Cap, fifteen feet out, shoulder-deep, alone.

Danny dug in, water surging past to his hips. Jack hunched just ahead, knuckles white on the rope, arms shaking. At the front, Ava planted her feet and leaned hard, the line cinched tight around her forearms.

They moved as one, no words, no signal, only the animal agreement of bodies bracing to pull.

"Now!" Cap shouted.

Danny hauled. So did Ava. So did Jack, the rope burning into their palms as it came tight.

The line went rigid, humming like a live wire. Cap's body snapped backward, yanked out of the shallows in a violent surge that tore his cap free and sent it skittering across the water.

The force staggered them.

Ava was wrenched sideways first, feet sliding out from under her.

Jack collided into her with a sharp cry as his grip faltered. Danny slipped too, the sand liquefying beneath him as he fought to keep one hand on the rope, the other locked around the shotgun…

And then he saw her.

Judy surged up in the shallows where Cap had been, her head breaking the surface in a rush of white water and shadow.

She was impossibly close, fifteen feet, maybe less, close enough for Danny to see the depth of her, the sheer breadth of her skull, the way the water seemed to bend around her mass.

A sharp, metallic reek rode the spray, blood and salt and something deeper, animal and cold, filling his nose before he could turn away. Her open mouth yawned black and cavernous, rows of teeth flashing like something unfinished, not meant to be seen in daylight.

She was bigger than his fear had allowed for. Bigger than anything he'd ever pictured.

Not fast.

Not frantic.

Just there - solid, ancient, undeniable.

For a split second, Danny forgot the rope. Forgot the gun. Forgot to breathe.

They went down together, limbs tangled, water crashing.

Ava and Jack dropped to their knees, but Danny fell back, falling to his ass, then elbows. The shotgun slipped from his grasp. For a moment, he saw it but could only watch as it disappeared beneath the water. Gone.   Still on their knees, Ava and Jack shook water from their eyes and kept pulling the rope, desperate to pull Cap away from Judy's gnashing jaws.

Cap's scream followed almost instantly, torn from him, jagged and wrong, "No! No! No! Stop! Let go!"

Danny stood, coughing up seawater. He grabbed the rope and pulled.

Then it hit him.

They weren't pulling Cap away from Judy - they were pulling him towards her.

The line had caught somewhere, not around her, not under her, through her.

Inside her goddamn mouth.

"Shoot her, Danny!" Cap screamed. "Shoot her!"

Danny squatted, hands diving into the cloudy water, raking the bottom in blind panic. The sand was thick with blood and grit. His fingers swept past shells, shards, plant matter - nothing.

COME ON! COME ON! FOR ONCE IN YOUR LIFE…

Then - metal.

Smooth and cold. His fingers closed around the shotgun's stock, and he yanked it free like dragging a man from a grave. The weapon felt heavier now, soaked and swollen with consequence.

He surged to his feet, breath tearing out of him, and drove himself forward.

The water surged around his waist, tugging at his hips, the sand unsteady beneath his feet. Ahead, the shoal fell away, an abrupt slope into deeper water, and he knew one misstep, one slip, and he'd be in her world.

He leveled the gun.

Judy thrashed in the shallows, her bulk surging against the sand with brute urgency.

Her body twisted in heavy, sweeping arcs, tail flinging sheets of spray skyward. Jaws gaped and slammed shut in wild, sightless snaps, striking at nothing, striking at everything.

Her eye turned and locked on Danny.

No flicker of confusion.

No delay.

She saw the weapon.

Danny's stomach clenched. It wasn't fear. It was worse. A gut-level certainty that something in her, some deep, ancient process, recognized that he was the threat.

He flicked off the safety and racked the shell - clack-clack.

The sound cut clean through the water.

Confident.

Final.

Her eye shifted. A pale membrane slid across it, sealing the black beneath in a dull, milky glaze.

Danny didn't hesitate. He stepped in and brought the shotgun up one-handed, arm locked, the barrel steady, aimed straight at the eye.

Less than a foot away.

The surface of it was blank now, ancient and unreadable, cartilage and skin holding fast where thought should have been.

No hesitation.

Do what's right, Danny.

He pulled the trigger.

CLICK.

Not a bang.

No kick to the shoulder.

A hollow, mechanical click.

A dead trigger.

A fucking dud.

His breath caught. For a beat, he didn't move, he stared at the gun like it might fix itself. Another twitch of her tail sent a wave crashing up his thighs. He stumbled, caught his balance, teeth clenched, heart pounding.

He racked the pump with trembling hands, slid it back, felt the action catch and tried to chamber the next shell. It jammed. Wouldn't seat. Too swollen with water. Too old.

Or maybe it was him.

His fingers were slick, his grip too tight or not tight enough. He worked the slide again, faster now, the weapon clacking and grinding in his hands.

Judy surged.

Her body rolled, tail flinging a curtain of spray across the shoal.

Danny flinched as her flank slid towards him, broad as a boat hull, dense and unstoppable. The ground tilted under her weight. He stumbled, shoulder knocking against her.

He wrenched the pump again. Another shell ejected, useless, wet.

He slammed the next one in - *Please, God* - and racked it forward.

Nothing.

No click.

No weight behind it.

The chamber was empty.

The gun was done.

Danny stood trembling in the churn, foam curling around his knees.

Judy twisted three feet away, her massive flank rolling like a capsized world, tail cleaving the air in great, frothy arcs.

She'd moved past him, hadn't even registered him.

He stared down at the shotgun. Dead weight. A soaked, useless thing.

But it was still a weapon.

With a roar, raw, from the base of his spine, he flipped it in his grip, clutched the barrel with both hands, and swung.

The stock smashed into the crown of her head with a dull, meaty crack.

The scarred skin split on contact, thin gashes opening across her snout, blood beading along the ridges where old wounds met new.

Danny swung again.

And again.

The blows thundered through his arms, jarred his shoulders, shot up his spine like electricity.

Flecks of paint and wood chipped away with each strike. Salt and spray flew, and somewhere in it all came a sound, a guttural yell, part rage, part grief, ripped from his chest before he knew he was screaming.

"Get off him!"

The gunstock split at the seam on the fifth strike, splinters biting into his palm. He lifted it, raised it over his head.

Judy didn't flinch.

Didn't bolt.

But her head shifted slightly, eyes turning away, body rolling off to one side, leaving behind a dark streak of blood in the foam.

From the corner of his eye, Danny saw Cap slide out from under the shark.

A voice cut through the roar.

"Danny!"

He turned.

Ava clutched Jack, arms locked around his chest.

The boy's heels skidded through the churn, bare feet dragging.

Tension had cinched the rope around his arm - tight, tangled -
and it was pulling.

Hard.

Jack's face was twisted in panic, mouth open in a silent scream.

He slid another foot, knees buckling, the rope drawing him closer
to Judy's gaping mouth.

Closer to death.

CHAPTER 55

Cap clawed at the bottom, fingers raking through grit and broken shell.

He tried to twist, lever, anything but the water surged over his face again. He turned his chin up, coughing, barely catching breath before it spilled over him again.

A firestorm of pain tore through his ankle, bones ground together, tendons frayed and useless, nerves lit like wire. It blinded him.

Nearly stopped him cold.

He gasped for air. Kicked at the shark. Strength bleeding fast.

Through the blur, he caught a flash - Danny, circling in with the shotgun, eyes wild.

But no boom.

No recoil.

Only panicked shouting.

"Get off him!"

The shark shifted. Not off but wild. Her body thrashed, head snapping toward Danny, tail slamming the shoal. A wave reared and fell. In that instant, her weight lifted, barely, but enough.

Cap kicked.

A scream tore loose, raw, guttural, torn straight from the center of him, as the crushed ankle slipped free. Skin tore against the grit. He lurched backwards, the pain flared white, too bright for thought.

Half-blind with pain, chest heaving, he staggered upright, barely more than vertical, but breathing.

The rope across his chest yanked hard again, alive with tension. It jolted him a step toward Judy.

He followed it forward with his eyes.

She had the rope in her mouth, clamped between jagged teeth,

twisted deep near the corner of her jaw. The middle of the rope.
She'd bitten it when she lunged. Now she was the anchor point,
pulling from the center.

Cap on one end…

The other cinched around Jack's arm, tight, being yanked straight
toward the open jaws, rows of teeth flashing like shattered glass.

Ava fought to hold her son back. Both arms around his waist.
Shoulders locked. Face tight with panic.

Danny skidded in, wrapped his arms around both of them, and
pulled back.

Where's the damn shotgun!?

Cap thought to shout, "Don't pull!" - the warning already forming
in his throat.

But he swallowed it.

They had to pull.

Every inch they dragged Jack back bought him breath, bought
him ground, bought him life. And if that same rope was hauling
Cap closer to her jaws, then so be it.

There was no time left for anything else.

He reached into his pocket by feel. Found the knife. Drew it free.
The blade flashed once as he snapped it open, the motion
automatic, muscle memory older than fear.

The rope crossed his chest, taut as a drawn wire.

Cap wrapped his fist around it, felt the strain humming through
the fibers, felt the lives tied to the other end.

Then he brought the blade down.

Not a hack.

A committed stroke, hard and clean, steel biting through braid
and tension together.

The rope parted.

The line snapped.

Cap staggered backward, chest heaving, the ends of the rope
slithering into the surf.

* * *

Danny clung to Ava from behind, arms locked around her waist, his chin pressed to her shoulder. He couldn't see Jack's face, just the blur of his limbs, the panic in his body.

Ava's grip never let up, both hands clasped around Jack's chest, legs planted wide as the tide surged. They were losing ground. Inch by inch. Jack's heels scraped across the submerged sand, dragging small wakes behind them.

Danny tried to dig in, shift his weight, hold tighter. But it was no use. Judy was too strong. Jack was being pulled toward that gaping, thrashing blur.

Out of the corner of his eye, Danny saw movement…

Cap.

He'd risen. Somehow.

He limped through the knee-high water, dragging his ruined leg. He waded straight to Jack's side and dropped hard to one knee, breath hitching, eyes already on the rope.

Danny saw the knife flash, short blade, red at the hinge.

Cap clutched the rope where it extended from Jack's arm, pinning it above the knot. With his other hand, he sawed.

Fast.

Hard.

No wasted motion.

The rope fought him, swollen nylon, slick with seawater and tension but he kept at it. One stroke. Two. On the third, the fibers gave with a harsh snap, and the rope spilled free.

Jack tumbled backward into Ava. Danny caught them both, and the three of them crumpled in a spray of water and sand.

Cap straightened, instinct driving him to stand, to flee.

But his crushed ankle gave out.

Cap's leg crumpled beneath him, sending him sprawling. He dropped sideways into the shallows, one hand breaking the fall, the other flinging the knife as he went.

Danny saw his face twist, jaw clenched, eyes wide, before he hit the water. The pain was obvious, sudden and sharp, flashing across him like a warning Danny couldn't unsee.

Judy didn't lunge.

She didn't need to.

Her head swept sideways through the tide, jaws open, not fast, but low and wide, terrifying in their precision.

Her teeth found his leg, bare, pale, half-buried in the sand.

Her bite yanked Cap flat. He twisted once, hands clawing at the bottom, mouth wide. Danny saw the shape of it, a silent gasp, more breath than sound, as the water surged over him.

Then Judy twisted.

A single, brutal wriggle and she came loose.

Her bulk rolled free from the shoal in a massive shrug, lifting off the sand in a low surge. Water rushed in beneath her. Her tail kicked once, dragging her backward, deeper.

Cap went with her.

His body skidded across the shallows, one leg stretched taut where her jaws held firm.

Then he was pulled under, arms flaring wide, vanishing in the churning water.

Blood followed, thick and dark, blooming outward, caught in the tide.

Then nothing.

Cap didn't surface.

The rope, cut clean, drifted in slow, lazy coils beside them.

CHAPTER 56

Ava clutched Jack against her chest, his heart fluttering like a bird's.

He was sobbing, but the rope was gone. The tension had snapped. The violence had moved on, for now.

Ava dropped to her knees, sinking into the churned sand.

The water climbed to her chin, slapped cold against her jaw. Her body shook in small, uncontrollable bursts.

Danny knelt beside her and pulled them in, one arm around Ava, the other firm and careful at the back of Jack's head.

His breath hitched, chest rising too fast, his eyes fixed on the empty water where Cap had been.

No one spoke.

Jack went rigid in her arms. Ava tightened her hold, turned his face into her neck, murmured something she knew wouldn't help.

Danny leaned forward until his forehead touched hers.

They stayed like that, pressed together, soaked and stunned, three bodies bracing against the space Cap had left behind.

Jack's breath broke.

Then thinned.

Then fell into a small, shaking quiet that hurt worse than the sound ever could.

Out west, the sun sank toward the horizon, staining the sky with streaks of orange and bruised red.

The tide rose.

CHAPTER 57

Ava stared at the sky and hated how beautiful it was.

Streaks of orange and bruised purple burned along the horizon, the kind of sunset people stopped for, framed, tried to keep. Clouds caught fire at their edges, gold slipping into red, while the sun sank low and heavy, pressing itself to the water as if reluctant to leave.

It was too perfect.

Too composed.

A painted lie hung over a world that had bled all day. The sort of beauty that dared you to forget what waited beneath it. Ava thought of those old John Boorman films, Excalibur, the battlefield washed in green and gold, bodies cooling under a sky that never acknowledged them. Lush. Impossible. Gorgeous enough to make ruin look ordained.

She couldn't stop thinking how wrong it felt.

That nature could look like this after everything. Like the ocean and the sky had moved on, cleaned themselves up, forgotten what they'd done.

Less than twenty-four hours ago, a hurricane had torn through, the wind howling like wolves, the rain coming down in violent sheets. Now the Sound shimmered, calm and glassy. As if the world had turned its face away from their suffering.

An hour had passed since Judy dragged Cap under.

One long hour.

An hour of staring at the water.

Jumping at every ripple.

Every shadow.

The quiet gnawed at her, scraping raw every nerve. Ava kept scanning the darkening surface, her mind spinning in tight, panicked circles.

Maybe Judy had gone, slipped back out to sea, swallowed by the Atlantic, her hunger finally sated. But that didn't feel true. Not really. More likely, she was out there in the deeper water.

Circling.

Watching.

Waiting.

But maybe not.

Ava shifted constantly, as if movement alone might keep them safe. Beside her, Danny clenched and unclenched his fists. Jack pressed his face into her stomach, arms locked tight around her waist like he could hide there.

Like she could shield him.

The red smear of Shel's blood, the mark Cap had drawn, was gone, swallowed whole by the tide. The sea pressed against Ava's ribs, midway up her chest.

It reached Jack's armpits. It lapped at Danny's stomach. The cold had settled into them, bone-deep. With each passing minute, the Sound rose around their bodies, slow and unshakable.

No rush.

No mercy.

Shallow water wouldn't stop Judy now.

She and Danny stood side by side, arms draped over each other's shoulders like rafters in a crumbling house. Jack was wedged between them, trembling. His breath warmed her side in uneven bursts.

They stood together, bruised, wrecked, but breathing.

Jack murmured something, his words muffled against her body.

"What, honey?" Ava asked softly.

She tilted his chin up with her fingers.

"Maybe she's gone," he said, voice thin, too quiet. "Maybe she went away."

There was a flicker of hope in his face, something small, bright, and impossibly fragile.

"I never wanna go fishing again," he added, voice breaking.

A child's plea for a world that made sense again.

Danny let out a short, tired laugh, "Yeah... that makes two of us."

"Three," Ava said. "Next time, we'll curl up on the couch and watch a movie."

* * *

Danny's mind flickered to the last time the three of them had curled up on the couch together.

It had been months ago, maybe longer, back when things had seemed repairable. Jack had picked Finding Nemo, something sweet and harmless, or so Danny had thought.

He remembered watching that little clownfish navigate the ocean's endless animated dangers, all for a chance to be reunited with his family. At the time, it hadn't meant much.

But now? Now it felt like a warning. A quiet reminder of how easy it was to get separated. Of how hard it could be to get back.

"Like a family?" Jack asked, his voice muffled and small.

Danny looked down. Jack was peering up at Ava, his eyes wet, searching her face for something solid.

Ava bent down and brushed his damp hair from his forehead. "We'll see," she said softly.

Danny swallowed, "Yeah... we'll see."

He meant it. Or at least, he wanted to.

Sometimes 'we'll see' was filler, something you said when you didn't want to lie but didn't want to crush hope either. But sometimes it was more. A hinge. A breath held at the edge of something new. He hoped this time it meant the latter.

Jack gave a faint, fragile smile, the first since Cap had gone under, "Not Shark Week, though."

Danny chuckled, low and tired, "No. Not Shark Week. No more Shark Week."

They stood like that for a while, arms around each other, the tide pushing higher, cold and insistent. Water lapped at their ribs, numbing skin, stealing breath.

But where their bodies touched, hip to hip, shoulder to shoulder, there was warmth. Not from the water, but from being held. From being together. Danny closed his eyes for a moment and let the feeling wash over him.

The sky had gone molten at the edges, streaks of deep orange fading into purple. The sun had almost vanished, a thin band of fire on the horizon. Stunning. Violent in its beauty. The kind of thing people flew across the world to see.

And here they were, half-submerged, watching it without joy.

Devildam's stern was underwater now, her bow tilted skyward like a hand reaching for help. The old boat looked broken. Twisted. Her hull groaned as water filled spaces never meant to hold water, dragging her down inch by inch.

Her cabin windows caught the last light and glowed faintly, orange fading to nothing. Barnacles clung along her lower hull like stubborn reminders of the life she'd lived. It wouldn't be long, now. She'd go under.

And when she did, Cap wouldn't be alone down there.

"Look," Jack whispered.

Danny followed his gaze.

Between Devildam's half-sunken hull and the edge of the sandbar, something floated on the water, dark, round, and slow.

A hat.

Cap's hat.

It turned in lazy circles, caught in the tide, its brim sagging and soaked through.

Something twisted in Danny's chest.

He'd barely known Cap. Less than a day. But the man had stepped forward, no hesitation, no theatrics, and done what no one else had. A man who didn't belong to them, who owed them nothing.

And he'd done the unthinkable.

Walked into it.

Cap wasn't perfect. He'd made mistakes, real ones.

But this?

This wasn't really on him. It was the hurricane that had reshaped the Sound, shifted the bottom, changed what used to be safe. The tide. The grounding. All of it started with that storm.

And yet Cap had never pointed to the sky or made excuses. He hadn't looked away. Hadn't passed the blame or vanished into the background. He stood in it. Owned it. Tried to make it right, even if it meant going under with the rest of them.

Danny didn't know if he could ever be that kind of man.

But right now, chest-deep in water, watching that ruined hat drift through the foam, he wanted to try.

The hat spun once, tossed in the current.

Behind the cap, Judy's dorsal fin broke the surface as clean and silent as a scalpel, black and jagged, slicing through the stillness.

It moved slowly, casual and unbothered. Each stroke of her tail sent the dorsal weaving side to side, a quiet declaration of presence.

She wasn't hunting.

She wasn't rushing.

She was there.

Claiming the water as hers.

Danny tensed. His arm pressed harder against Ava's back.

She inhaled sharply beside him, "Oh God..."

Jack's small hand clutched hers, tight.

No one moved.

No one spoke.

They could only watch as the hat, and the nightmare that followed it, drifted closer.

CHAPTER 58

The shallows peeled away from the top third of her body, water slipping from her scarred snout in rippling sheets.

She cut the surface like a warship's prow, slow, exact, unbothered.

The twisted stump of her dorsal fin knifed through the wake, jagged and puckered at the edges, the skin around it torn and pitted.

Beneath it, the fist-sized shotgun wound glistened, its edges dark with clotted blood. The injury oozed blood, but it didn't slow her. If anything, it lent her a terrible authority, wounded but undeterred, shaped by survival.

The small red light on her SPOT tracked blinked once, sharp, mechanical, then vanished beneath the churn.

Each slow sweep of her tail erased the distance between them.

No urgency.

No hesitation.

She advanced with a presence that needed no permission.

Water parted around her like it had no say in the matter.

* * *

Ava froze, breath caught somewhere between a gasp and a sob. Her mind locked, not from panic, but from certainty. This was it. The end. No way out. No rope to pull, no tricks left to try.

She yanked Jack to her side, clutching him like a lifeline. Her arms wrapped tight around his small frame, her body forming a wall between him and the thing in the water.

She couldn't speak. Couldn't pray. Her mouth opened, closed, nothing came out.

Only terror, thick and dry in her throat.

Danny moved into her field of vision, stepping in front of both of them. He spread his arms wide as if he could somehow shield them with his body alone. There was nowhere left to retreat, the sand beneath them thinned to nothing, falling away into open water.

Jack stumbled.

He grunted, catching his foot on something beneath the surface. His balance faltered, and he went down hard, water splashing up into his face.

"Jack!" Ava cried out, grabbing him under the arms, heart hammering.

"I'm okay!" he sputtered, coughing.

She saw him kneel again, shoulders hunched, hand groping in the water. Then he pulled something free, slick, clear plastic catching the light.

A bag.

For a heartbeat she didn't recognize it. Then her stomach turned.

Inside it, the severed baby shark head glared through the folds of cloudy film.

"Oh Jesus! Get rid of it!" she snapped, her voice high and shrill.

Jack raised the bag to throw, but his arm stalled in the air. He stared at it.

Ava opened her mouth to shout again but stopped.

Jack's eyes had narrowed. Something was happening behind them. She could see the spark, the strange lift in his face.

"Remember Shark Week?" he said suddenly, looking not at her, but at Danny.

His voice had shifted, no longer frightened, but urgent.

* * *

The sand pressed close to her belly. Each stroke of her tail met resistance now, water thickened with silt and rising grit.

But she advanced, slow, deliberate.

Water funneled along her flanks, tugged at the edges of her gills. Pressure tremors pulsed through the substrate, three shapes ahead, clustered tight. Muscles twitching. One smaller than the others. Its signal sharp and fast. The magnetic flicker of a heart too quick, too near.

The current thinned. The land pushed back beneath her. Her pectorals flexed. She adjusted, lifting slightly, enough to keep moving.

Not fast.

Not stealthy.

Simply forward.

The water changed, warmer, crowded with mammal breath and blood trace. She drank it in.

Not decision.

Not hunger.

Only response.

She kept on. Because something moved ahead. Because it had not yet stopped moving.

Because this was the only way she knew.

* * *

"A dead shark... is like shark repellent. They can't stand it."

Jack's voice was shaky but certain, his eyes locked on the severed shark head in the plastic bag.

Danny's brow furrowed.

Then it hit him, something half-buried from a Shark Week marathon he and Jack had watched a few summers back. He could see it: glowing TV light, Jack curled beside him on the couch, popcorn spilled between them.

One of the scientists had said it, calm, clinical, how sharks avoided their own dead.

How the scent repulsed them.

Some ancient instinct.

Survival hardwired deep.

It had sounded like trivia then.

Now it felt like salvation.

He dropped to his knees beside Jack and took the bag from his hands, the severed shark head inside. His fingers were clumsy but fast, tearing small holes in the plastic.

"Hurry, hurry, hurry," he muttered, breath sharp in his throat.

"What are you doing?!" Ava shouted from behind, her voice sharp and tight.

Danny didn't look back. He could feel the water around them change, the energy, the weight of it. He risked a glance up.

She was coming straight at them now, body low in the water, her dorsal fin cutting a slow arc through the fading light.

Danny heard Ava's breath hitch beside him. She pulled Jack closer, whispering something he couldn't make out.

No time.

The shark was thirty feet away.

Twenty. Less.

"She's coming. Oh my God…" Ava's voice cracked.

"Back up! Back up!" Danny shouted, pushing to his feet, shark head in one hand, his other arm flung wide across Ava and Jack.

"I love you!" Ava cried. "I love you both!"

Danny didn't answer. He couldn't. He stepped forward and plunged the bag into the water, stirring it hard, letting the foul, rotting scent bleed into the current.

Judy surged forward.

Danny could see her now, really see her, those blue-black eyes locked on him, the torn rope from Cap's final act hanging from her mouth.

Her snout rose, teeth parting, the water bulging outward from her mass. The pressure wave hit Danny's legs, nearly knocking him off balance.

Her mouth opened wide - red and endless.

He extended the shark head like a shield.

Judy punched into the fouled water.

And flinched.

The scent hit her.
Not blood.
Not prey.
Rot.
Shark.
Wrong.
It flooded her snout, thick and foul, riding the current like oil through water.
Not fresh.
Not alive.
The chemical signature coiled into her brainstem, bypassing everything else. Nerve endings flared. Jaw twitched. Her whole body hesitated.
Danger.
Disease.
A rival destroyed.
A trap.
In the deep time etched into her body, that scent spoke with absolute clarity: *leave.*
She veered.
Hard left. Tail drove deep. Her body twisted sideways, slipping from the shallows in a single heavy stroke.
Pectorals flared. Gills flexed wide. The pressure behind her exploded as she rolled into deeper water, abandoning the unnatural taste.
She didn't weigh it.
She didn't choose.
She fled.
The current snapped behind her, boiling the surface as her mass disappeared into the dark.

The water calmed.

Ripples from her sudden turn faded, smoothing out into glass. What followed wasn't sound or motion. It was the hush of water closing in behind her.

Danny stood frozen, chest heaving, ears ringing. The silence felt wrong. The kind of quiet that came before something broke. He scanned the surface, heart thudding against his ribs.

She could come from any direction. There'd be no shape to watch for, no sign to brace against, just the blur and bite of teeth.

The surface gave him nothing, no dorsal fin, no ripple, no sign.

A wide, empty shimmer of water swallowing the last of the light.

Behind him, Ava shifted, took a step.

Too far.

Danny heard her gasp.

He turned in time to see her heel slide. Her foot caught nothing. She'd reached the edge. The sandbar was gone beneath her.

She toppled backward, arms flailing, eyes wide. One hand shot out and caught Jack by the arm. He yelped, and then they were both under, plunged into deeper water in a flurry of limbs and spray.

"Ava!" Danny shouted, but they were already kicking, already fighting to stay up.

Then he saw it.

Judy's fin - behind them, cutting the surface like a blade.

So close.

No time to think.

"No!" he roared, charging forward, swinging the severed shark head high.

He brought it down hard, slamming it into the water with everything he had, churning rot and death into the current.

CHAPTER 59

The rhythm of approaching rotors swelled in the distance, heavy, measured, unmistakable.

The sound spread across Pamlico Sound like a warning, steady and rising.

The helicopter cut low over the water, a sleek MH-65 Dolphin, painted in the unmistakable red and white of the Coast Guard.

Its fuselage gleamed under the moonlight, streaked with salt spray from hours of search. As it banked, its wide bubble windows caught distant flashes of light below.

A searchlight hung beneath its belly, sweeping in slow, deliberate arcs across the black expanse. The beam stabbed forward like a spear, slashing side to side through the gloom. The cabin doors remained open.

Crewmen leaned out, harnessed and alert, spotlights in hand, calling coordinates to the cockpit above the roar of blades.

* * *

Below them, a U.S. Coast Guard motor lifeboat pressed forward, forty-seven feet of steel, grey-hulled and salt-scoured, the red diagonal slash along her side stark against the dark water. She advanced at a measured pace, bow lifting and settling with each swell, movement deliberate rather than hurried.

The superstructure rose square and solid, windows fogged from within, metal grates bolted over the glass. Coiled lines hugged the rails. Everything about her spoke of weather endured and weather expected.

Built for storms, she rode low and sure, engines rumbling deep, a steady, resonant growl that traveled through the water like purpose made audible.

Antennae and radar bristled above the bridge, silhouetted against the night sky. At the bow rail, four Coast Guard crew stood shoulder to shoulder, night vision binoculars pressed to their faces. None spoke. Their posture told the story, alert, silent, shaped by the rhythm of missions like this one.

The bow-mounted searchlight swept wide across the surface, its beam slicing white into black. It tracked over open water, then caught on scattered debris, an overturned foam cooler, a dented bucket, the mangled frame of a crab pot spinning in slow circles.

It all floated like the aftermath of something freshly broken, the sea not yet finished with it.

"Surface clutter ahead," a voice called from the wheelhouse, calm, clipped, unmistakably Coast Guard. "Visual on debris field. Slow her down."

The helm acknowledged with a short nod. The cutter's twin diesels throttled down to idle, shifting the rhythm of the boat into a low, mechanical thrum. Their wake flattened behind them.

"Radar contact," the tech added. "Bearing zero-eight-five. Thirty meters. Holding steady. Could be debris, low return."

His fingers tapped across the screen, adjusting gain. A soft green blip pulsed on the display, slow, ambiguous.

"Mark it," the coxswain said. "Let's bring the light back."

The searchlight swept again, this time slower, more precise.

A few more feet of drift, and the light caught it full, a sliver of Devildam's bow jutting ten feet from the Sound like a crooked monument.

No rail, no deck, nothing but hull.

The fiberglass skin looked warped in the beam, bruised by tide and impact, salt-scrubbed and streaked with grime. Water sheeted down her sides in slow, slick veils. A fine fracture traced the curve above the waterline, hairline, barely visible, but long as a man's arm. Below that, darkness.

She didn't move. Not with the wind, not with the current. Like she was pinned there, impaled on the sea itself.

At the rail of the rescue vessel, Rachel Delgado, the Coast Guard photographer, compact, sharp-eyed, ponytail tucked under her cap, stepped into position and raised her camera.

The flash burst, white and sharp, again and again. Each whine and snap seared the moment into digital memory, freezing wreckage in harsh, pitiless light.

The strobe lit the bow, tilted, defiant, the last piece of her refusing to go under. Rachel adjusted her footing, braced against the slow roll of the deck, and shot another frame.

Flash.

Whine.

Snap.

Cold light.

Black water.

The searchlight continued sweeping, undeterred.

* * *

Kid stood near the bow of the rescue boat, hands wrapped in fresh gauze, the fabric stiff from the dried blood beneath. Salt air stung his cracked knuckles. He barely noticed. His thoughts looped in uneven circles, stuck somewhere between exhaustion and disbelief.

He remembered the metronome beat of rowing, the pull of his arms, the lock of his shoulders, the dinghy scraping forward in uneven lurches.

The sun had baked his chest and shoulders until they blistered and peeled, salt drying into white crusts along every rib. His hands bled where the skin had rubbed raw, but the pain had slipped somewhere distant, submerged beneath repetition and need.

He hadn't paddled with hope, or courage, or any thought of making it out. He paddled because stopping had never presented itself as an option. Because the next stroke was always there. Because as long as his body kept moving, the rest of it didn't matter yet.

He remembered something shifting beneath him.

A scrape.

A jolt.

The bow of the dinghy caught on something solid.

Land.

He stared, blank, not quite understanding. Then he stood and stumbled out, legs stiff, knees folding with each step. Wet sand sucked at his heels like it wanted him back. The air felt different. Trees in the distance. Homes. People.

Everything after came in shards, blurred faces, voices he couldn't hold onto.

A family, he thought.

Dragging post-storm wreckage into a pile. Splintered siding. A mangled lawn chair. A crushed doghouse.

He couldn't remember what he'd said to them, only that he'd said something. His mouth had moved.

The words had come out slurred and shaking, "You have to call 911. There's a shark. They're out there. They're going to die."

Now he stood on solid footing again, eyes following the spotlight as it tracked the surface.

It crawled methodically across the water, wide, slow arcs carving order into the dark. The beam swept over the depth marker, lighting the orange shaft in stark relief.

Kid remembered when the water had barely climbed two feet up its length, when there'd still been room to stand, room to breathe. Now the tide lapped at the four-foot mark, swallowing the pole a little higher with every surge.

It felt less like the water had risen than that it had decided to, advancing with intent, patient and absolute, taking back what it had loaned them for a while.

Sinking them all.

Then…

"There!" he shouted, voice raw.

His finger jabbed toward the water, "There - port side!"

The spotlight caught it a second later. Three shapes huddled together in the waist-deep water.

Danny stood with one arm locked around Ava and Jack, the

other clutching a torn plastic bag that sagged with the baby shark's bloated head. Ava leaned into him, soaked and streaked with something darker than mud. Jack clung to her hip, limp but upright.

But they were alive.

Battered, soaked, filthy - but alive.

"Here! We're here!" Danny yelled.

His voice cracked, the sound ripped away by the wind, but the spotlight locked onto them and held.

Kid's stomach twisted.

Cap wasn't with them.

He stared into the light, waiting, hoping Cap might appear wounded, maybe, but alive.

Nothing.

Just the three of them. Three survivors. Drifting like wreckage.

Judy must have taken him.

The thought landed like an anchor, solid and cold.

Cap, who'd trained him, who'd taught him how to tie a cleat hitch and how to listen for engine trouble without a gauge.

Cap, who never got tired of yelling at him, then laughing five minutes later like it hadn't happened. He'd been a bastard sometimes, short-tempered, sarcastic, but he'd been fair. He'd been there. Always had something to teach. Always made sure you were paying attention.

He'd been a boss.

Then a mentor.

Then something like a father.

Kid's eyes drifted to Jack. The boy was trembling, face pinched white with cold and shock. Something sat crooked on his head, dark, soaked, barely clinging to his scalp.

Cap's hat.

The brim curled gently upward, soggy and beaten, like an old flag waving goodbye.

* * *

Rachel snapped another picture.

The flash lit the darkness, freezing the moment mid-breath: three figures huddled in the water, waist-deep and windblown, held together by exhaustion and instinct. Jack's arms were wrapped around Ava's neck, his face pressed to her shoulder.

Danny stood behind them, one arm across both, the other holding the torn plastic bag, the severed shark head blurred by the low light. Cap's old hat crooked on Jack's head.

The image was raw. Unguarded. Ava's eyes were half-lidded with fatigue, but her body leaned into both of them, protective. Danny's jaw was clenched, his face streaked with grit and salt, but his stance said one thing: *you're safe now.*

Jack, pale and shivering, was silent. Alive.

The photo would come to define the story. Raw. Immediate. Impossible to forget.

It would run in newspapers, on websites, on glowing television screens across the country. People would stop and look, not because of the violence, but because of what remained afterward.

A family, torn apart and somehow reassembled. Not whole. Not untouched.

But changed, stronger in the way that only survivors can be.

Americana, some called it.

Not the glossy kind with flags and front porches.

The kind forged in saltwater and held together by what didn't break.

EPILOGUE

In the weeks after the events in Pamlico Sound, Judy made her way up the East Coast.

Her SPOT tracker pinged at regular intervals, digital breadcrumbs that traced her silent path. She pushed two hundred miles offshore, vanishing into the black Atlantic before curving back toward the continent.

For days, she disappeared, a ghost in the deep, before surfacing north of Virginia Beach. There, she lingered in the mouth of the Chesapeake, circling the brackish waters for nearly a full day before slipping once more into open sea.

Her next ping came less than a mile off the glittering resort hotels of Ocean City, Maryland. Tourists played in the shallows, laughing and splashing, oblivious.

Two more pings followed a few miles north, offshore from Bethany Beach, where the wealthy skimmed across the surface on high-dollar jet skis and sleek speedboats.

Judy passed beneath them all, unnoticed, unseen. A shadow under their joy. A silence beneath their noise.

When news of the North family's ordeal broke, the world turned its gaze on her.

The shark.

The killer.

The one that had terrorized a fishing charter in Pamlico Sound. The beast that had taken lives and, somehow, spared one small family.

Fear spread faster than fact.

Aquavantis, the research team that had tagged her the day before the attacks, tried to explain: Judy wasn't evil.

She wasn't rogue.

She wasn't broken.

She was simply what the sea had shaped her to be.

A hunter.

A survivor.

A creature of instinct and anatomy, not cruelty.

She was doing what sharks had done for millions of years - moving, striking, enduring.

As Ava had told Jack, "Judy's just doing what Judys do."

But reason was no match for fear.

Outrage followed.

Demands to track her, kill her, mount her as a trophy.

People wanted vengeance, as if nature owed them balance.

Aquavantis pushed back.

They called Judy essential - a living relic of a system older than cities, older than memory.

She was not a villain.

She was weather.

A current.

A storm rolling through with no awareness of what stood in its path.

Killing her wouldn't bring justice.

It would bring ignorance.

But fear doesn't reason.

It acts.

Worried some weekend warrior might decide to hunt her, Owen Dyer quietly boarded Aquavantis, logged into his shark tracking app, and disabled her tracker.

One keystroke.

That was all it took.

Judy disappeared.

No more pings.

No trail left behind.

She drifted out into the open sea, directionless but not lost. There was no plan. No memory. Only instinct, current, and motion.

Somewhere below the thermocline, the world turned quiet again.

She did not vanish.

She returned to what she'd never truly left.

Not hunted.

Not hunting.

Just gone.

The ocean breathed, and she was part of it.

* * *

It wasn't fast. It wasn't clean. But they got better.

Jack started sleeping through the night again sometime in October.

Ava didn't notice it at first. She opened her eyes one morning and realized she hadn't heard his voice. He curled up against her most nights, checked the locks twice before bed, but he was smiling more.

Drawing again. Sharks, at first, cartoonish and wide-eyed, but then birds, boats, sunlight on water. Lighter things.

Danny started running again. At first, short jaunts around the block, then longer stretches.

One morning, he came back flushed and winded, grinning like he hadn't in months, not at anything in particular, the kind of grin that came from being alive, from moving, from feeling something shake loose inside.

Ava watched him from the kitchen window, his shirt dark with sweat, his chest rising and falling.

She thought of the Sound.

The water.

Cap's hat.

She pressed her palm to the glass and said nothing.

Some things they didn't talk about.

Cap's name still caught in their throats. Sometimes Danny would stop mid-sentence, eyes drifting out toward the backyard like he was watching something move.

Sometimes Jack would ask about him out of nowhere, on the way to school, brushing his teeth, and Ava would have to pause, breathe deep, and find words that didn't fall apart in her mouth.

They never had good answers. But they always answered.

The dinghy got patched up and tied to a tree behind the house. Danny had thought about burning it, but Jack had cried when he mentioned it.

So, they kept it.

Let the rain collect in its hull. Let it grow moss and memory.

In early November, they went to the beach.

The air was cool, the sand windblown and empty.

Jack held Ava's hand the whole time. Danny carried a towel under one arm, though none of them planned to swim.

They walked. The tide low. The sky gray. The waves slow and even.

They didn't talk much.

But they walked.

Together.

And that was enough.

ACKNOWLEDGEMENTS

Every book begins in private, but it does not reach the world alone.

My sincere thanks to Dark Anthem Press for believing in *JUDY* and giving this story a home.

I am especially grateful to Nicola Pittam and James Moorer for their guidance, patience, and care in helping bring the book from manuscript to finished work. A novel changes when it begins to leave the writer's hands, and I am thankful mine was met with such thoughtfulness and enthusiasm.

Thank you to Alexander Robb, who always pushed me creatively to do more with less. That lesson stayed with me through every page of this book: to trust restraint, to leave room for silence, and to let the dark water speak for itself.

I am deeply grateful to Larry Kealy for sticking with me through the long process of writing and rewriting, and to Patti Lee for keeping me honest and straight on the facts. A story like this depends on tension and imagination, but it also depends on accuracy - the weight of a boat, the pull of tide, the shape of a coastline, the things that either ring true or don't. Any mistakes that remain are mine alone.

To Jennifer, my wife, thank you for the love, patience, enthusiasm, and steady belief that carried this book forward. You lived with this story long before anyone else could read it, and I know how much of its existence belongs to you.

And to Maddy, my bright light in dark seas: thank you for reminding me, always, why stories matter.